American Exit Strategy

Book One of the Economic Collapse Chronicles

Mark Goodwin

ACKNOWLEDGMENTS

I would like to thank Jesus Christ, the Messiah, for lifting me up out of the miry pit and giving me a firm place to stand.

Thanks to my mom, whose prayers protected me in dark times.

Thanks to my beautiful wife for all of her help and support in getting this book together.

Thanks to those who helped awaken me to the need to prepare through blogs, podcasts and books, especially Ron Paul, James Wesley Rawles and Jerry Robinson.

Foreword

American Exit Strategy is a work of fiction, but the threats that materialize in the book are real. Many of the numbers stated in the book are forward projections made by the author and based on real numbers. *American Exit Strategy* looks at the current financial problems our country is facing and simply does the math. Plan accordingly.

The steps taken by the Bair family to prepare are based on extensive research by the author to prepare for an actual economic collapse and are included for educational purposes and to convey realism. The author shall not have liability nor responsibility to any person or entity with respect to any loss or damage caused, or allegedly caused, directly or indirectly by the information contained in this book.

For more information on preparing for a financial meltdown or other natural or man-made disasters, visit the author's website at www.PrepperRecon.com

Except for a few people and one cat whose real names were used with permission, all of the characters, places and incidents are products of the author's imagination or are used fictitiously. Any resemblance to actual people, places or events are entirely coincidental.

If you would like to be notified when new books by Mark Goodwin are released, send an email to **prepperrecon@gmail.com** with **New Book Notification** in the subject line.

CHAPTER 1

"A wise and frugal government, which shall restrain men from injuring one another, which shall leave them otherwise free to regulate their own pursuits of industry and improvement, and shall not take from the mouth of labor and bread it has earned. This is the sum of good government."

Thomas Jefferson

Texas Senator Paul Randall plopped down on his hotel bed. Exhausted, it was all he could do to loosen his tie. He thought, *once this campaign is over, I promise myself I will never return to New York*. He hated the hustle, the bustle, the crowds, the traffic and most everything that made New York, New York. He had been in New York for three days now and had spoken at two banquets and given seven interviews. There were only three more weeks until the election. After that, win or lose, it would be over and he could get some rest. For now, his body ached, his head pounded and he was too tired to sleep.

There was a knock at the door. "It's open," Randall called.

Sonny Foster, Randall's campaign manager, opened the door and stuck his head in the room. "Sir, you look bad. Are you going to be okay? Should I have the doctor come check you out?"

"I am tired Sonny, not dying," Randall snapped.

"Yes, sir, but we have to keep you well, or I won't have a campaign to manage. All the staff is ordering Chinese. I took the liberty of ordering you some barbeque wings, ribs and crab rangoon," Foster stated.

"I thought you were trying to keep me well," Randall smirked.

"Comfort food, sir," Sonny replied. "Tomorrow is a long day. We're heading to New Hampshire for a rally."

"What happened to the NYC Police breakfast and that Central Park thing tomorrow?" Randall asked.

Sonny walked over to the writing desk near the bed and sat in the chair. "New York is a lost cause, sir. We're spinning our wheels and wasting valuable time here. It's time to cut our losses. Besides, New Hampshire will be a bit more relaxed for you. You're running on empty. You just have to give them twenty minutes of face time at the rally then a fifteen minute interview with the local Libertarian talk show host; you can rest for the remainder of the day. While we're on the subject, dodge the abortion questions. I don't have to tell you that you are losing a huge chunk of the Libertarians to New York Governor Howe on that issue."

Paul Randall sat up—Sonny had just struck a nerve. "They shouldn't claim to be Libertarians if they don't stand up for everyone's liberty. A woman's right to choose what she does with her body ends when that unborn child's life begins. That unborn child has the same God-given rights to life, liberty and the pursuit of happiness as anyone else."

Sonny replied, "I agree with you, sir, but I just think we should have fought that battle after you got into office."

Paul looked at Sonny. "America tried that in the Revolution. Everyone went along to get along. Several states looked the other way on the issue of slavery to get a consensus on the Constitution. That wicked infection festered until it erupted eighty years later in the bloodiest war our nation has ever seen. You knew when you took the job that we were going to do this right or not at all, Sonny."

"I know, sir," Sonny conceded. "It's just that you're fighting an uphill fight as an Independent. You need all the alliances you can get. No one has ever won an election doing what you are doing. You are neither a Democrat nor a Republican."

Randall shot back, "I am a Republican, Sonny. I'm a true Republican. It's the Republicans that aren't "'Republicans.'" The party's been hijacked by the neocon warmongers and the mealy-mouth big government liberals. The true Republican Party began as the Jeffersonian-Republicans. Small government, state sovereignty, non-intervention and no federal bank that can tax the citizens through inflationary money creation to be spent on the profligate lifestyle of an obese state. What we now call a Constitutionalist is the true Republican. I'm the true Republican candidate, not Juan Marcos. Juan Marcos is the corporate fascist candidate."

Neocon was short for neoconservative. They were also referred to as RINOs, which was an acronym for Republican In Name Only. Neocons were the wing of the Republican Party that had forsaken traditional Jeffersonian ideology. Their magnanimous ambition to export democracy around the world through military force was actually only a thin veil that concealed their true motives. Their true intention was to have global control of resources and to dictate to the world through military might. Their biggest campaign contributors were defense contractors who worked with that branch of the party to pilfer the riches of the once great nation. Together, this wicked alliance formed what became known as the *military industrial complex.*

Sonny said in a tired tone, "Be that as it may, sir, Congressman Marcos is the one wielding the full power and might of the Republican political machine. And whatever you may call it, it is a power to be reckoned with."

CHAPTER 2

"I think myself that we have more machinery of government than is necessary, too many parasites living on the labor of the industrious."

Thomas Jefferson

Matthew Bair arrived home from his job as a financial planner a bit earlier than his wife, Karen. He gathered some fresh field greens and a few bell peppers from the small garden in the backyard. It was the first small crop of the year. Late October was the beginning of growing season in South Florida. Matthew got a quick shower and started dinner. He looked at his phone to be sure the ringer was on. Karen was a bit later than normal, but he didn't get concerned as she frequently stopped by the grocery to scoop up special deals that were often time sensitive. Karen was something of an expert couponer. She had managed to feed the two of them and their small cat for under $50 a week. This was a phenomenal feat, especially with the excessive inflation that had nearly doubled grocery prices in the last three years.

Just as he turned away from the phone, it rang.

"Karen?" he answered. "Are you okay?" He was a little jittery as the neighborhood had twice been locked down by police searching for suspects in the past week. Even in their middle-class neighborhood, there had been a carjacking and a home invasion in the past seven days.

"I'm fine," she replied. "But I have a flat."

"We can handle that." Matt was relieved to hear it was nothing more serious. "There is a can of Fix-A-Flat in the trunk. Just shake it up and screw it on the valve stem. Push the button on the top and the tire will re-inflate."

"I did that already," she said. "All the air just came right back out of the side of the tire."

"I'll be there in 15 minutes," Matt said. "Wait for me inside. I don't want you standing around outside in that neighborhood. And take your pistol with you."

"We can't have guns in the school, Matt. I could get fired for even having it in my car on school grounds," Karen said.

Matt said firmly, "Please don't argue with me about this; there are a lot worse things than being unemployed."

Karen agreed to follow his instructions and went inside. Karen was a high school counselor for the public school system. Her school was far from the worst in their county, but none of them were really safe. The second downswing in the economy had taken effect just after the implementation of the new health care law. Many counties around the US had gone bankrupt. Several schools closed, class sizes nearly doubled and schools were little more than holding cells for students as teachers and administrators were overwhelmed and understaffed.

The mass school board layoffs of the first round of the recession had been replaced by mass "no-show" firings in this, the new depression. Rather than give a resignation, hordes of teachers had simply not shown up for a few months, then filed for unemployment stating they were fired. The teachers had seen how the welfare class manipulated the system day in and day out. Many of their students bragged about how they didn't need an education because the government would take care of them, just as it had done for their parents and their grandparents before. With recent tax increases and inflation, the teachers were risking their lives to live on the exact same level as those who did nothing but milk the system. Why risk getting shot or having your throat slit? They weren't making any difference in these kids' lives. There was no discipline, the very few students who had an interest in learning received no attention because of the behavior of the rest. In fact, many of the good kids dropped out to get GED's, which they could earn online, in the safety, peace and quiet of their own home.

Matt pulled into the lot of the school and got out of his Dodge Ram pick-up truck. Karen walked out to meet him. Matt looked at the flat tire. "Someone knifed your tire. Did you have any of these kids locked up lately?"

"No," she said. "The police don't come to arrest them anymore. They say they don't have the resources to send officers unless there has been a murder or rape. There are metal detectors at the door where the kids go in. I doubt they could get a knife in here."

"They can sneak in a ceramic knife. They won't set off a detector," Matt said. "Why would anyone slash your tire?" Matt popped the trunk to pull out the jack and the spare tire. As he looked down at the bumper, it clicked in his head. "I bet it's your 'Paul Randall for President' sticker."

"What about it?" Karen asked curiously.

"Some liberal probably slashed your tire because of your bumper sticker. It's nice to see the kids even know who he is," Matt answered.

Karen rolled her eyes. "It was probably one of the teachers. They mostly all support Howe. Most of them carry knives to 'open boxes' since that's the only form of self-defense they can have. There may be 20 boxes to open all year, but we all have a knife if that box makes it to our desk. They say some really hateful things about Paul Randall—things that would probably be illegal to say if he were president."

These types of vandalism were to be expected. The county had voted 2-to-1 Democrat in the last presidential election. This city was a liberal septic tank. While they preached a message of tolerance, the liberals around here were anything but tolerant.

Matt changed the tire and they headed home.

Over dinner, Matt was quiet. He didn't look up from his plate.

Karen tried to console him. "The car is fine, Matt. Don't let it bother you."

Matt spoke for the first time since they sat down to eat. "It's not the car. It's work. I lost another company account. It was the last one. So many companies are closing their doors. Businesses can't stay open. This depression is killing everybody. The few places that can keep their heads above water are forced to shell out what they would have contributed to employee retirement plans onto government health plans. The government taxes them to pay for everyone else's health care. After the health care law bankrupted all the health insurance agencies, the government took over. There is no alternative to paying what they demand. It's the law. Without company matches, no one invests their own money into a 401k. I don't blame them. Retirement plans are just money pits now. I only have a few individual accounts left. No financial planner in the world can protect people's wealth in this market. Everything is going down the toilet."

Karen tried to encourage him. "You still have your furniture restoration hobby, and I still have a job. The house is paid for; we don't need much."

"I know, baby. But it will be hard to save much money just buying and selling used furniture on Craigslist," Matt replied. "And I hate your job. It's not safe at all. You shouldn't be there."

"We have to be grateful for what we have, Matt," Karen said.

"I am grateful. I just wonder if I'm fulfilling my job as a husband by staying in this area. The crime just keeps getting worse and worse. There are few prospects and little hope of things getting better. It's a social decay that comes from the people who live here. The mentality around here is like a cancer. People are mean, rude and they all have the entitlement attitude. People aren't like that back in Kentucky. There is a much larger percentage of people that believe in Jesus, and that makes a huge difference. You can feel it when we go home to visit my folks."

Matt knew Karen didn't like the people around their town either, but he also knew she hated the cold winters in Kentucky even more. That's why he stayed.

CHAPTER 3

"The general principles on which the fathers achieved independence were the general principles of Christianity. I will avow that I then believed, and now believe, that those general principles of Christianity are as eternal and immutable as the existence and attributes of God."

John Adams

Boise, Idaho, church pastor, John Robinson walked out to the pulpit of Liberty Chapel on Sunday as the last worship song finished. The congregation lowered their heads as he prayed. "Father, our country has strayed so far from your side. We have kicked you out of our school system and out of our courtrooms. We have done things our own way and become our own gods. Just as you promised in your Word, we are reaping the consequences of those choices. Our schools have a dropout rate of nearly half. Those who do finish school have little hope of finding employment. Violent crimes have spiked in recent years to the point that it's not safe to go out after dark in many of America's cities. We need your help, God. We need you to intervene in the coming election. We must choose a leader that will set an example by following your Word and your way. Thy will be done, Father, in Jesus' name, Amen."

He looked up at the congregation. "Church, we have filed the proper forms with the IRS to forfeit our tax-exempt status. I have prayed and fasted about this decision. It did not come easy and it certainly won't be without a cost, but I refuse to be held hostage by a tax break. Jesus said you cannot serve God and money."

Applause broke out that drowned out the sound of the murmuring. Everyone could still sense a large portion of the congregation disagreed even though they couldn't hear it.

Pastor John continued, "The non-profit tax exemption has been held over the heads of God-fearing church pastors for too long. It has been used as a tool of Satan to keep us quiet on perhaps the most important topic of our day. I believe that if we are to affect our culture, pastors must be free to offer biblical perspective about specific candidates. We need the freedom to tell our congregations why each candidate measures up or is found wanting when they are held up to our plumb line, the Bible. As Paul Randall is the only candidate that has taken a stand to defend the life of the unborn, and as he is the only candidate that has taken a stand to protect the Constitution, the document that guarantees us our God-given right to worship our Creator here today, I will be laying out my case today for why I believe Senator Paul Randall most correctly represents God's Word. He has the type of character that can lead us back in the direction from which we have fallen."

The auditorium was nearly full. The twenty or so people who walked out after the announcement were barely noticed because of the nearly unanimous standing ovation that Pastor John Robinson received. Pastor John's church was well south of the Idaho panhandle where patriotism was as thick as pea soup, but his church was well known for taking the Bible and the Constitution as meaning exactly what they say. The church even had a shooting range where firearms safety courses and concealed carry classes were given on Saturdays.

The rest of Pastor John's sermon focused on the importance of the church's involvement in politics. He spoke for some time about the pastors who had been involved in the American Revolution.

CHAPTER 4

"When governments fear the people, there is liberty. When the people fear the government, there is tyranny."

Thomas Jefferson

Two weeks before the election. Presidential Election Debate on Cable News Channel, CNC.

New York Democratic Governor Anthony Howe gave his closing statement. "If we want a truly civil society, we must care for the less fortunate. If we want a truly civil society, we must keep firearms out of the hands of criminals. If we want a truly civil society, we must protect women's rights to make their own decisions. If we want a truly civil society, we have to forge a new America where equality is not just a buzzword, but is guaranteed by the state. If we want a truly civil society, those who have more should expect to kick in their fair share. How many houses can you live in? How many cars can you drive? We have a huge public obligation to provide food, shelter, and health care for our citizens and to keep our streets safe. We cannot accomplish our mission while the greedy hoard their pennies in their castles and the rest of America goes without. Senator

Paul Randall speaks of a fair tax. What is fair about the level of income inequality in America? If he abolishes the IRS, what recourse will the oppressed have against their oppressors? Congressman Marcos advocates a tax cut for the rich in the face of dire economic shortfalls that threaten the basic services every government owes to its people: nutritional programs for the poor, Social Security for the disabled, health care for the young who can't find jobs and housing for those who just need a helping hand. Will they really rob poor Americans to line the pockets of those who have more than they need? Will you give them that power, or will you stand together in solidarity and demand what you deserve?

"We have come so far under the leadership of President Al Mohammad. He has brought us into the civilized world by implementing a health care plan that is the envy of the nations. Unemployment is the lowest it has been in over a decade. But we need those who have made their riches on the backs of the poor and middle class Americans to help out a little bit more. My tax plan asks people who earn $100,000 or more to contribute to a sixty-percent tax. It is a fair and equitable way to sustain our American Dream.

"Our dream will not be turned into a nightmare by guns. I intend to sign an executive order banning all semi-automatic firearms upon my inauguration. Citizens who consent to our strict registration and monitoring programs will still be allowed to have single-shot and pump-action shotguns as well as revolvers and bolt-action rifles for hunting and home defense, but military weapons belong on the battlefield not on the street. I challenge you to share in making this dream a reality."

The moderator, CNC correspondent Amy Stein, betrayed her feelings as she wiped a tear of inspiration while she thanked the Democratic New York Governor for his participation in tonight's debate. "And now we will hear the final words from California Republican Congressman Juan Marcos."

"America, all is not lost," Marcos began. "We can work together to find a middle ground. We can reinvigorate our economy by reducing corporate taxes that will allow companies to hire more workers. Those workers can buy homes and prop up our housing market, which is deflating once again. We can find a middle ground on abortion laws. By limiting abortions to early-term pregnancies and by offering counseling to pregnant women, we can reach a compromise.

"I intend to work with Congress, to come up with responsible gun laws similar to the ones we have in California. It is a middle ground that will limit the capacity of magazines while still allowing sportsmen and gun enthusiasts to enjoy responsible gun ownership. We are not two nations. We are not the extremist-left nation of Governor Howe and the extremist-right nation of Senator Randall. We are one nation under one flag. Extremism seeks to alienate and destroy your opponent. A democracy seeks to find a path that we can all travel on together.

"I also have a plan to reform the health care law to get it back on a sustainable track. My plan will shore up our national security. Our defense budget has been devastated by the austerity measures placed on us by the UN and IMF in our bailout agreements. I am working with representatives from the IMF even now to begin paying back our obligations to them so the restrictions on military spending can be lifted. Once that is done, we can begin to build ships and planes and repair our military infrastructure. This will create jobs for everyday Americans like you. It will reaffirm our presence as a global force for good. We will work to sustain the intelligence networks that have kept our country safe from terrorism for so long.

"Once these new economic engines are in place, we can begin to scale back the level of support that we are required to expend on social programs that have been draining our budget for the past eight years. We will pass new work bills that will get everyone in America a job to do. We will get our roads and bridges back up to standard. We will reopen our schools and put teachers back to work, training our next generation. We will rise from the ashes and return our country to its former glory by our American spirit."

The camera caught Amy Stein as her eyes were rolling at the congressman's speech. "Thank you for your participation in tonight's debate, Congressman."

"Thank you for allowing us this opportunity," Marcos replied.

"Now we will hear the closing statement from Texas Republican Senator Paul Randall... I'm sorry, Senator, I meant to say 'Independent.' I have gotten so used to calling you a Republican over the years," the moderator exclaimed.

Randall said, "That's alright, Amy. Technically, I'm still a Republican senator, but I am running as an Independent in the presidential election."

"That's because I won the Republican nomination, Amy," Juan Marcos interjected.

Senator Randall bit his lip to keep from saying something he would regret. He knew Marcos was baiting him. Juan Marcos had been using these tactics on Randall all night. Paul Randall sat silent for a minute. Amy Stein reminded him, "You may proceed whenever you are ready, Senator."

Paul finally replied, "Yes, thank you, Amy. I had an excellent speech that we had worked on all day, but the closing remarks made by Governor Howe and Congressman Marcos have hit me harder than I expected. These two men do not represent what our forefathers had in mind when they risked their lives to build this country, America. Our forefathers had in mind to build a nation on faith that was anchored by morality and law to ensure liberty. The framers of the Constitution spent years creating a document that would ensure our liberty and guarantee our God-given rights. They had just thrown off the chains of tyranny and hoped to guard you against that same oppression. Governor Howe and Congressman Marcos sought to put this document behind them—the document upon which the entirety of our legal system is founded. Without the Constitution, we have nothing but anarchy. All the powers of government are defined and prescribed by that document. These two men go beyond nullification of the Constitution; they seek to take away the rights given to you by your Creator.

"Let's look at just a few of the infractions these two have made against our founding principles. The Declaration of Independence so eloquently speaks of the right to life. Yet both of these men have infringed upon that right for millions of unborn children. They condone murder of the most defenseless. I know they don't think that it's a life. They think that it's just a blob. Have you ever seen an ultrasound, Governor Howe? Does that look like a blob to you? It looks like a person to me. I see tiny arms, legs, a head, fingers and toes. So when does life begin? I say at conception. You say at some other time, but you can't tell me when. If you can't tell me when, then you cannot say definitively that it does not start at conception. Therefore, you can't tell me definitively that abortion is not murder. If we're going to pick a time that's convenient to say when life begins, let's just say it starts when you wake up from being a liberal or a neocon.

"Both of these men have been involved in passing laws that infringe on your Second Amendment rights. The amendment says 'A well-regulated Militia, being necessary to the security of a free State, the right of the people to keep and bear Arms, shall not be infringed.' What part of 'shall not be infringed' don't you gentlemen understand?

"Our country has been reduced to begging for handouts from the IMF and UN because of the continued welfare spending proposed by Governor Howe and the warfare spending proposed by Congressman Marcos. If we want to regain our national sovereignty, we're going to have to cut defense spending to a sustainable level. That will not include Congressman Marcos 'jobs' plan that pilfers the taxpayer to enrich the military industrial complex. It also won't include the constant growth of the surveillance police state that 'protects' us from terrorism. Do you know the odds of dying in a terrorist attack, Congressman Marcos? It is 20,000,000 to 1. Do you know the odds of being struck by lightning? That's 6250 to 1. Lightning is 3200 times more likely to kill you than a terrorist. Do you know how many lightning rods and rubber shoes we could buy with the $300 billion dollar intelligence budget that we use to spy on our own citizens through programs like Prism? But that doesn't matter, because it's not about saving Americans from terrorism; it's about controlling them.

"We need to turn welfare back over to the Church. Government can't handle welfare, and it is not their job. This is the job of the Church. When a person is in need of financial help, there are usually other factors at work. Sometimes it may be drugs or it may just be poor money management. Sometimes it's just that they need help through a hard time. But they need the Church to counsel them and find out what the issue is. The Church can then help them get back on their feet. If they're just freeloaders, the Church can discern that and kick them out the door. Government can't do those things. They get people stuck in a cycle that they can't or won't get out of. Government has no ability and no desire to help people who are down. The liberals get dependents to give up their freedom for an Electronic Benefits Transfer card and ensure their votes and our nation's demise.

"Health care? Ironically, the heath care bill dubbed "Al Mohammad Care" was the disease that completely collapsed our economy into the ruins we see today. Governor Howe brags about the unemployment rate. It's a manipulated number that doesn't count millions of people who've dropped out of the workforce over the years because there were no jobs to be had. The number also neglects all the people who are working part-time because they can only find part-time work. If you calculate those folks into the total, the number is much closer to thirty percent than the seven percent that's reported by the BLS. Millions of part-time jobs popped up when the health care law forced many service sector businesses to cut employees to twenty-five hours per week to avoid being required to provide health care insurance for their workers. For many companies, the added costs of insurance would've put them out of business. New part-timers were hired to take the hours of the employees whose hours were cut. That goosed the U3 unemployment number to make it look lower.

"My plan is not an economic stimulus plan. It is not the lie-in-the-sky bill of goods these other two candidates are offering. My plan is painful, but it takes us back to a sustainable path. The future will be painful. The only question is, will we salvage what we have and rebuild or will we burn it to the ground, to a point from which there is no coming back? My plan will prevent significant loss of life. Howe's plan or Marcos's plan will most certainly end in a complete collapse of our government and economic system. Depending on how much charity we receive from other nations, we should expect a die-off of between ten percent and forty percent of the US population. There's no more sugar coating the facts. It's just simple math. We're out of time and the collapse is at hand. The IMF is low on funds and unable to bail us out much further. To continue to print money through quantitative easing will collapse the little value the world still places on our paper currency. My plan will take us through a revaluation and reinstitute a 100-percent-backed, bi-metal monetary system backed by physical silver and physical gold. Gold and silver have been used as stores of value since the very beginning of time. Genesis 13:2 states 'Abram had become very wealthy in livestock and in silver and gold.' That, my friends, is the beginning of time. The metals-backed system will replace the Federal Reserve and the central planners with a free market that regulates monetary supply through scarcity. It protects the citizens from inflationary taxation through new money creation, which robs savers. The value lost by savers through inflation is reallocated to the government for them to waste and buy votes.

"My plan is not a new one. It's the same plan our forefathers handed us more than 200 years ago. It's a plan that worked, so let's get back to it."

Marcos proclaimed with a loud voice, "Nobody is going to die, Randall! Your fear mongering is a new low for you, Senator. I find it disgusting!"

Paul Randall walked out from behind his podium toward Marcos. "I find your willingness to lead this country into an early grave in order to line your pockets and the pockets of your cronies disgusting, Congressman!"

Marcos stepped back with a look of fear and shock. Security flanked Senator Randall, but he returned to his podium on his own.

"Well, that was certainly a debate for the history books!" Amy Stein exclaimed. "Join us right here on CNC for the poll results coverage on tonight's debate right after this short break."

.

CHAPTER 5

"In the house of the wise are stores of choice food and oil, but a foolish man devours all he has."

Proverbs 21:20

Matt shut down the computer and went into the living room to watch a few minutes of the news with Karen. She was relaxed on the couch with their cat, Miss Mae. They were watching *DC Live*, the prime-time political show on CNC.

Ed Nolan, the lead correspondent for *DC Live*, turned to his guest Amy Stein. "Amy, what was that high school locker room scene at the end of the debate last night? Your job was to keep things civil."

Amy replied, "Marcos and Randall were so far behind in the polls before the debate, it couldn't hurt, so why not pull a publicity stunt?"

"If it was a stunt, it worked for Randall. He's up five points in the polls today," Ed countered.

"He's going to need a lot more than five points to pull ahead of Howe. Even with Randall's barbarian bump, Howe was still in the lead today by seventeen points," Amy said.

"Is that what we're calling it, the *barbarian bump*?" Ed inquired.

Amy answered, "He got a five-point bump by acting like a barbarian, hence the term barbarian bump."

"His supporters evidently thought it conveyed passion," Ed responded.

Amy smirked, "Well, they may be a bit barbaric as well. What does President Al Mohammad call them, the 'Guns and Religion Caucus'?"

Ed tried to redirect the conversation before Amy's mouth got them into any more trouble. CNC flew the flag of trying to remain in the center, but the center had moved quite a ways to the left over the past decade. "I think President Al Mohammad can't wait to turn over the keys to the White House, no matter who wins. It's been a rough eight years."

Matt threw his hands in the air. "I can't listen to this, Karen. I get worked up, and then I don't sleep well."

"Change it." She tossed him the remote.

Matt's phone rang and he picked it up. "Hey, Cousin."

"What're ya'll doin'?" Adam Bair asked. Adam was Matt's cousin in London, Kentucky. Adam had served in the US Marines in Iraq and Afghanistan. When he returned from the war, like many vets, he had a very hard time adjusting. He tried to silence the anger and the sadness with drugs and alcohol. It almost cost him his life. Adam blacked out when he was on his way to deliver 100 pills of

OxyContin. He was high on them himself and nodded out while he was driving. The police found him in the wrecked car on the side of the road. He was not seriously injured and he hadn't hurt anyone else. It could have been a lot worse. Because of the amount of drugs the police found in his car, Adam was looking at a lot of time. A Christian judge in London, Kentucky, gave him the choice of prison or a Christian rehabilitation center called Teen Challenge. Despite the name, the center worked with people of all ages to overcome addiction through the power of Christ. Adam chose rehab to stay out of prison. His motivation was to do his time in a better environment and to eat better food, but he learned the true depths of God's love for him while in the program. When he finished with Teen Challenge, he was a radically changed man and was reunited with his wife and two daughters.

His wife, Janice, left him shortly after he returned from the war. She didn't feel safe around him and wasn't sure it was safe for the girls. Since his conversion, she loved him more than ever and only felt truly secure when he was home.

Matt replied to Adam's inquiry, "We were just watching the coverage of last night's debate. Did you watch it?"

"That's why I'm callin', Cousin," Adam said. "Paul Randall said some things that got me thinking. I really like the guy and he has my vote. I took an oath to defend the Constitution. That didn't stop when I left the Corps. I think Randall will defend the Constitution as well. I think he's the best choice we've had in my lifetime. What he said about a bunch of people dying, do you think that's realistic? Could that really happen? And do you think he believes that or do you think Marcos was right? Do you think it's possible that he's trying to scare people into voting for him? I know you spend a lot more time reading about economics and finance than I ever could. I understand economics; it just bores me to tears."

"I think he's spot on," Matt said. "Our system is fragile and interdependent on every other part of the system. It's also extremely complex. The complexity increases the chances of something going terribly wrong, and it makes it more challenging to fix. We're in such an economic pit that there is literally no way out. Consider the Great Depression. Ninety percent of the population lived on farms or at least in rural areas. Only ten percent of people lived in cities, yet even with most everyone living on farms and all the good will people had toward their fellow man, Americans still starved to death. Now, people will slit your throat for a pair of tennis shoes and the exact opposite demographic is true. Ninety percent of people live in cities and only ten percent of people live in rural areas or farms. What would those people eat if the system came crashing down? If the currency collapses, how will the farmers sell their produce to purchase seeds and fuel to produce the following year's crop? And it all just cascades downward from there. Our cities are filled with violent people just waiting for the police to not get paid and quit going to work. Once that happens, it doesn't matter how much charity we get from other nations in the form of food, because no one will deliver it into a war zone ran by gangs and criminals."

Adam asked, "Couldn't the military deliver food and aid? They've done it all over the world."

Matt explained, "They're still all over the world. They're not here. Even if we brought them home, there aren't enough to do the job. That's the only thing the lobbyists from Northrop Gruman, Boeing and Booz Allen Hamilton don't lobby for: more troops. As long as there are enough soldiers to sign the delivery invoices, they don't care if there are enough pilots to fly the planes.

"Back to Paul Randall's estimate, I think a ten-to-forty-percent die off is very possible. Grocery stores only stock about three days' worth of food. If there is a run on grocers, the shelves could be empty in six hours."

Adam said, "I suppose we haven't thought about it much,

because we're out here in the sticks. If we lived in the city, I guess we'd be preppers, too. But I guess if folks get scared, they'll panic all over. I don't expect riots in London, Kentucky, but they could probably clear out the shelves at Kroger pretty quick."

"I think that's a good assessment of the situation," Matt stated.

Adam asked, "So if I decide that I want to get ready for some type of event like that, what should I do? Where do I start?"

Matt was glad that Adam asked. He loved to help people get prepared. "I recommend you start with some long-term food storage—six months' worth at a minimum. The easiest and cheapest way to kick start it is with dried beans and rice. Even with this radical inflation, they're still relatively cheap. If you seal rice in a Mylar bag with some oxygen absorbers, it'll last twenty years or more. Make sure you get white rice. While brown rice is more nutritious, it still contains the bran which has fat. The fat has proteins that'll rot. You can only store brown rice for about a year. Most types of beans will last at least ten years if they are sealed in Mylar. Then, I would make sure you have a good water supply. Are you on a well or city water?"

Adam answered, "They ran the pipes from the city about five years ago. We hooked up because the well dried up a couple times during droughts. I can still run the pump on the well. We also have a good creek."

Matt stated, "I would put a hand pump on the well. Just use it once in a while to keep it primed. Also, get some rain catch barrels to catch the run-off from your roof's gutters. It wouldn't cost much to put gutters on the barn either. The barn roof has a large surface area. It won't take much rain to fill up barrels from the barn roof. You also want to keep some stored drinking water for droughts or contamination of the water table. Start filling up your old juice and soda bottles with water when you empty them. You have plenty of storage space in the barn, so use it."

"Wow, you think we would lose power and need a hand pump?" Adam asked.

Matt said, "If the currency collapses, there are no paychecks. Maybe the guy at your power plant will work for the joy of doing it, but I wouldn't count on it. He's going to have to think of some way to feed his family, too."

Adam pondered all of the advice Matt gave him. "So I guess I should look at alternative power sources, also; maybe a generator?"

Matt said, "A generator makes a great yard ornament, but it won't be good for anything else when we run out of fuel. I'd go with solar. You can start small and build on with solar. Keep in mind, the power going out is probably an extreme example and may not be likely, but you never know. In Argentina, they had brownouts and low voltage when their currency collapsed in 2001."

"That's a lot to digest. Do you know a good site where I can learn a little more about prepping?" Adam asked.

Matt suggested, "Check out SurvivalBlog.com. It is loaded with tons of great information. The Survival Podcast has tons of information on homesteading and self-sufficiency. You can download all of the past episodes. I read PrepperRecon.com. That guy is pretty thorough. Go back and listen to some of his archived shows on prepping."

"Thanks, I'm going to let you get back to that beautiful wife of yours," Adam said. "Thanks for the info and take care."

"You too," Matt closed.

CHAPTER 6

"I am for doing good to the poor, but...I think the best way of doing good to the poor, is not making them easy in poverty, but leading or driving them out of it. I observed...that the more public provisions were made for the poor, the less they provided for themselves, and of course became poorer. And, on the contrary, the less was done for them, the more they did for themselves, and became richer."

Benjamin Franklin

Pastor John Robinson was a few minutes early to the meeting with Ron White, the head of the benevolence ministry at Liberty Chapel. He waited patiently and sipped his coffee. Ron was right on time as usual.

"Good morning, Pastor," Ron said.

"Good morning, Ron," Pastor John replied. "I spoke with Steven, and the title is clear on the Young farm. Mr. Young wanted the church to have it when he passed. He worked that farm since he was twenty years old. I want to use it in a way that will honor his memory. It's a fully functional farm with machinery and out buildings. I think the highest and best use is food production."

"Pardon me for saying so, sir, but isn't that mission creep? Do we want to get into the farming business?" Ron asked politely.

Pastor John replied, "I understand your point, but we're already in the feeding people business with the benevolence ministry. If we can get these people involved in producing food and feeding themselves, I think it'll pay for itself. We'll have to pay a few staff members, but we'll be producing the food instead of handing out grocery store vouchers. It'll give those in need a sense of integrity to be involved in providing for themselves. You can't put a price tag on that. It'll also be a good outlet for the troubled youth program. The boys can be around some of the strong men in the church and be mentored while they learn some useful skills. Single moms can come in through the week when the Fellowship Grill is closed and use the kitchen for canning. A couple of the moms can take turns watching the children. This ministry will also quickly weed out the freeloaders. Paul wrote in II Thessalonians 3:10, 'The one who is unwilling to work shall not eat.' "

The pastor and Ron continued to iron out the details of how they would implement the plans for the new property. Making sure they made the most of all the resources God blessed them with was always their highest priority.

CHAPTER 7

"The democracy will cease to exist when you take away from those who are willing to work and give to those who would not."

Thomas Jefferson

Matt woke up late. He had started working from home two days a week. The office was closed on Tuesdays and Thursdays to conserve electricity and support staff expenses. He did his morning routine, which consisted of a few minutes of prayer before he got out of bed. Next, he listened to a couple of worship songs as he did his morning stretches. He started his coffee and sat down to have cereal with some fruit, usually an apple or blueberries. As he ate his cereal, he would read a chapter or two from the Bible. This morning he was reading Deuteronomy 28.

Blessings for Obedience

28:1 If you fully obey the LORD your God and carefully follow all his commands I give you today, the LORD your God will set you high above all the nations on earth. [2] All these blessings will come on you and accompany you if you obey the LORD your God:

³ You will be blessed in the city and blessed in the country.

⁴ The fruit of your womb will be blessed, and the crops of your land and the young of your livestock—the calves of your herds and the lambs of your flocks.

⁵ Your basket and your kneading trough will be blessed.

⁶ You will be blessed when you come in and blessed when you go out.

⁷ The LORD will grant that the enemies who rise up against you will be defeated before you. They will come at you from one direction but flee from you in seven.

⁸ The LORD will send a blessing on your barns and on everything you put your hand to. The LORD your God will bless you in the land he is giving you.

⁹ The LORD will establish you as his holy people, as he promised you on oath, if you keep the commands of the LORD your God and walk in obedience to him. ¹⁰ Then all the people on earth will see that you are called by the name of the LORD, and they will fear you. ¹¹ The LORD will grant you abundant prosperity—in the fruit of your womb, the young of your livestock and the crops of your ground—in the land he swore to your ancestors to give you.

¹² The LORD will open the heavens, the storehouse of his bounty, to send rain on your land in season and to bless all the work of your hands. You will lend to many nations but will borrow from none. ¹³ The LORD will make you the head, not the tail. If you pay attention to the commands of the LORD your God that I give you this day and carefully follow them, you will always be at the top, never at the bottom. ¹⁴ Do not turn aside from any of the commands I give you today, to the right or to the left, following other gods and serving them.

Curses for Disobedience

[15] However, if you do not obey the LORD your God and do not carefully follow all his commands and decrees I am giving you today, all these curses will come on you and overtake you:

[16] You will be cursed in the city and cursed in the country.

[17] Your basket and your kneading trough will be cursed.

[18] The fruit of your womb will be cursed, and the crops of your land, and the calves of your herds and the lambs of your flocks.

[19] You will be cursed when you come in and cursed when you go out.

[20] The LORD will send on you curses, confusion and rebuke in everything you put your hand to, until you are destroyed and come to sudden ruin because of the evil you have done in forsaking him [21] The LORD will plague you with diseases until he has destroyed you from the land you are entering to possess. [22] The LORD will strike you with wasting disease, with fever and inflammation, with scorching heat and drought, with blight and mildew, which will plague you until you perish. [23] The sky over your head will be bronze, the ground beneath you iron. [24] The LORD will turn the rain of your country into dust and powder; it will come down from the skies until you are destroyed.

[25] The LORD will cause you to be defeated before your enemies. You will come at them from one direction but flee from them in seven, and you will become a thing of horror to all the kingdoms on earth. [26] Your carcasses will be food for all the birds and the wild animals, and there will be no one to frighten them away. [27] The LORD will afflict you with the boils of Egypt and with tumors, festering sores and the itch, from which you cannot be cured. [28] The LORD will afflict you with madness, blindness and confusion of mind. [29] At midday you will grope about like a blind person in the dark. You will be unsuccessful in everything you do; day after day you will be oppressed and robbed, with no one

to rescue you.

[30] You will be pledged to be married to a woman, but another will take her and rape her. You will build a house, but you will not live in it. You will plant a vineyard, but you will not even begin to enjoy its fruit. [31] Your ox will be slaughtered before your eyes, but you will eat none of it. Your donkey will be forcibly taken from you and will not be returned. Your sheep will be given to your enemies, and no one will rescue them. [32] Your sons and daughters will be given to another nation, and you will wear out your eyes watching for them day after day, powerless to lift a hand. [33] A people that you do not know will eat what your land and labor produce, and you will have nothing but cruel oppression all your days. [34] The sights you see will drive you mad. [35] The LORD will afflict your knees and legs with painful boils that cannot be cured, spreading from the soles of your feet to the top of your head.

[36] The LORD will drive you and the king you set over you to a nation unknown to you or your ancestors. There you will worship other gods, gods of wood and stone. [37] You will become a thing of horror, a byword and an object of ridicule among all the peoples where the LORD will drive you.

[38] You will sow much seed in the field but you will harvest little, because locusts will devour it. [39] You will plant vineyards and cultivate them but you will not drink the wine or gather the grapes, because worms will eat them. [40] You will have olive trees throughout your country but you will not use the oil, because the olives will drop off. [41] You will have sons and daughters but you will not keep them, because they will go into captivity. [42] Swarms of locusts will take over all your trees and the crops of your land.

[43] The foreigners who reside among you will rise above you higher and higher, but you will sink lower and lower. [44] They will lend to you, but you will not lend to them. They will be the head, but you will be the tail.

[45] All these curses will come on you. They will pursue you and

overtake you until you are destroyed, because you did not obey the LORD your God and observe the commands and decrees he gave you. [46] They will be a sign and a wonder to you and your descendants forever. [47] Because you did not serve the LORD your God joyfully and gladly in the time of prosperity, [48] therefore in hunger and thirst, in nakedness and dire poverty, you will serve the enemies the LORD sends against you. He will put an iron yoke on your neck until he has destroyed you.

Today's scripture and the reality of what was happening to America hit Matt like a ton of bricks. The Bible was clear on what a nation should expect when it rejects God. The scripture pointed out many things that were already happening to America, and the promise of the curses to come were even more disagreeable.

The sad thing was that it didn't have to be this way. If the United States had just been faithful to God, if they had continued to serve God faithfully, they would still be enjoying the blessings of obedience. But now, America was certainly reaping the curses of disobedience.

Matt muttered to himself, "Now the sky above is bronze and the earth beneath is iron. We're borrowing from many, yet lending to none."

The Bible text for the day felt like a harbinger of doom. Was it a premonition? The overwhelming tragedy of the entire situation unsettled him. Indeed, it seemed it would not be long before many more people would be in hunger and thirst, in nakedness and dire poverty.

Matt shook off the unpleasant thoughts and poured his coffee. He went to his office and, as usual, started his morning news routine with Drudge Report. The top story was the Federal Food Stamp program. SNAP benefits had been slashed in half with no advance warning. There was simply no funding to fully resupply them. Users whose cards ended in the digit "1" had their EBT cards reloaded with the SNAP benefits on the first of each month. Today was November 1st. Matt figured the administration had not mentioned anything prior to today because they were obviously trying to push the event past the election. All the midnight backroom deals could not buy them one more week. Exactly seven days to Election Day and the mother of all financial disasters had just hit.

Matt and Karen were preppers, but there was no way to prepare for what was coming. Matt didn't hesitate. He texted Karen with an abbreviated version of the news report. He told her to tell everyone at work that she was not feeling well and to come straight home. He preceded the message with the term "CODE RED." They had predetermined that this meant to get home right away.

Matt opened the safe and took out two credit cards and a few hundred dollars in cash. He stuck his Ruger LC9 in the holster, grabbed the extra magazine and headed out the door. The Ruger was small and compact. The pistol only held eight rounds with one in the pipe, but he liked the fact that it was chambered in 9mm. It was a relatively large round for a concealed carry gun.

Matt's first stop was the Winn-Dixie just around the corner. He had no idea what to expect when he walked in the door. Surprisingly, it looked like business as usual. However, there was someone yelling at the cashier because her EBT card didn't have as much as she expected. She was throwing the groceries on the floor to bring her balance down to the amount that was on her card. Evidently, this was the first she heard of the benefits reduction. Other people were stopping to watch the action between the irate lady and the cashier. Not Matt though; he headed straight for the canned meat section. He loaded up the cart with canned tuna, canned chicken, canned beef and canned turkey. When the cart was nearly full, he headed for the checkout. He paid with his credit card without any issue. He unloaded the canned goods into the passenger seat of the truck. He returned to the store with the cart and went straight to the rice and beans. He bought 5 twenty-pound bags of parboiled rice and 100 pounds of dried beans. He bought various sizes and varieties of beans. Black beans and red beans were the most abundant, so he bought more of those than the other varieties.

Matt made a quick pass down the coffee aisle and loaded up on several pounds of coffee as well. Matt and Karen weren't coffee snobs. Matt's favorite was Eight-O-Clock, but it had risen in price faster than other brands over the past few years. They often drank Folgers and Maxwell House, depending on what Karen had coupons for. Winn-Dixie had Chock Full O' Nuts coffee on a buy-one-get-one sale, so Matt placed several large cans of that in his basket.

Matt breezed through the checkout lane again, loaded his haul into the bed of the truck and headed home.

As he was unloading, Karen pulled into the driveway. "More beans and rice? I thought we were all stocked up on that stuff. What's going on?" Karen asked.

"I think it just hit the fan." Matt continued to unload the groceries into the living room floor as he explained. "The government was only able to replenish EBT cards with half of what the recipients have been receiving. There was no advanced warning."

"What's the government saying?" Karen inquired.

"I don't know yet," Matt replied. "I saw the headline on Drudge, texted you, and ran straight to the grocery store. There are a few more things I want to do before we sit down and watch it all unfold. I need you to go fill up your car with gas. Then go to PNC Bank and close that account. Withdraw it all in cash. If they can't give you all cash, take what they'll give you in cash and leave the rest. Call me when you know, so I can decide what to do about the Bank of America account. For now, I'm planning to keep it open to pay our bills with. Take your gun out of your purse and put it on your waist. You need to be able to get to it fast today. I don't want to scare you, but I want to take every precaution. I'm going to Auto Zone to buy a couple of gas cans. I'll fill the cans when I gas up the truck. Meet me at Publix when you finish at the bank."

Matt could tell that Karen thought he was overreacting. He was glad she didn't say it. He thought he might be overreacting as well. But if his initial instinct was right, things were going to go downhill fast.

Matt arrived at the Publix grocery store before Karen. He gave her a quick call to see how it was going. Karen answered her phone. "They're giving me the cash, but it may take a while. They have to get the manager to go into the safe. I can't believe they don't have $4000 in the cash drawer!"

"Okay, baby, call me when you get to the store. I'm going to go inside and get started," Matt said.

Matt went in and saw things were not quite as pleasant as they were at Winn-Dixie. There were several people arguing with cashiers. It seemed most of the EBT card holders were finding out about the benefits reduction at the checkout. They seemed to have never heard the term "don't shoot the messenger," because they were taking out their frustrations on the cashiers and store managers. The lines were backed up into the aisles. It looked like a scene from Black Friday. One manager was catching a rant about discrimination because he'd opened two checkout lanes with handwritten signs that said, "No EBT cards in this lane." There were two other people jumping on the bandwagon about the "discrimination" issue, so the manager took the signs down.

Matt proceeded to the pasta aisle. He filled the cart with several boxes of angel hair pasta and cans of sauce. These were items that took very little fuel to prepare. Angel hair cooks faster than any other pasta because it's so thin. He bought several cans of canned pasta. This is something they would usually never eat, but if things get really bad, they could eat it right out of the can, and it's very high in fat, carbs and calories. Normally, that's not a positive attribute, but in a survival situation, it's getting the most bang for your buck.

Matt grabbed five gallons of bleach in case they needed it to purify water. Eight drops purifies one gallon of clear water, and sixteen drops purifies one gallon of cloudy water. It won't taste great, but it will be free of bacteria that can cause illnesses.

Next, he headed to the bread aisle. Once there, he threw in ten loaves of bread. He picked up several packages of cookies and several bags of candy. "The next few days have the potential to be stressful," he said to himself. "I better load up on some comfort food." He grabbed some peanut butter and several large jars of jelly then headed to the checkout. His cart was just big enough to handle his haul.

When he arrived at the front of the store, there were two new signs. One lane said, "Credit Cards Only." The other lane said, "Cash Only." The store manager outsmarted the whiners. Since there was no mention of EBT cards, they couldn't make a valid claim that they were being discriminated against. Matt surveyed the lines. The credit-card-only lane had eight people in it. The cash-only lane had only one man. Matt chose the cash-only lane. Just then, his phone rang.

"I'm here," Karen said over the phone.

Matt spotted her walking in the door and waved her over. Karen made her way over to him and looked in the shopping cart. "Matt, we're already prepared for this. We have at least six months' worth of food at home."

"We also have a lot of neighbors," Matt replied. "I doubt any of them have more than a few days' worth of food. We may need to help them out if things fall apart. A few hundred bucks is a small price to pay to be able to help out. Besides, we may need help from them as well. If we share what we have right now, our stockpile won't last two weeks."

The energy inside Publix was similar to the mad rush to get supplies just before a hurricane. Everyone in South Florida was well acquainted with dwindling stocks on store shelves the day before a big storm was due to hit.

Karen looked around at the chaos in the other lines. "Maybe you're right about all of this. I know you keep your ear to the tracks when it comes to economics and these sorts of things."

Matt replied, "Even if I'm wrong, I need you to be with me on this. If I'm right, the consequences of being unprepared may be death."

"I'm with you." Karen smiled at him as she gave him a big hug.

They checked out, took their cart and loaded it into the trunk of Karen's car. Next, they went back with two more carts. They filled them with toilet paper, rice, beans, canned meats, canned vegetables, powdered milk and other dry-good staples. Once the carts were filled to the top, they returned to the cash-only lane.

Three lanes down from them, four EBT card users were in a physical confrontation with two male stock clerks and a male manager. One cart overturned and groceries, including a busted two liter of soda, scattered all over the floor. The larger stock clerk pinned the main trouble maker to the floor. Three others attacked the clerk to try to get him off the pinned trouble maker. The other stock clerk and the manager tried fighting them off.

People were trying to get away from the madness. Several customers walked out of the store and left their filled carts sitting in the aisles. The cashiers watched the action. Progress froze in the slow moving lines. No one seemed to mind as they were engrossed in the ongoing commotion.

"Don't get involved," Karen said sternly.

"Don't worry," Matt replied. "I have my mission and I'm not planning to be distracted from it. The people who walked away from their carts will be sorry tomorrow."

Matt and Karen finally checked out and proceeded towards the parking lot. As they were leaving, five police cars arrived to address the fight. All of the attackers fled except the primary trouble maker. The big stock clerk still held him in a total submission hold.

"Why are they blaming the cashiers and the store for their benefits being cut?" Karen asked. "It's not their fault. They had nothing to do with the shortages."

Matt walked briskly through the parking lot, pushing his cart as he addressed Karen's question. "The majority of those people have been trained for generations that they're not responsible for anything, but that everybody else is responsible for taking care of them. The store employees are part of 'everybody else.' The wicked politicians who rely on these people to continue to get re-elected have worked hard at convincing them of that idea."

They loaded the contents of the carts into the bed of Matt's pickup and headed home.

CHAPTER 8

"I, however, place economy among the first and most important republican virtues, and public debt as the greatest of the dangers to be feared."

Thomas Jefferson

Sonny Foster busted through the door of Paul Randall's Kerrville, Texas, office. "Sir, you must turn the television on now!"

Randall's Kerrville ranch was the base of operation for Randall Ranches Cattle Corp, the family grass-fed beef business.

"Sonny, settle down! What's happening?" Paul was surprised by the interruption. "Are we at war?"

"Yes, sir, but we've been at war for fifteen years. That's not the news." Sonny scrambled for the remote.

Paul found the response to be amusing and couldn't help but smile to himself. This reminded him of why he liked Sonny's quirky personality so much. They had gone through a lot together over the past few years. In the same way marketing campaigns for Christmas now started in late August, unofficially, presidential campaigning began in the back rooms the week after the previous inauguration. Sonny had been with Paul Randall for over three and a half years now. He did great work on getting information about the timing of the other candidates' announcements to run for the office of President of the United States. All of the strategies, social media campaigning, and even a large part of the fundraising were coordinated by Sonny Foster.

The television sprang to life and "News Alert" scrolled across the bottom of the screen. CNC reporter Patrick James was reporting from the White House Rose Garden. "We're awaiting a statement from the president at any minute. Millions of Americans depend on SNAP, the Supplemental Nutritional Assistance Program, to meet their basic dietary needs. This morning, they went to their grocery store to find that only half of their usual benefits had been reloaded to their EBT cards. No advance warning of the cuts were issued by any government agency.

"The unannounced shortfall triggered a massive sell-off in the markets this morning. Wall Street saw the biggest plunge on record. About an hour after the market opened this morning, the Dow was down 975 points. This represented an eight-percent decline and the SEC made the decision to invoke the circuit breaker rule and close the markets at 11:00 am today. Among the stocks hardest hit was Howe Clancy. Howe Clancy is the investment firm co-founded by Governor Anthony Howe's father, Porter Howe. The firm processes all the transactions for the SNAP program and earns a transaction fee for every swipe. With the huge withdraw from corporate and individual investment accounts over the past few years, the loss of the SNAP benefits revenue could be catastrophic for Howe Clancy. Their stock was down thirty-one percent when the SEC made the decision to close the markets.

"Beyond the woes of Wall Street, Main Street is seeing troubles of its own. Main Street is without a circuit breaker rule and life goes on despite the calamity. Reports are flooding in of violence erupting in grocery stores all over the country. Police have been called into several big box retailers and grocery stores in major metropolitan areas. We've learned of eleven shootings at food retailers and grocers reported across the nation, all in large cities. There have been numerous arrests and too many reports of violence to count. The reports continue to flood in and we're still waiting for the president, who was scheduled to issue a statement at 2:00 pm Eastern Standard Time."

"What happened?" Paul Randall's face had a look of complete shock.

"My source at the Treasury says there was a deal to get the program funded by midnight last night and it didn't happen," Sonny answered.

"You mean they've been running things that close to the edge? Why didn't they let the people know there would be a benefit reduction?" Paul quizzed.

Sonny explained, "They're still scrambling to get it funded. From what my source understands, Treasury Secretary Melinda Chang is trying to put together an emergency bond auction as we speak. Her advisors are telling her there aren't enough buyers and it could spike interest rates on the ten-year Treasury note to sixteen percent."

Paul put his hand over his mouth in utter dismay. "The ten-year is around 13.25 percent. They believe one auction could push it up 275 basis points? What about the Fed—they won't buy the emergency bonds?"

Sonny rattled off his analysis, "Fed Chairwoman Jane Bleecher would do it in a heartbeat, but there's no consensus. Including Bleecher, there are five doves and five hawks on the FOMC. New York Fed President Sydney Roth and Ted Rosenthal, from the Board of Governors, are both toss-ups. The Fed independent oversight committee is screaming Armageddon if they raise current levels of monetary creation even one more dollar. Roth and Rosenthal tend to follow their advice."

"I have to hand it to you, Sonny, you certainly have your finger on the pulse. I couldn't do it without you." Paul knew compliments were very important to Sonny, even though he would never admit it.

"You would never have to, sir," Sonny stated faithfully.

Paul continued, "We're printing a total of $275 billion every month, $3.3 trillion a year through the combined quantitative easing programs. I can't believe we can't scrape $21 billion a month out of that to fund SNAP. Don't get me wrong, I think the program is bloated and a completely bad idea. The government has no business in charity, even if it were charity. But it's hard to use the term 'charity' to describe robbing one man of his hard-earned cash to support another that contributes nothing to society. Charity is when he gives it freely, of his own accord. Nevertheless, you can't shut a program like SNAP down overnight. It has to be phased out over time to avoid a systemic collapse."

Sonny explained, "Nearly half of the $275 billion in monthly QE is going to service the debt. We owe $26 trillion dollars on the national debt. With an average interest payment of eleven percent, that's $238 billion a month. No one is purchasing new bonds. Most of the remaining $37 billion left over after interest every month is going toward rolling over existing bonds. If the Fed doesn't buy the roll over debt, rates will go to the moon and the interest on the existing debt will become unserviceable."

The two of them turned their attention back to the television. Patrick James was still talking. "Security personnel are coming out of the White House door in the Rose Garden. That probably means the president will be out directly behind them. A crisis like this couldn't have come at a worse possible time for the election. The administration will want to carefully craft the damage control. I see Treasury Secretary Melinda Chang coming out the doors right now. White House Press Secretary Armando Sanchez is directly behind her. It appears he's going to give some opening remarks before President Al Muhammad makes his statement. We'll listen in now."

White House Press Secretary Armando Sanchez walked to the podium. He was flanked by Treasury Secretary Chang and Secretary of Health and Human Services, Gerald Brown. Sanchez positioned the microphone and began his speech. "We are issuing a brief statement for now and will hold another conference tonight where we'll be taking questions from the press, but we will not be taking questions after this statement.

"Late last night, unforeseen events caused a temporary setback in funding for the Supplementary Nutritional Assistance Program. Despite the glitch in the system, we were still able to fund the benefits at a reduced rate. SNAP benefits that are allocated to EBT card holders whose card number ends in the digit one, received their reduced benefits at midnight last night. Tonight at midnight, card holders whose cards end in the digit two, will be credited at the reduced rate as scheduled. Holders of cards ending in each subsequent digit will receive their reduced benefits on the corresponding day of the month. Let me be clear, funds are available to pay out the reduced rate benefits to each card holder on the day they are scheduled to receive their benefits credit. We anticipate having the funding complications ironed out by the 15th of the month. At that time, the balance of the funds promised to each American who depends on the SNAP program will be credited to their EBT card account. There is absolutely no reason for people to panic. Statements made in last week's debate have caused much confusion and anxiety. President Al Mohammad has promised that everyone will get the benefits they have been promised. We're simply asking the American people to remain calm and be patient as we work through this minor difficulty.

"If your normal benefits typically last you the entire month, you should have no problem getting to the 15th of this month on the reduced rate. At that time, you'll receive the balance of your benefits.

"Once again, we want to emphasize how important it is to keep a cool head and not get caught up in the rhetorical fear mongering that was so rudely displayed in last week's debate. This irresponsible language has triggered some hysterical behavior across our nation. There is absolutely no need for it and no truth to the statements made by Senator Paul Randall. No one is going to die. We will get through this just as we have always gotten through trying times. I thank the members of the press for coming out and we will let you know what time tonight we'll hold the conference for questions and answers."

Sanchez quickly turned his back to the reporters and walked inside as they demanded, "Where is the president?"

"Did he just blame this on me?" Paul Randall's mouth was wide open and his brow furrowed. "They've blamed every problem for the past eight years on the previous administration and now they're trying to pin this one on me! They can't admit responsibility to anything. This entire administration never knows what is going on and it's never their fault. And what happened to Al Mohammad? I thought he was supposed to be making the statement. He just drove this country over the cliff and then sends his henchman, Sanchez, out to blame it on me. Are you serious?"

Sonny was smart enough to know when not to engage. This was one of those times. He kept silent, poured himself a glass of water and walked over to look out the window. It was best to let the senator digest this allegation for a while.

CHAPTER 9

"Be courteous to all but intimate with few, and let those few be well tried before you give them your confidence; true friendship is a plant of slow growth, and must undergo and withstand the shocks of adversity before it is entitled to appellation."

George Washington

Matt paced back and forth from watching the television in the living room to the office computer checking his list of alternative news sites. Karen sat on the couch in the living room with Miss Mae.

"Come sit down by us," Karen said firmly. "You are making me dizzy. Watch the news with us for a while, then go check your computer for a while. You're just walking back and forth right now. You're not going to stop whatever's going to happen. You've done your best to prepare, so just relax. Besides, Sanchez is claiming that the balance of the SNAP benefits will be reimbursed on the 15th. I don't think it's going to be that bad."

"I hope you're right," Matt said doubtfully. He walked over to his easy chair and sat down next to Karen and Miss Mae to watch the coverage on CNC.

Ed Nolan was on earlier than normal to head up the special coverage of today's events. "We'll be bringing you a live feed from KWXT in Detroit, Michigan. Detroit Mayor Melvin Jones is giving a press conference from the Wayne County Courthouse in just a few minutes. Detroit Police have just calmed a riotous situation at a Detroit Walmart. The discount chain store is located in a predominately urban area where eighty percent of the population relies on SNAP benefits to make ends meet. Police had to use tear gas and rubber bullets to subdue the crowd. Those arrested during the melee were loaded into buses and transported to a processing center. A source working for the Detroit Department of Corrections told CNC that the jails were filled beyond capacity prior to the outbreaks of civil unrest today. The informant said he expects the perpetrators of today's violent reaction to the benefits reduction to be processed and released by tomorrow morning. Patrick James will be broadcasting live from downtown Detroit to get the reaction of residents to the cuts tonight at eight o'clock.

"We'll direct you back to the live feed from the Wayne County Courthouse. Mayor Jones is stepping to the podium now."

The mayor looked up at the camera from his notes on top of the podium. "Detroit will be imposing a dusk 'til dawn curfew effective immediately. We're asking all Detroit businesses to cooperate with city officials and to close their doors until tomorrow morning. Beginning tomorrow, we'll have officers staffed at the entrances and inside all grocery stores and large retailers to help maintain an environment of peace and safety. Thank you for your cooperation. I'll open the floor for a couple of questions."

"Mr. Mayor," a local news reporter, Sam Evers, called out. "What about the Walmart on Eight Mile Boulevard? It was the location of a very rowdy incident today. Will it reopen tomorrow?"

Mayor Jones chuckled and smiled. "A rowdy incident is a very kind description of the event, Sam. Thank you for that. To answer your question, I do not expect that particular Walmart to open tomorrow. There was some fire damage. Detroit Fire and Rescue did come out to extinguish the fire or fires. It's my understanding that there will be a cleanup effort there for several days. The Detroit Building Department will be working with Walmart management to ensure the store is up to code, safe and ready. As soon as possible, Walmart will resume meeting the needs of the people in that community. Next question."

The next reporter asked, "Mayor Jones, the Detroit Police Department has already been severely understaffed since the bankruptcy. How will you be able to effectively enforce a curfew when crime is already tearing this city apart?"

Not quite as amused by this question, Jones said, "Our City Law Enforcement Officers have been doing more with less for some time now. They're among the best trained and most loyal officers in America. They know what's expected of them and they consistently deliver a high level of service. I didn't intend to announce this until all the details were ironed out, but to put the residents of Detroit at ease, I'll go ahead. We're finalizing an agreement with the Michigan National Guard to help us enforce the curfew. If all goes well, they should be here by midnight tonight." The mayor had been pushed into saying more than he wanted to say, so he closed the press conference abruptly. "That will be all for tonight. Thank you."

Matt looked over at Karen. "Sounds like Jones just declared martial law in Detroit."

"Martial law is when the military takes over?" Karen asked.

"Yes, it's when the military takes over enforcing the law," Matt answered. "The military is trained to kill people. They lack a certain 'finesse' that one would like to see in a civilian law enforcement agency."

"Doesn't that violate Posse Comitatus?" Karen asked.

"The way the law reads now, the Posse Comitatus Act doesn't prohibit the National Guard from stepping into a civilian police function as long as they're acting in their own state or are invited by the governor of a neighboring state," Matt answered.

Matt turned his head as he heard a vehicle drive by. "I think Jack's van just pulled in. I'm going to see what he thinks about all this."

Jack Mason was the Bair's next door neighbor. He was a general contractor and liked working with his hands. Jack was a very intelligent guy but paid little attention to news and politics. He was stocky, had a beard and very friendly. If he saw anyone in the neighborhood working on a project, he always offered to lend a hand or to let them borrow a tool.

"Jack," Matt yelled as Jack stepped out of his work van.

"How you doing, buddy?" Jack responded.

"I'm good. What do you think about what's going on?" Matt asked.

Jack looked around. "Why, what's going on? Did someone else get robbed?'

Matt proceeded to fill him in on the recent news. He had tried to engage in topics of this nature before with Jack, but he had shown very little interest. Now that it was happening, Jack listened a bit more intently.

"Okay, some of that was over my pay grade, but it sounds bad. Still, I don't think anything like what happened in Detroit will happen here," Jack concluded.

Matt filled him in on his adventure at the Publix grocery store earlier. He explained the situation with the separate lanes and the fight involving the stock clerks and the manager against the trouble makers. Matt could tell that Jack was starting to come around to reality.

Jack said, "I still have a week's worth of stuff left over from what we bought when it looked like Hurricane Lucinda was going to hit us."

"That's a start," Matt said. "But this situation has the potential to cause problems for more than a week."

"Maybe I'll head over to Winn-Dixie after dinner," Jack stated.

Blaine Phelps was walking his two Huskies and came over to greet Matt and Jack. "You guys see what's going on in Detroit?"

Jack gave Blaine the abbreviated version of Matt's Publix story. Matt figured Jack wanted to appear to know what was going on, so he let him tell the story.

"No kidding!" Blaine responded. The conversation turned to provisions, and Blaine explained that he had a couple of weeks' worth of dry goods. Like Jack, Blaine's food stocks were things he bought for hurricane season.

Blaine stated, "I have a revolver and a shotgun if things get nasty."

Matt smiled and gave a nod but didn't tip his hand. Part of the prepper code was to maintain operational security or OPSEC, which entails keeping your mouth shut about what you have and how much of it.

"Are you guys all set?" Blaine asked.

"We can get by for a while," Matt said.

"Can you take care of yourself if things get bad?" Blaine inquired of Matt.

"We have a pistol," Matt said. *And then some*, he thought to himself.

Jack looked pensive before he spoke. "Things are getting kinda rough around here anyway. Maybe I should get something. What do you guys recommend?"

Blaine started, ".357"

Matt commented, "A .357 is a nice gun, but it only has six rounds. And it takes a while to reload. Glock makes a .45 that takes a thirteen-round magazine plus one in the pipe. Once the magazine is empty, it's a matter of seconds, not minutes, to reload. Glock is a popular gun, making it easy to get extra magazines and parts for it. They're also the gun of choice for many law enforcement agencies and militaries around the world because of their dependability."

"Wow!" Blaine added, "I hope I never need fourteen rounds."

"I hope I never need one round." Matt chuckled.

The men said their good-byes and returned to their respective homes.

CHAPTER 10

"The prudent see danger and take refuge, but the simple keep going and pay the penalty."

Proverbs 22:3

Matt went to the shed and retrieved the steel hurricane shutters. He started to place them on all of the windows that were facing the back fence.

He said to himself, "I should have just enough time before all the daylight is gone."

He started on the side of the house with no lights. If night fell before he finished, he would have the security lights on the other side of the house to work by.

Karen came out and asked, "What are you doing?"

"Just putting up the hurricane shutters to harden our house. It will make it harder to get into. Additionally, the shutters are bullet resistant to most handgun and shotgun ammo," Matt replied.

"Do you think it's going to get that bad here?" Karen asked.

"I don't know. Do you put your seat belt on because you expect to get into an accident?" Matt inquired.

"Good point," Karen said.

Matt finished with the back shutters and took the panels for the front windows in the house. He put each set of steel shutters next to the corresponding window. "I'll put these up inside if we see any signs of violence in the neighborhood. It'll just take a few minutes to screw them into the walls. I don't want to put them on the windows outside or do anything that would mark us as having something worth taking. It's a delicate balance between looking like a hard target and looking like you're fortifying because you have something to protect. Besides, the shutters will be harder to get through if they're on the inside."

Karen asked, "Will they leave holes in the walls?"

"There are worse places that could end up with holes than the walls." Matt kept working on his project.

"You mean us," Karen said.

After he was finished with the shutters, Matt and Karen started to move all of the extra food they purchased earlier that day into the office. They didn't have a huge house and all of their storage areas were full. They stacked the bags of rice on top of each other, then stacked the beans on top of the rice. The canned goods were stacked along another empty space on the wall.

They completed their tasks and started dinner. They enjoyed a great meal of steak quesadillas and fresh greens from the garden that evening. Police sirens were a common sound around their home these days, but this evening they were more prevalent than ever.

Karen cleaned up the table and dishes and Matt went to the safe. He loaded an extra magazine for his .45 caliber Glock 21 and one for

Karen's 9mm Glock 19. He put fresh batteries in both of the gun's tactical lights. The pistols had been their nightstand guns. He was using his subcompact Ruger LC9 as his concealed carry weapon and she had been carrying her Kel-Tec .32 auto. From now on, they would be wearing looser clothes and carrying the Glocks. Different times called for different tactics. The new nightstand guns would be the Mossberg 12 gauge for her and the AR-15 for him. They were each equipped with tactical lights as well. Matt topped off three extra 30 round magazines for the AR-15 and set them on the nightstand.

There was a knock at the front door. Matt looked out the front window for a car in the driveway. He didn't see one. He walked past Karen and put a finger over his lips to signal to be quiet. He drew his pistol from the back of his jeans and signaled for Karen to go to the bedroom to get a weapon. They had been over this a few times, so she knew exactly what to do. He walked to the side door, which would allow him to surprise the person at the front door. The locked gate was between the side door and the front providing a safety zone that would slow down any would-be home invader. With one hand, he opened the door while concealing the loaded Glock in the other hand, still inside the doorway. It was only Jack, the next door neighbor.

"Jack!" he yelled, which also signaled to Karen that everything was safe. "I'll be right out." He stuck the pistol back into the small of his back, walked to the front door and opened it.

"What's happening?" Matt asked cheerfully.

"I just wanted to give you a heads up," Jack said. "I went to Publix and it was chaos. The police were there arresting people left and right, but they couldn't get a handle on it. It was like everyone thought the end of the world was coming or something. I finally got in, but there wasn't much on the shelves. I just started filling my cart with whatever I could find. I got hot-dog buns, but there were no hot dogs or any other meat left. I got some pasta sauce, but there was no pasta left. I bought some mixed fruit jelly because that was the only flavor still in stock. There was nothing on the shelves. This is worse than before a hurricane.

"Next, I tried to go to Winn-Dixie to see if they might have a few more items. They were closed and there were two cop cars parked in front of the doors with their lights on. I didn't see any action in there. It didn't look like it was a crime scene or anything, it was just closed. There were several people standing around yelling at the cops, but they just stayed in their patrol cars. They kept calling over the loud speaker for the people to disperse. The people backed up a few yards then started closing back in. I've never seen anything like it. I'm going to get a pistol tomorrow."

"There's a three day wait on handguns. You should probably pick up a shotgun, too. That will cover you 'til you get the pistol," Matt said.

"Wow, I don't really want two guns," Jack replied. "Three days, huh? I don't know. I'll think about it tonight."

Matt said, "Outdoor World is still open; you could pick up a shotgun right now. People might be scrambling for guns tomorrow like they're scrambling for groceries right now."

Jack looked at Matt intently. "You might be right. Can you ride over there with me?"

Matt's answer was sympathetic, but firm. "I can't leave my wife here with all of this going on. I certainly don't want to say I told you so, but I've tried to talk to you about this stuff before and you blew it off. I can't put myself at risk because you failed to prepare. I'm not judging you; I'm just telling you how it is."

"What can I say? You're right and I don't blame you at all. Can I at least call you when I get there if I have any questions?" Jack inquired with concern.

"Absolutely," Matt replied with a smile.

Jack left and Matt joined Karen on the couch to watch the coverage of Detroit. The sun was setting and aerial footage showed fires all over the city. There were reports of several shootings, carjackings and massive looting. The cops had lost all control and the criminal element was running wild.

"So much for Mayor Jones's curfew," Karen said with a faint snicker.

Patrick James had just arrived and was starting his on-the-scene coverage. CNC hired a private security firm for the news team's protection while they broadcast. Normally, you would never see the security personnel in the camera shots, but there were so many, you could easily spot a couple on the side every few minutes. These guys weren't mall cops either. They were decked out in full riot gear with folding-stock shotguns and semi-automatic pistols in cross-draw holsters on tactical vests.

Patrick James was commenting on the chaos. "Folks, many of you may remember when I was embedded in Syria with the rebels during their civil war a few years back. I do not feel any more secure right now than when I was in that war zone. In Syria, there was some feeling of knowing who was behind you. We had a pretty good idea who wanted to hurt us and who didn't. Tonight, I'll tell you, this is a completely volatile situation."

Patrick called to a passerby to tell him what he thought of the situation. The young man stated, "This is crazy. The government can't just let all these people starve to death. They have to do something. They have to bring in food. These people are going to die! This ain't no joke, man! We gonna die!"

Patrick replied to the man, "But there is money on the EBT cards. No one should die. Everyone is going to get half of their SNAP benefits credit on the day they were originally supposed to get it. The White House has promised the balance of the benefits will be paid on the fifteenth."

"Come on, man," the passerby objected. "They lyin'! They ain't no mo money! It's gone. What they gave 'em today was it. Ain't nobody gettin' no money tonight, tomorrow, on the fifteenth, never. If they had it, it would've been there today. They take care all these rich people and leave us out to die. I'm tryin' to tell you, man!"

Patrick inquired further, "So, is that the consensus? Everyone in your community believes the White House is lying about the benefits that will be loaded over the next few days? Where is this information coming from?"

"Everybody know it, man," the interviewee replied in a hostile tone. "Why you don't know? You the news! Ya'll believe them? Ya'll better wake up. We goin' get ours!"

The man walked off. He seemed to be insulted because Patrick didn't agree with his perception of reality. Patrick turned back to the camera. "All the comments we have heard since we arrived appear to confirm that a mob mentality has taken over. The local residents give the impression that they don't believe anything the press or the government spokesmen say. By not getting in front of this issue before the benefits cuts appeared, the government has lost all credibility with this community."

An armored police vehicle pulled up to the news crew. An officer dressed in riot gear got out and addressed Patrick on camera. "Folks, you need to leave the city immediately. It's not safe for you here."

Rapid machine-gun fire rang in the distant background.

Patrick argued with the man, "We have our own security, and the American people have the right to know what's going on. You have to honor the freedom of the press."

The officer responded, "I understand all of that, but you're hindering our ability to keep the streets of Detroit safe. Your crew being here distracts us from what we need to be doing."

The camera kept rolling as Patrick James called his producer. The officer tried to avoid facing the camera. Two minutes later, the lead police officer received a call over his radio. He returned to the armored vehicle and pulled away without saying anything else to Patrick.

A security team member told Patrick they should relocate. Patrick James relayed the information to the camera, "Our security team is friendly with some officers in the Detroit Police Department and we're getting information on what's happening and where the threats are located. We just received a warning that a large mob is heading this way. They're burning cars, breaking windows and looting every store in their path. We're going to take a short break in order to relocate to a nearby parking garage. When we come back, we'll continue our live coverage from Detroit."

CNC ran commercials for a few minutes, then Ed Nolan came on to recap the events of the day.

In less than twenty minutes, Patrick James was broadcasting live again. The camera was set up on the fourth level of a parking garage, which gave a tremendous vantage point. From the corner of the garage, television viewers could see down several blocks to where the mob was creating all the havoc.

Patrick jumped right into action, "The sight you see behind me is a mob that has lost all hope in their government. They feel betrayed and feel they have no other recourse but to go out and take what they need. If we zoom in, you can see several of the people in the group carrying various types of makeshift demolition instruments. They're bashing cars, windows, trash cans and anything that gets in their way. We see flashing lights from police vehicles right now coming together two blocks in front of where the mob is. The police are setting up a barricade with patrol cars to try to head the mob off. The officers are forming up into a phalanx with tear gas guns."

Matt and Karen were immersed in the scene on the television as the camera focused on the line of police. They watched as the mob continued toward the police line undeterred.

The police began firing tear gas. The mob covered their faces and ran forward to the barricade. The rioters soon reached the barricade and began beating the police officers. Next, several officers began firing their side arms. Simultaneously the armed individuals in the crowd fired back at the police. Unarmed members of the mob fell back while the armed elements of the mob continued to engage the police in a firefight. The camera continued broadcasting while several police and rioters were shot before they cut away from the horror.

The coverage went back to the CNC studios with Ed Nolan. "Folks, we just saw some very horrific sights of people being shot. We're going to continue to get footage of the events occurring right now in Detroit. We're going to edit through that footage so not to disturb our sensitive viewers and we'll get it right back to you. We're also getting reports of smaller riots, fires and looting of large grocery chains from cities all over America tonight, but nothing compared to what we just saw in Detroit."

Karen looked up from the television. "Can you believe they just showed that on TV?"

"Everybody is watching it," Matt said. "They know they're going to get viewers glued to the television now."

Shots rang out from a few streets over from the Bair's house.

"Was that gunfire?" Karen asked.

"Sounded like it," Matt said. "I am going to listen in on the scanner." He didn't have an actual police scanner, but he did have the city police scanner bookmarked on his internet browser through Broadcastify.com. One quick click and he could monitor whatever went over the regular channels. A lot of the high priority incidences went to the police tactical channels, but in the event of widespread civil unrest, the tactical channels would be overrun with traffic. They would have to use the regular police channel. Matt downloaded the Scanner Radio app, which also used Broadcastify.com, to his phone. It could be helpful to know the streets that were being blocked off in manhunts.

From what Matt could pick up, it sounded as if people were looting the Winn-Dixie located a few blocks away from the house. Evidently, they overran the two patrol cars Jack saw earlier. SWAT was being called in with orders to shoot on sight. One of the officers parked at the store was injured, so the rubber bullet courtesy had been suspended for this incident.

Matt couldn't understand everything that came over the scanner. He was starting to recognize the 10 codes the police used, but he still needed to refer to his cheat sheet. This took time and caused him to miss a lot of information while looking up the translation of the 10 codes.

Matt's phone rang. It was Jack. "Hey, Matt, it's chaos in here. I had to take a number. I've been waiting almost an hour. They just called my number. They have a Glock .40 caliber and a Sig Sauer 9mm. Those are the only two semi-automatic pistols still available.

All the other guns left in stock are revolvers. Which one should I get?"

"Do they have ammo for the .40?" Matt inquired.

"I don't think they have any ammo for anything. The shelves were pretty low when I got here, but they look like they've been completely cleaned out now," Jack replied.

Matt said, "Then get the Sig. I will spot you a box of 9mm ammo. I can't help you with .40 caliber ammo and you may not find any for a while. A few years ago, when we had the gun ban scare following the school shooting, there was no ammo for about six months. What about a shotgun? Are you going to get one to hold you over until the waiting period is up and you can pick up the pistol?"

"They only have one. It's a semi-automatic Benelli 12 gauge. It's $2100. I was expecting to get something for around $600 or less," Jack explained.

"If you had been watching what is happening in Detroit right now, you'd give the guy $5000 and tell him to keep the change. I can spot you a box of 12 gauge shells if you get it. I'm sure they're out of those, too. Whatever you think your life is worth, that's your cap on how much you should spend," Matt said with conviction.

Jack said, "Okay, I'll get the shotgun. I'll come by when I get back."

Matt replied, "Call to give me a heads up, so I'll know it's you. Keep your head down when you get by Winn-Dixie; they're going nuts over there right now. There was an officer injured while looters were breaking into the store. They won't be playing nice over there. And tell Tina to come over here and wait for you if she gets scared. There's a lot of gunfire coming from around the neighborhood."

"Thanks, buddy." Jack hung up to complete his purchase.

Karen asked, "Is Jack going to buy a gun?"

"He is trying to get one," Matt replied. "From the sounds of things, he almost waited too long."

Matt and Karen continued watching the news coverage of Detroit and the rest of America descending into ruin and disarray. There was nothing they could do to stop it. Matt had done his best to construct his plan to get them through whatever was coming. All that remained was to sit back and observe the collapse.

CHAPTER 11

"To disarm the people is the best and most effectual way to enslave them."

George Mason, Father of the Bill of Rights

Sonny called Senator Randall the evening the riots started. "Dina Fitch is calling an emergency session in the Senate tomorrow to approve emergency powers to handle the riots. They're meeting tomorrow to vote on suspending firearms sales until the crisis dies down. They're also going to vote on allowing the Army to provide logistical support to the National Guard in areas where martial law has been invoked."

Paul Randall replied, "That's par for the course. Their motto is, 'Never let a crisis go to waste.' Every time something goes wrong, they manage to take a hole puncher to the Constitution. The problem is, there's barely an area of the Constitution or the Bill of Rights big enough for them to get a grip. This is one of the times people need to be able to defend themselves the most, and they want to suspend gun sales. I'll book a flight out to DC tonight. I'll call you tomorrow during lunch and let you know how long the vote is going to run. It will probably go late into tomorrow night, so you can just take care of things here rather than fly out."

"Thanks," Sonny replied. "I have no shortage of things to do here. Howe is down five points since this morning. Even though he has little to do with this mess, the Howe Clancy connection to the EBT card processing fees is reflecting in people's opinions of him. It's his constituents that are feeling this. None of those folks were going to vote for you anyway."

Paul said, "I just got off the phone with Commanding General Allen Jefferson. The National Guard is just outside of Detroit. They've canceled plans to go inside and try to restore order. They determined it's an unlikely objective and are now coordinating an effort to quarantine the city. FEMA will be there tomorrow to start taking refugees to camps. They'll start with women and children and families. Basically, males over eighteen who don't have ID to show and live with a wife or family won't be allowed to leave the city until more FEMA camps are set up. The first one is going to be in Lansing, and from what General Jefferson described, they are almost like minimum security detention centers. I would hate to have to pick between that FEMA camp and Detroit."

Sonny was starting to grasp the magnitude of the ordeal. "I'll pray for those folks tonight. Most of them didn't ask for this."

"Pray for folks all over, Sonny," Paul added. "We're even hearing of Walmarts that are getting looted in cities in Texas. Dallas has reported three stores that have been ransacked and one burned to the ground. The people who are doing this are cutting off their own feet. They're destroying their own communities."

Sonny replied, "Unfortunately, sir, they haven't done much to build those communities. What little they have has been given through government handouts for generations. When you don't work for something, you generally don't put much value on it."

"Very well said, Sonny," Paul replied.

Sonny said, "Thank you, sir. I'll let you get to work, booking that flight."

"I'll talk to you tomorrow. Maybe it will be a better day." Paul hung up the phone and started looking for a flight to DC.

CHAPTER 12

"But you are a shield around me, O LORD; you bestow glory on me and lift up my head. To the LORD I cry aloud, and he answers me from his holy hill. I lie down and sleep; I wake again, because the LORD sustains me. I will not fear the tens of thousands drawn up against me on every side."

Psalm 3:3–6

Matt answered his phone. It was Jack calling.

"I'm pulling in my driveway now," Jack said. "I'm going to get Tina and bring her over so you can show both of us how to work this thing. That's better than me trying to repeat your instructions."

"Good call," Matt said. "See you in a bit."

Jack knocked at the door, but Matt still went out the side as a precaution. It was overly precautious, but if ever there was a time to be on your toes, this was it.

"Is your front door opening properly?" Jack quizzed as he and Tina walked in.

"Yes, but the way the peephole is situated, I can't get a very good view of my surroundings before I open it. I feel better going out the side and having the gate as an extra obstacle," Matt explained.

"That's clever thinking. I guess I don't think like that. I probably need to start training myself to be more cautious, like you," Jack said.

Tina and Karen went to start some tea in the kitchen. They chatted about the events that were unfolding in the neighborhood and around the country.

"So, we have a gun now," Tina exclaimed. "I guess we're buying another one whenever the legal thing goes through. I don't like guns at all. They scare me, but I don't know what to think about what's happening. Don't guns scare you?"

Karen replied, "Not unless it's pointed at me. My gun actually makes me feel quite comforted, especially today."

"Have you shot it?" Tina asked.

Karen answered, "Yes, we go to the range once in a while, but the range is pretty strict. Matt's cousin has a farm in Kentucky. When we go there, we shoot a lot."

"So would you say you are good at it?" Tina asked with a hint of surprise.

"I can hit a soda can at twenty-five yards with a pistol. People are a lot bigger than soda cans. So, I guess I'm good enough," Karen said confidently.

They poured the tea and walked back in where the guys were.

Matt was checking out the shotgun as Jack looked over the

instructions.

"You paid more than you wanted, but you have the Cadillac of shotguns," Matt complimented. The Benelli Vinci had a camo finish with a tactical pistol grip full stock. This made it look that much more intimidating.

The girls sat down and Matt explained the basic operation of the gun. He had Jack pull the trigger on the empty chamber several times to feel where the slack ended on the trigger before it actually released the firing pin. He demonstrated the proper stance and went over basic safety rules, such as never, ever letting the barrel of a gun point at a person you don't intend to shoot. Jack picked it up pretty quickly.

Next, Matt started working with Tina. He had to remind her not to point it at people a few times as she kept inadvertently letting the muzzle sweep his stomach or leg. Finally, he got her to be somewhat comfortable with aiming the gun.

After the quick lesson, Matt brought out a box of steel buckshot shells. "Number-two shot is a good middle of the road shot. It's big enough to do some damage, but there are enough pellets in there to give you a decent pattern. If you shoot someone at close range in the house with these, they're going to be splattered all over the walls and floor."

Matt handed the box of shells to Tina.

"Is there anything that wouldn't be as messy?" Tina joked.

"I guess I aim for their head, right?" Jack quizzed.

Matt explained, "Typically, you want to aim for the center of gravity. Right in the middle of their body, because this space is loaded with vital organs. A close range blast with this gun will be a kill shot every time."

Matt began loading the weapon for them.

Tina asked, "Should we be keeping that loaded? Can't we wait until we need it to load it?"

"People are killing each other all over the country tonight, Tina. You need it now," Matt answered firmly.

She seemed to understand. "Thanks for the lesson," Tina said.

Jack said, "We'll let you guys get some sleep. Thanks for everything."

"One of us will be up all night to keep watch," Matt said. "I would recommend the two of you take turns staying awake and keeping watch. I'll check out the window every so often, but it's hard for me to know if something is going on over there."

"Thanks, I suppose we'll both be up all night," Jack said.

Matt and Karen walked the neighbors to the door.

After Jack and Tina were gone, Karen said, "I feel like they didn't completely get it."

"It'll take them a while to come around," Matt said. "Why don't you try to get some sleep for a while and I'll take the first shift. I'll wake you up at 6:00 am. Then, you can keep an eye out while I get some sleep."

"Okay," Karen said, "but I hope we don't have to do that for long. I hate when you aren't in the bed with me."

"If things don't calm down tomorrow, I'll try to get a block watch organized," Matt promised.

Karen went to sleep and Matt sat down in the quietness for a few minutes. His head was full of the turmoil of the day. He whispered a prayer to God. "Lord, our country has walked away from you. America has strayed so far away from your protection and your shelter. Please watch over Karen and me, God. The wolves are out tonight. Send your angels to watch over this property and to keep us safe. Hide us in the shelter of your wings. You always do. Thank you."

Matt didn't say, "Amen." He thought of it as a sort of signing-off with God. He didn't really have anything more to say, but he took comfort knowing the conversation line was still open.

After he had sat quietly for about an hour or so, he got up and began to gear up for his night watch. He picked up an extra magazine for his Glock and stuck it in his pocket. He also opened up the radio scanner app on his phone. He plugged the headphones in and stuck one side of the headphones in his ear. This would allow him to listen to what was coming over the police frequency and stay aware of the immediate surroundings. Matt took the walkie-talkies out of the safe as well. They weren't that expensive, he just thought if there were ever an EMP or coronal mass ejection, the walkies would be protected from the electronic pulse in the metal safe. He brought the charger base for the walkies into the bedroom and let Karen know that he was setting it up next to her. If he had to go outside and needed her to back him up, he would call her on the walkie. She nodded that she understood and slipped back to sleep.

Matt scratched through the closet to find a pair of cargo pants. With a full-size pistol, phone, walkie, flashlight and an extra magazine, he was gathering quite a collection to haul around. It would be nice to wear a holster and a magazine pouch on his belt, but he was trying to keep a low profile right now. He took out a pair of khaki cargo pants and changed into them. He put on his hiking boots and checked his pockets. "I don't have a knife," he whispered. "Why do I need a knife? I don't really. I'm watching for intruders, I'm not hiking." He always carried a knife and didn't feel complete if it wasn't there. "I guess it's a type of security blanket." He stuck a folding blade Gerber Kiowa in his pocket and started to make his first round.

The first thing Matt did was kill the inside lights. This allowed him to crack the Venetian shades just enough to see outside without allowing anyone to see back in. He took a close look down the street. He didn't see anything. He double checked the lock on the front door and walked to take a look out the kitchen window. Just then, he heard something around the side of the house. Adrenaline shot to his heart. He drew his gun and shut the earphone off from the radio scanner, which was playing on his phone. He checked to see that the walkie was on in case he had to call Karen. *Maybe I should wake her up first. No, I'll check it out. I'll let her sleep*, he thought.

Matt switched on the light mounted to the tactical rail on his Glock and stepped out the door. He scanned the yard with the light. Slowly, he stepped around the side to the laundry room door. He turned the knob and pulled it open. He stepped back as he did so to draw down on anyone that might be inside. No one was there. He closed the door and locked it. He stepped around to the bike racks and something shot out from the shrubs!

It happened so fast. Fortunately, it was only Buster, the cat from up the street. The cat frequented Matt and Karen's yard. Buster belonged to Chicken Elvis. The man's first name was really Elvis. They lived in a decent area, it wasn't a trashy neighborhood. There was no community association telling you what type of flowers to plant, but you wouldn't expect people to have chickens in this neighborhood. Chicken Elvis had chickens. He also had two roosters. Those roosters were up every morning at 4:30. The nickname Chicken Elvis was the way Matt and Karen differentiated him from the guy who owned the gun store where they shopped. Oddly enough, the gun store owner's name was also Elvis. As a form of soft retribution for the roosters waking him up from time to time, Matt referred to the man as Chicken Elvis to the neighbors, even though they required no distinguishing adjectives.

Matt thought about the cat running out from the bushes. What a start it gave his heart. *What if it had been an intruder? Would I have been able to take aim and shoot? Maybe I should check the corner from a greater distance.* He was overanalyzing the event. *Just keep your head and be alert. I'll also come up with a few things to make this fence harder to get over tomorrow morning,* he thought.

As Matt walked back around, he heard the exchange of gunfire in the distance. "Somebody found more than a tomcat," he whispered.

CHAPTER 13

"Are we at last brought to such a humiliating and debasing degradation, that we cannot be trusted with arms for our own defense?"

Patrick Henry

The day after the riots started, Matt's phone rang. It was his cousin Adam from Kentucky.

"How're y'all doing?" Adam asked with concern. "Is everything okay there?"

"We made it through the night without any incidents, but it sounded like a war zone outside most of the night. I was listening to the police scanner over the internet and it sounds like the good guys just barely held on. The criminal element thrives on this type of volatile environment," Matt answered.

"You guys should pack it up and head on up here," Adam said. "You can have the pull-out bed in the office for as long as you need it. We have plenty of storage space in the garage for all of your stuff. Rent a trailer, hitch it to your truck and come on up."

Matt replied, "Thanks for the offer, but I don't think the roads are all that safe right now. We'd have to come through Jacksonville and Atlanta to get there. There are large scale riots in both of those cities. It's worse than what we have here in South Florida. We're pretty well set to hunker down for a while."

"Did you hear about the bill Senator Dina Fitch is sponsoring?" Adam asked.

"Actually, I just woke up. We had to take shifts last night. Karen slept 'til 6:00 am, then she got up and stood guard while I went to sleep," Matt explained.

Adam continued, "Fitch is asking Congress to put a 'temporary' moratorium on all gun sales until the crisis is over."

"There's been a crisis of some type for the past year. If they pass this bill, they'll never lift it. There'll always be a crisis if the government needs there to be one," Matt said.

"I think that's the point," Adam said.

"How's your brother? Does he like teaching at Berea College?" Matt asked.

Adam answered, "He likes it alright. We'll see how long this lasts."

"Why do you say that?" Matt inquired.

"They're forbidden to date students. Wesley is twenty-five and most of his students are juniors, around twenty or twenty-one. Being off-limits makes him forbidden fruit. He gets a lot of notes," Adam explained with a laugh.

"He shot a big ol' buck yesterday," Adam continued. "We'll have plenty of meat all winter. We could live off of deer meat. People who don't like venison don't know how to cook it."

"That's great; what did he take it with?" Matt questioned.

".308" Adam replied.

"His .308 battle rifle? Is that legal?" Matt inquired.

"As long as it has a five-round magazine, it's legal," Adam said.

Matt asked, "How are you guys set for ammo? This gun bill will probably start a panic buy if it hasn't already. Outdoor World was completely out of every type of ammo last night. Empty shelves as far as the eye could see."

Adam said, "Between me and Wesley, we probably have over 5,000 rounds. Mostly .308, 5.56, .40 caliber, shotgun shells and .22 long rifle. I stocked up after it came back on the market from the last Fitch gun bill scare. If Al Mohammad is the number one firearms salesman in America, Fitch takes the gold medal for selling the most magazines and ammo. We should really send them a thank-you card for helping America get so prepared, if it all goes to the devil."

"What would we do without them?" Matt asked with as much sarcasm as he could stomach. "Did you guys get some extra dry goods?"

Adam answered, "Yep. I got beans, rice, sugar, coffee, flour and we also bought several country hams. We hung them in the cellar. You don't even need to refrigerate them. They have enough salt to last 'til Jesus comes back!"

"That might not be that far off," Matt added.

"I hope it isn't far off," Adam said. "The Marines made me as tough as a bag of nails, but I wish Mandy and Carissa didn't have to grow up in this kind of world."

Matt thought about the tragedy of the children who had to get by in the chaos going on around the world. It broke his heart.

"Those girls have a good family," Matt stated. "They're going to be just fine. I'm glad to hear you guys stocked up. Have you heard of any trouble around there?"

"No," Adam said. "Business as usual. There are quite a few people on food stamps. From what I hear, they were all well behaved. They went to the store and used up the credits they had on their cards. They'll go back when the cards get reloaded."

"So they believe they'll get the balance reloaded to their cards on the fifteenth?" Matt asked.

Adam answered, "I don't know, but if they would've acted a fool like they're doing in Detroit, they'd got shot. I suppose that's good motivation to behave."

"I guess Detroit and London, Kentucky, are two different worlds," Matt said. "I'll call in a few days to let you know how things are going around here. Take care."

"You too," Adam closed.

Karen stayed home from work. The public schools were closed due to the civil unrest. The sounds of gunshots and sirens died off during the early morning hours. They all but ceased by the time Matt went to bed at 6:00 am. It was just after 1:00 pm and he was still drinking his morning coffee. Karen was doing her normal routine. She finished a load of laundry and was checking her coupon sites for deals.

Matt said, "You know you're not going to be able to go to the store and use your coupons for a little while, baby."

"I know," she replied. "It helps me feel normal to keep up my routine. I can only watch the replayed footage from last night's riots for so long."

"Have there been any new developments this morning?" Matt

77

asked. He had not gotten around to the news yet.

Karen replied, "Things look terrible in Detroit. The military has blocked all the roads that lead in and out of Detroit. FEMA is there processing people who are asking to leave. They're taking people away on buses to a FEMA camp in Lansing, Michigan. It looks like a Nazi concentration camp. It's fenced in with ten-foot chain-link fences topped with razor wire. It even has guard towers."

"How horrible. Why would anyone elect to go there?" Matt asked.

Karen answered, "That's the only way they're allowed to leave Detroit. The government doesn't want refugees sprawling all over the country, especially trouble makers. They can't tell who is and who isn't going to be a trouble maker."

Matt said, "I suppose we've been heading in this direction for a while. Our phones have been tapped for years by the NSA, our gun rights have been assaulted at every turn, and we're treated like criminals every time we travel. It's just the natural progression of things. Once a tyrannical government starts to taste power, it's like a drug addict that can't get enough. Very few people have said anything about the destruction of the Constitution all these years. It'll soon be too late to say anything.

"I'm going over to Jack's to see if we can get a block watch started tonight. If we can get a few people involved, we won't have to stay up all night."

Matt knocked on Jack's door. Tina answered and let him in. Jack was watching the news as was most of America. Not since the days following the 9/11 events had so many people been glued to their televisions.

"Did you get any sleep last night, buddy?" Jack asked.

"I slept a few hours," Matt said. "How about you?"

"We both sat up till about four o'clock, then we fell asleep on the couch watching the news," Jack responded.

Matt thought about how vulnerable they were during the worst part of the night. He remembered some of the calls that were coming across the scanner last night at about that time. He thought, *Ignorance is bliss...at least until it is unfathomable horror.* Matt didn't say anything about it. He had made his recommendations. Jack and Tina were old enough to make their own decisions.

"How do you feel about setting up a block watch tonight? I was thinking dusk 'til dawn," Matt said.

Jack said, "The worst seems to be over. I hope things will be getting back to normal."

"Let me know if you change your mind." Matt let himself out the door. He wasn't going to get anywhere, so he went to Blaine's house across the street. Maybe Blaine would be a bit more receptive to the idea.

Blaine and his wife Annie came to the door. They discussed the events in Detroit as well as what had been going on in the surrounding areas. They considered the block watch but, like Jack, hoped that the worse was behind them.

On his way home, Matt saw Trevor Smith who lived directly behind him. He was at the end of the street talking to Chicken Elvis. Trevor normally had little to say to Chicken Elvis, but times like these brought people together. Matt walked over and joined the conversation.

Trevor said, "I think this might be the end of the world as we know it." While not quite a prepper, Trevor was fairly well tuned in politically.

Trevor continued, "I have no love for the Democrats nor the Republicans. They both played their part in creating this mess. I've been watching the demise of the dollar for decades, and I was expecting some type of event like this a long time ago."

Trevor was a landscaper. He maintained a very nice garden as well as a variety of fruit trees. Matt figured the reason he was talking to Elvis was most likely to establish communications for future trade involving some chickens. If it had just hit the fan, Chicken Elvis was going to be a popular guy.

Matt asked, "How would you two feel about putting together a block watch?"

Trevor and Elvis both acknowledged that it was a good idea. Since it was only the three of them, they set up a triangular perimeter that included their three homes. They decided to split the evening into thirds. Each guy would pull four hours outside patrol and four hours inside on call, in case the outside guy needed backup. The on-patrol and on-call guys would use Matt's walkies. Each of them would get four hours to sleep during the night. They agreed on that plan for the night and would evaluate the schedule as needed.

Matt headed home. He took some old boards and ran three-inch wood screws in various places all along the boards. He laid them, screws facing up, along the perimeter of his backyard fence. Anyone jumping his fence would have a rough landing. He ran a few long screws facing both directions on the tops of the wood plank privacy fence. Anyone who was stupid enough to try to navigate between the screws sticking out on the outside of the fence was likely to get caught on the screws facing inside.

Matt continued to think of ways to harden his property without marking it as overly prepared. He put two metal hurricane shutters on the inside of each of the windows facing the street. He positioned them to the sides of each window leaving the middle of the window exposed. This left enough space to see out of, or if necessary, to shoot out of. The thick metal shutters offered a much higher level of protection than just the glass.

Lastly, he parked the car catty-corner in the yard. This created a fallback position if there was trouble from 9th Avenue. Matt Bair's property was near the end of Oak Street, where it terminated on 9th Avenue. 9th Avenue was a neighborhood access street. It was not a main artery; however, it did get a significant amount of traffic. There was a much higher probability of trouble approaching from that direction than any other.

Having worked off some of his nervous energy, Matt washed up and prepared a nice lunch of pasta and salad for his wife and himself. Karen cleaned up the dishes, and Matt sat down to watch the news until his shift for block watch came up.

CHAPTER 14

"The battle, sir, is not to the strong alone; it is to the vigilant, the active, the brave."

Patrick Henry

"The emergency session just ended," Paul Randall told Sonny Foster over the phone. "I'll be staying in DC tonight. I have a lot of work to do. The Senate passed both of Fitch's bills. The gun-sales freeze they labeled the Right to Security Bill. The authorization for the military to assist the National Guard and local police is called the Liberty Bill. The en vogue thing to do on Capitol Hill is to try to label bills exactly the opposite of what they do."

"Oh yeah, kind of like the Patriot Act was the most unpatriotic piece of legislation ever passed. And the Affordable Health Care Act made health insurance prohibitively expensive for millions," Sonny said.

"Exactly," Paul replied. "I'm going to try to get some support in the House to reject the bills."

Sonny inquired, "The House won't pass the freeze, will they?

Even the neocons respect the Second Amendment. Any Republican who votes for that will get killed by the NRA in the next election."

Paul answered, "Republicans only hold the House by seven votes. If four Republican congressmen sway on this, it will pass. I know Marcos will cave on it. He's based his whole campaign on the middle ground. I'm sure he'll vote for the freeze. That means if three more cave, it passes. Forget about the military-powers bill—it will pass with flying colors. President Al Mohammad will be waiting at the back door to sign it into law. How's everything back home?"

Sonny replied, "Anthony Howe is getting destroyed in the polls. You're up six points. It seems people think you saw this mess coming and your prediction of failure is coming true. Even though many don't want to subscribe to the pain involved in your plan, they'd rather have someone who knows what's going on at the wheel."

Paul said, "I wish I were wrong, but I think this is just the beginning—the first big crack in the facade. It's too late to save the system now. I just feel like we could do a better job of managing the collapse. Perhaps we could save some lives if we had the opportunity. There will be no glory to the next president. Whoever wins will be blamed for the collapse. In many ways, I dread winning; I'm truly in this because I feel it is my duty."

Sonny added, "If they would've promoted a new captain on the Titanic after it hit the iceberg, it would've still sunk. I suppose we're just trying to get everyone to the lifeboats."

Paul Randall ended his conversation with Sonny and headed to a nearby deli called Capitol Dill for a quick sandwich. Due to its close proximity to the Capitol building, it was a regular lunch meeting place for senators and their staff. Paul grabbed a seat at the counter to blend in with the crowd. He had been around these people enough and needed a break before he spent the next few hours trying to convince members of the House to defend the Constitution.

"Paul," someone called from behind.

Not recognizing the voice, Randall winced. He knew his moment of solitude was to be cut short. As he turned around, he was pleasantly surprised to find that the voice belonged to his friend, General Allen Jefferson. General Jefferson was the Commanding General, US Army Forces Command, or CG FORSCOM for short.

Sonny had tried to get Jefferson to run as Randall's VP to attract the black vote. Regardless of the general's race, Sonny genuinely respected the man. But Sonny looked at everything in the light of political capital, even skin color. It was his job. Despite what their mouths may say, the American public proved skin color mattered to them through their votes. The general was too dedicated to his duty in the Pentagon for such a frivolous pursuit as vice president.

"How are you, General?" Paul stood to shake Jefferson's hand.

"Better now that I ran into you," Jefferson said with a grin. "I'm heading back over to the Pentagon to start working out the logistics of this foolish Liberty Bill. I've been advising against it all day. I spoke with the Senate Armed Services Committee, then I spoke with the Senate Homeland Security and Government Affairs Committee. In two hours, I have to give my opinion to the House Committee on Homeland Security. None of them listen. They ask questions to try to get me to stamp their card. Each side is trying to get me to prove their points to the other side. It's such a horrible bill. It goes right up to the limit of suspending Posse Comitatus. I feel sorry for the American people, but these are the fools they sent up here. It's very frustrating, Paul."

Paul Randall replied, "I've done everything I know to wake people up. They seem to not care. I don't know when they'll start caring. I don't know when they'll open their eyes and start thinking for themselves."

The General said, "There's a lot of hostility from the ranks on this one. I have several high level officers that are going AWOL if the military is ordered to assist in the efforts to enforce a blockade around Detroit. Many others have simply stated that they'll refuse any orders that are unconstitutional."

"Does the term 'unconstitutional' have any common understanding among them?" Paul inquired.

The general informed him, "There's an organization known as Oath Keepers. Their primary purpose is to unify the patriots among the ranks of the military as well as law enforcement officers. Members specifically pledge to disobey orders to enforce martial law or to blockade a city, such as what is being done to Detroit as we speak. There are several other orders that they have taken an oath not to follow, including confiscating food or provisions, detaining or disarming the American people, or assisting foreign troops on American soil. This movement has spread like wildfire over the past few years. We are talking about twenty or thirty percent of the entire military has taken this oath. The percentage is even higher among the older officers. Many of them have even put the Oath Keepers patch on their uniform. "

"What is your opinion of them, General?" Paul inquired.

"I may not wear the patch, Paul, but I have taken their oath." Jefferson replied in such a tone of conviction that it sent chills up Paul Randall's neck.

"God bless you, Allen Jefferson," Paul said. "You are a patriot in a manner that gives definition to the very term."

The two men finished their lunch and returned to their respective tasks. Each of them was encouraged by the other. They worked in a town where their views were considered radical and unwelcomed. It was as refreshing as a drink of cool water in the desert to be around another patriot after being submerged in a sea of ignorance, day in and day out.

CHAPTER 15

"By removing the Bible from schools, we would be wasting so much time and money in punishing criminals and so little pains to prevent crime. Take the Bible out of our schools and there would be an explosion in crime."

Benjamin Rush, signer of the Declaration of Independence

Karen came to sit down by Matt. "If things settle down this weekend, do you think they'll reopen the schools on Monday?" Karen asked.

Matt responded, "I don't know. I don't know what the world will look like Monday. Even if they do, it doesn't mean you'll be going back. If things stay volatile, you can't go back to work until they settle down."

"I can't sit in the house all the time. I have to get out and move around," Karen countered.

Matt said, "Go sit at the neighbors or find a hobby. You have to be safe. That school wasn't a good place even in the best of times. Most of those kids have no sense of right and wrong. They've just witnessed the world starting to crumble. They won't be safe to be around when things start to come unglued.

"It absolutely breaks my heart, but a lot of those kids are beyond helping until they realize they need help and ask for it. The schools have taught them that there is no such thing as God. Schools have used the myth of evolution to tell these kids that they just happened. They believe there's no plan and there's no purpose for them to be here. They've been taught that they evolved from an animal, so why wouldn't we expect them to act like animals? A large majority of the kids in your school are treated like animals by their mothers. The reason they had children in the first place was to milk the welfare system. They get SNAP benefits, housing, an Al Mohammad phone, Al Mohammad care, help from the utility companies, and everything they need to live a life of leisure by having four kids. These welfare queens have zero expenses and they get a tax credit for each kid. Every year the free-money tax credit goes up. It's currently around $4200 for each kid. They can get a credit for up to four kids. That comes to $16,800 a year. That's tax-free money that could go straight in the bank. Most of them choose to blow it on flat screens, purses and nights out on the town. All of their day-to-day expenses have been taken care of. You never see a welfare mom with five kids. The benefits caps out at four. Many of those moms see their kids as cattle, reinforcing the idea to the children that they're nothing more than animals.

"The federal government has effectively subsidized irresponsible pregnancies. Any time a government subsidizes something, you get more of it. It's a basic economic principle. If they subsidize corn, the economic benefits encourage farmers to grow more corn. Washington has subsidized bad behavior. The economic benefits encourages more bad behavior, and now our society is suffocating under the weight of it.

"We have an entire class of people who are second and third

generation welfare dependents with no moral compass. They offer nothing to society in return for what they take. In fact, each mother offers a negative return by creating an average of two more welfare mothers and an average of two more sperm donors to inseminate the next generation of mothers. The new welfare mothers perpetuate the problem and the sperm donors fill up the prisons."

Karen added, "It costs a lot of money to create that problem. Simply by not spending the money and not giving the tax credit, many of them would've never had children they couldn't afford. Even if the government capped benefits at one child, being a welfare queen would never be lucrative enough for people to make a living out of it."

Matt said, "Well, those chickens may be coming home to roost. I think the nanny state has just about tapped out on funds to support this nonsense. The horrible thing is that the people who have bought into it for generations are the ones who will be most hurt by it."

Matt's patrol didn't start until 10:00 pm. After his shift, he was the backup guy for the 2:00 am to 6:00 am shift. It was just after 7:00 pm and the sounds of sirens were already starting to become more prevalent. Distant gunfire was getting more frequent. Shortly after 8:00 pm, a loud succession of gunfire rang out from just a few streets over. It lasted for several minutes and it was obvious that it had involved several shooters.

"That sounded like it was close by," Karen said.

Matt responded, "I think it was about two streets over. Try to stay away from the windows. Even with the hurricane shutters covering most of the windows, a stray bullet could still slide in. You should keep your Glock on you at all times. Wear it in your holster if that's more comfortable."

Shortly after the intense gunfire, there was a knock at the front door. Matt and Karen knew the night protocol by now. Karen went to the hallway and stood with her gun trained on the front door while Matt came out the side door to confirm who it was. He kept his gun in his right hand, hidden inside the doorway.

Matt called out to let Karen know who it was. "It's Blaine, but better safe than sorry." Matt walked to the front door and let their neighbor in. Matt locked the door behind Blaine once he was inside.

Blaine looked serious. "I spoke with Jack a few minutes ago; we decided we probably should have a block watch. It sounded like World War III over there."

Matt replied, "I've already set up a watch with Trevor and Chicken Elvis. I'm sure they'll be fine with expanding the watch zone since we'll get more guys to patrol. Why don't you and Jack go door-to-door and see who else you can recruit from our street. I'll start thinking up another patrol zone to present to Trevor and Elvis. Do you have your pistol on you?"

"It's in the house," Blaine answered.

"Get it first, then go recruiting," Matt said with a hint of authority. He had no desire to be bossy, but he was somewhat annoyed to be redrawing the battle plans at the eleventh hour.

"Okay," Blaine responded. "I'll be back in a few." Blaine took the command with a good attitude.

Matt spoke with Trevor and Elvis.

Trevor said, "That's great! The more people we have to work into the rotation, the better show of force we'll have."

Soon, they had nine men from the neighborhood standing at the point position in front of Elvis's yard which was closest to 9th Avenue. It was decided that since Elvis and Trevor had already been watching, one on guard and the other on backup, they would finish their shift at 12:00 pm.

Matt explained the schedule to the new recruits. "Starting tomorrow, we'll have four guys from 6:00 pm to 12:00 am. We'll have five guys from 12:00 am to 6:00 am since that tends to be the most active part of the night."

Matt and Jack took the intersection of 9th Avenue and Oak. Blaine and another man from the block, Arthur Pendleton, took the other end of the street. The fifth man, Dan Cleveland, was the runner. He was stationed with Matt and Jack, but would be responsible for giving breaks or waking the other off-duty men in case of an event. Matt parked his truck perpendicular to the road. He would have to move it in order for anyone to gain access to the street.

The sirens were constant for most of the night.

Jack commented, "I can smell fire, but I can't see any smoke to say for certain where the fire is coming from."

The men kept the walkie-talkies with them, but tried to avoid using them as much as possible. To request Dan to come and give a break, the men at the other end of the street texted the front station. Phones were working about eighty percent of the time. The other times, an all-circuits-are-busy message would come up. Text messages ran slow, but if you sent one, it went through within five minutes.

The beginning of Matt's shift passed without incident. Their first sign of action was a visit from the police. A patrol car pulled up to the checkpoint and the officer inside asked, "Why is the truck in the road?"

Patrol cars had been whizzing by all night, but they all had somewhere else to be.

Matt replied, "We all live here and we're trying to maintain a perimeter around our homes."

"Do you fellas have identification?" the officer asked.

Matt, Jack and Dan produced their IDs to show they were the residents of the street. The officer verified the addresses and handed the IDs back to the men.

"Are you fellas armed?" the officer asked.

Matt answered, "Yes." He began to pull his concealed-carry permit from his wallet that was already in his hand.

The officer never asked for the permit. He simply said, "Good, carry on," and pulled away.

Around 3:00 am, four rough looking young men approached on foot. They were walking up 9th Avenue and headed toward the checkpoint. Matt walked out with a smile and asked, "Can I help you, gentlemen?"

The one who looked like the leader said, "I don't know, can you help me?"

Matt dispensed with the pleasantries. He slid his hand to his back and let it rest on the grip of the pistol. Jack had his new shotgun laid across the seats of Matt's truck. He was already in position and placed his hand on the stock.

"You guys need to keep moving while you still can," Matt said.

The leader said, "We need to get through here. We goin' to see my cousin."

"What's your cousin's name?" Jack inquired from behind the truck door.

The men decided to end the conversation and tried walking past Matt and Jack. Matt and Jack produced their guns as Dan walked up behind them with his revolver already leveled at the leader's head.

"Moving any further in our direction will be considered an act of aggression, and we will kill you!" Matt shouted.

The three other men were already moving out of range by the time the leader looked behind him to see what they were going to do.

"I'll catch you later, homeboy," the thug mouthed off as he retreated.

The following night, the patrols went without incident. Several more bands of rough looking individuals passed by on foot and in cars, but they decided against a confrontation with the neighborhood patrols.

The news reported that most of the riots were dying down. Detroit was still under siege and fires roared through the city unchecked. The majority of the Detroit firemen had left the city. There was little they could have done. Several fire stations, themselves, were burned out inside.

Los Angeles and Atlanta were the other two holdouts. Police were still putting up a good fight in those cities, but only because the riots would calm in the daylight hours. This respite gave the police an opportunity to regroup and reorganize for the following night.

CHAPTER 16

"But a Constitution of Government once changed from Freedom, can never be restored. Liberty, once lost, is lost forever."

John Adams

Kimberly Randall opened the door to let Sonny Foster in the Randall's Texas farmhouse. His BMW looked a bit out of place sitting out front with all the trucks and SUVs. He came in and exchanged pleasantries with Mrs. Randall. She was always kind to Sonny when he stopped by the house.

Kimberly said, "Sonny, sit down and eat something. Let me make you a ham sandwich."

Sonny always looked a bit frail. "Thank you, Kimberly," he said.

The Randalls had a maid that came twice a week, but Kimberly insisted on doing most of her own housekeeping. She loved to cook. On occasion, when they entertained, she would hire a kitchen assistant and servers, but she handled the menu and most of the preparations herself. Kimberly was the former Miss Texas. She had aged very gracefully and still looked stunning.

"Sonny, are you stealing him away already? He just got home from DC" Kimberly said with a playful smile. She was being nice about it, but she really did have to fight resenting Sonny for the time he spent with her husband. She knew it was not his fault, but who could she blame for all the lonely times since the campaign started?

"I'm afraid so, Mrs. Randall," Sonny replied, "but your country appreciates your sacrifice."

"I hope so," she replied. Normally she would have laughed off such a comment, but she was really starting to feel the pain of being separated from Paul so much over the past months.

Paul Randall walked into the huge kitchen where they were.

"Sir, you're continuing to gain favor in the polls," Sonny said.

Paul said, "That's good, Sonny."

Paul made himself a sandwich and sat down to have a snack with Sonny. "Honestly, I'm getting tired of polls and the tiresome labor of politicking. I also feel guilty for the amount of time I'm spending away from home. It'll all be over soon. By the way, the House passed the Liberty Bill."

"Isn't that the bill to use the military to enforce martial law, or something to that effect?" Sonny asked for clarification. "Didn't General Jefferson say he expected that bill to cause chaos if it were signed into law?"

"He did say that," Paul said. "Al Mohammad signed it this morning, but the majority of the riots are dying down."

Kimberly jumped into the conversation. "So, why did he sign it if they don't need it?"

Paul loved her because she hadn't been totally corrupted by politics. She still had a certain pure, childlike quality to her.

Paul explained, "Once they get a new dose of power, they don't give it up. Even if it's not advantageous to use it now, they can keep it in their back pocket and use it at a more opportune time."

"What about the gun sales moratorium?" Sonny asked.

Paul replied, "Even the neocons know what side their bread is buttered on. The House Republicans did shoot that down. Of course, if it hadn't been for the pressure of the NRA, Juan Marcos would have talked them into passing that as well. Let's hear what you have to tell me about those polls."

Sonny reverted back to explaining the polls data. "You're now only trailing Howe by three points. That's a huge increase. You were seventeen points behind before the riots."

"What about Juan Marcos? Did he get a bump from the riots?" Paul asked.

"Yes, but not as much as you. He's still five points behind you. He was three points behind you before the riots," Sonny explained.

"So it's still any man's race," Paul said as he looked out at the cattle in the field.

"Yes, sir, it is any man's race," Sonny replied.

CHAPTER 17

"Were we directed from Washington when to sow and when to reap, we should soon want bread."

Thomas Jefferson

Matt was glad the schools were closed. This meant he didn't have to have a heated conversation about Karen not going in. She always went along with his recommendation on weightier subjects like this, but not without a serious discussion.

Even though things settled down, the schools were not yet reopened. Most of the schools had severe damage ranging from broken windows and stolen computers to burned out classrooms and missing air conditioning compressors.

Karen occupied herself in the garden while she was home from work. She began to meticulously weed the garden and even the shrubs in the front yard. She soon ran out of weeds and started some new tomato seedlings and bell peppers. Both took a while to get started. Hopefully, the new seedlings would be able to take over when the current plants petered out. She also started another several rows of green beans and mixed salad greens. These grew very well at this time of the year in Florida.

Many of the grocery stores that had been looted were still closed. The National Guard was bringing in some meals-ready-to-eat or MREs for short, but they were far less than what was needed and the lines were horrendous.

Matt and Karen were very well set for food. The fridge was still packed. The only thing they ran out of was milk, but they had some condensed milk and powdered milk, which was just fine for cereal.

Fortunately, no one lost power throughout the riots except for Detroit. The fires took out several electrical reducing facilities. Large swathes of the grid had to be shut down to keep the lines from becoming hazardous. Many of the utility poles actually burned down and left exposed power lines lying in the molten insulation.

The nightly gunfire and sirens died down gradually over the next few nights, so Matt and the others cut the neighborhood watch to 10:00 pm until 5:00 am. This allowed the block watch to run with one shift per night, and the watchmen to alternate nights off.

Matt was making a large pot of rice and a large pot of beans. He knew everyone on the block was not as well stocked up as he and Karen. He planned to take some of the rice and beans around to those who were getting a little tight on food.

Karen came in from the garden with a large plastic bowl filled with peppers, tomatoes and lettuce. "This will make a nice salad," she said. "Are you making those pans up for the neighbors?"

"Yes," Matt replied. "Blaine went over to St. Mark's and stood in line for five hours this morning to get four MREs from the National Guard. He must be getting pretty low on food to go through that much trouble."

"I thought Blaine said they were pretty well set on food," Karen said, somewhat surprised.

"They eat out all the time under normal circumstances. They have no idea how long a can of Spaghetti Os will last them. In their mind, two plastic bags of groceries from Publix will last a month. In reality, it will last about two or three days for two people, depending on what's in the bags, of course. Let's play a guessing game." Matt knew that she loved guessing games. It was something of a sport to her.

"Okay," Karen said.

"You know the five-gallon bucket filled with bags of dried beans and rice that I just opened? How long would that last you and me if that was all we had to eat?" Matt quizzed.

"Can I look in the bucket?" Karen tried to get as much information as possible before she made her guess.

"Go ahead," Matt agreed.

She counted out the contents as she rifled through the bucket. "We have four bags of black beans, three bags of red beans, two bags of chickpeas and two bags of black-eyed peas. And we have one 20-pound bag of white rice. I guess all of that would last the two of us about two to three weeks."

"Ten days," Matt replied, "but that was pretty close. You could stretch it to two weeks if we really reduced our calorie intake. The point is, it looks like a lot more than it is. Most people eyeball their food stockpile. I used relatively loose estimations, but I actually calculated the amount of calories that we needed to come up with how long we could last on what we had stored."

"What are you making for the neighbors?" Karen inquired.

Matt answered, "I'm going to open a couple cans of that chicken we bought and mix it in with the rice and black beans. I put a little blackened seasoning in it. It's not gourmet, but it will be better than an MRE. I'm also going to take the opportunity to talk about storing food. I don't want to just 'give a man a fish,' I'd like to give them some pointers on getting more prepared when things get back to normal."

"So, you think things will get back to normal?" Karen asked.

"Well, 'normal' may a bit of a stretch. It doesn't look like these food riots are going to trigger the end of the civilized world. I think we'll have grocery stores back up and running. I think I'll be able to start selling used furniture on Craigslist again. I couldn't say if we'll be able to go back to our regular jobs. The schools weren't safe before the riots and the stock market is probably not coming back, at least for a while. Wall Street opened for the first time since the riots this morning for two hours. The Dow actually opened up fifty points. An hour and a half later, it plunged 890 points. The SEC closed the markets to stop the free-fall. ZeroHedge.com says they don't expect the markets to reopen 'til after the election.

"I expect that this was the first crack in the veneer, and I would guess that the veneer is pretty thin. I don't know how long it'll be, but we'll probably see more events similar to this one, and I think they'll grow in intensity."

Matt and Karen sat down to eat their salad and a small plate of the blackened canned chicken with some of the beans and rice he had prepared. After they finished, Matt grabbed one of the aluminum pans containing the chicken and rice, then headed over to Jack and Tina's. He didn't spend much time there as he had several more stops to make. He was able to make a dish to take to all of the folks involved in the block watch. Everyone was very appreciative of the food and they all vowed to get on a food storage plan when the stores reopened.

CHAPTER 18

"The race is not to the swift or the battle to the strong, nor does food come to the wise or wealth to the brilliant or favor to the learned; but time and chance happen to them all."

Ecclesiastes 9:11

Election Day

One week had passed since the riots and things were starting to quiet down around Matt and Karen Bair's neighborhood. The block watch was terminated Sunday night. Sirens and gunshots faded to normal levels and people were getting back into the routine of things.

About half of the grocery stores in their immediate area reopened. The shelves were very sparsely stocked. The stores stocked most food items, but the selection of different sizes and brands were small. The store shelves didn't look like they belonged in a typical American grocery store. The top shelves and lowest shelves were completely bare. Grocers stocked all the goods at the center shelves to give the appearance of a full store. Many items were stocked only two or three deep to fill up empty space. The meat coolers held very low stocks. When a truck made a delivery of meat, it would sell out fast. The cheaper cuts of meat went first and the more expensive cuts lingered less than four or five hours from the time they arrived in the store. Chicken was also a prized commodity and didn't stay stocked long. Cheese and milk lasted a little while longer than the meats, but they were always out of stock by the end of the evening as well.

Then there were the lines. The stores were short staffed. Many people had not yet returned to work after the riots. A "Now Hiring" sign was in the front window. Matt grabbed an application while Karen waited in the line. They didn't have to be at the store, but they wanted to pick up some fresh milk, eggs and cheese. They went early in the morning and had no problem obtaining the things on their list.

"You're not going to work at Publix, are you?" Karen asked.

Matt answered, "I think I should probably take what I can find. I can probably get deals on things they're going to throw out like day-old bread. It'll also give me an opportunity to watch for signs of shortages. We don't need the money now, but if things don't return to normal, our savings will get depleted fast. If I'm right, things are really going to deteriorate and we'll be thankful for every dime we have."

They took their groceries home and headed for the polls. They each cast their ballot for Paul Randall. Now, there was nothing left to do but wait. They tried to explain the need for Randall's plan to the neighbors and actually convinced Jack and Tina to vote for Randall. Blaine voted for Anthony Howe. He was a dyed-in-the-wool liberal. Even though he believed in having guns, he toed the party line on all other subjects.

Matt and Karen invited Jack and Tina to come over to watch the poll results come in, but they declined. They voted, but they still weren't that into politics. It would've been torture for Jack and Tina to watch the election coverage.

Matt and Karen made some finger foods for themselves to eat while they watched the results. They ate celery sticks, chicken wings and spinach dip. Miss Mae, their cat, jumped up on the couch beside Matt. She also seemed to take interest in the election...or the chicken wings.

CNC's *DC Live* was running nonstop since 4:00 pm. Ed Nolan was full of energy. He lived for election night. The excitement of the polls sent adrenaline through his veins. Election results would be pouring in until the early morning hours of the next day, and Ed Nolan would be there for the whole thing.

The commercial ended and Ed Nolan announced "It's 7:00 pm Eastern Time and that means *DC Live* will soon be getting poll results on the most historical presidential election ever. This year, we have three contenders for the oval office. We've had third party candidates in the past, but none that have caused such havoc to the two-party system as independent candidate Paul Randall. This evening promises to be eventful, so stay with us throughout the night as we bring you the most accurate results first.

"You can see the numbers coming in county by county for the states whose polls have just closed. CNC is predicting that Paul Randall will take the eight electoral votes from South Carolina. We're also calling Vermont as we expect it to go to Anthony Howe. Virginia is very close and it may be some time before we're able to project a winner for that state. CNC is also able to project that Georgia will go to Paul Randall. The current total vote for the Electoral College is Anthony Howe with three and Paul Randall at twenty-four."

"Yee-haw!" Karen exclaimed.

"It's way too early to get excited, baby," Matt said with a somber tone.

"You have to be positive; that's a good start," Karen said. "We haven't had much to get excited about lately, so let me enjoy myself."

"I don't want you to get disappointed," Matt replied with a smile. Karen's optimism was a little infectious. He knew he should sit back and enjoy the show. Matt grabbed a chicken wing and cheered with Karen as CNC projected that Paul Randall would also take Kentucky and Indiana.

Back in Texas, the crowd was jubilant at Paul Randall's headquarters. The CNC coverage was being played on huge screens, there were balloons being tossed in the air and red, white and blue streamers draped every inch of the hall. The crowd became very quiet as the projections for North Carolina and West Virginia were both given to Paul Randall. The totals came up on the screen and the enthusiastic crowd went wild. The totals were Howe with three votes, Marcos with no votes, and Randall had sixty-three.

Paul Randall knew it was going to be a long night, but he couldn't help but be encouraged by the totals showing on the screen. Sonny didn't look as excited as the rest of the crowd. He had been studying the polls for months now.

Very gently, he reminded Paul Randall, "These are the easy ones, sir. There will be 172 electoral votes up for grabs in the polls that close at eight o'clock."

CNC correspondent Amy Stein was at the Governor's Mansion in Albany, New York. She had befriended Anthony Howe's wife, Jenna. They met at several fundraisers and events throughout the campaign. The banquet hall in the mansion was absolutely regal. It had patterned hardwood floors and each wall was flanked by a tremendous fireplace and columns that stretched to the top of the twenty-five foot ceiling. A grand staircase with marble spires poured into the room like a river. Tables were set up, but most people mingled around the front where the giant screen was setup.

Amy began her coverage. "The mood is very vibrant here at the Governor's Mansion. The champagne is flowing in anticipation of tonight's victory. CNC will be getting the results of the polls as they close tonight at eight o'clock. Anthony Howe expects to make up a lot of ground over the next hour."

Shortly after 8:00, the results began to roll in. CNC projected Connecticut, Delaware, Illinois, Maine, Massachusetts, New Jersey, Pennsylvania, Rhode Island, and the District of Colombia to go to Anthony Howe. Juan Marcos took his first state, Alabama. Paul Randall took Tennessee and Oklahoma. Florida, as usual, would be a close call. It could be hours before a projection could be made for the battleground swing state.

Meanwhile at Randall headquarters, Paul Randall saw what Sonny was talking about when the totals appeared on the sign. Howe quickly pulled into the lead with 100 electoral votes. Randall trailed with eighty-one and Marcos had nine. The night was young, but this was a very bad start for California Congressman, Juan Marcos.

At 9:00 pm Eastern Standard Time, another huge block of results began to trickle into the news desk. *DC Live* host, Ed Nolan knew the projection would most likely be made after these votes were tallied. Seven more states were projected to go to Paul Randall, including his home state of Texas, which carried thirty-eight votes alone. Anthony Howe picked up his home state of New York as well as three others. Enough data had come in from Ohio and Florida to predict they would go to Marcos, along with Arizona, Louisiana and Wisconsin.

Ed Nolan announced the latest data. "Folks, what we're seeing is the nightmare scenario that the pundits have been talking about for weeks. At this point, Paul Randall has 150 electoral votes. Anthony Howe stands in the lead with 162 votes. Juan Marcos only has eighty-five votes at the moment but every CNC poll is predicting that he will easily take his home state of California. It's just before ten o'clock here in the East and California's polls won't close for another hour. If, at that time, Marcos does take those votes, he will add the fifty-five votes from California to the eighty-five he now holds. That will give him 140 votes. That is a total of 452 votes taken. That only leaves eighty-six votes outstanding in the Electoral College. Those eighty-six votes cannot get any candidate to the required 270 votes in order to win the presidential election through the Electoral College."

In the Bair's living room, Karen looked at Matt with a look of surprise. "So, no one is going to win?"

"According to the Twelfth Amendment, it will have to be decided by the House of Representatives," Matt said plainly. "Several states have laws forbidding their electorates to vote for anyone other than the candidate who takes the most votes in the state. It would be impossible for the Electoral College to decide the vote because of those laws."

"Who will they pick?" Karen demanded.

Matt answered, "The Republicans have the majority in the House. I don't know. They may decide for whoever wins the popular vote. That would probably be the equitable thing to do. Of course, even if Howe wins the electoral vote, none of the Republicans would ever be reelected if they put him in office. I would guess they'll go with either Paul Randall or Juan Marcos. Marcos is the Republican candidate, but many of the Republicans openly supported Randall all the way through the campaign. I don't know. I suppose we'll be up for a while seeing who wins the popular vote. The House won't be meeting tonight. We probably won't know anything until at least tomorrow."

The rest of the night had a different feel. In the newsroom at CNC, at the Governor's Mansion, at Randall's headquarters, and in the Bair's living room, everyone had a sense of a long battle to come. After so many months of campaigns, America wanted closure on this night, but there would be none.

Juan Marcos did, indeed, go on to win his home state. His final tally was 160 votes. Anthony Howe ended the night with 185 votes. Paul Randall won the popular vote and also took the highest amount of electoral votes. He had 193 electoral votes when all the polls reported.

Back in Texas, Sonny approached Paul Randall. "I just spoke with the Howe and the Marcos camps. Neither is willing to issue a concession speech at this time."

"I expected that," Paul replied.

"You won the popular vote, sir. Congratulations," Sonny said.

"Thank you, Sonny. You worked very hard to make that happen. Congratulations to you as well. You know I want you on my staff if everything works out. Let me rephrase that—I need you on my staff if everything works out," Paul replied.

"Thank you, sir. It's always my pleasure," Sonny said with a smile.

Kimberly Randall hugged her husband, while their twin teenage boys, Robert and Ryan, surrounded them with more hugs. Kimberly also grabbed Sonny and pulled him into the group hug. Sonny was too busy for a family, so she did everything she could to make him feel like a part of theirs.

Everyone congratulated Randall on the win. They tried to be sincere, but everyone knew the next day or so would show if Congress would confirm or deny the will of the people.

CHAPTER 19

"In circumstances dark as these, it becomes us, as Men and Christians, to reflect that, whilst every prudent Measure should be taken to ward off the impending Judgments....All confidence must be withheld from the Means we use; and reposed only on that GOD who rules in the Armies of Heaven, and without whose Blessing the best human Counsels are but Foolishness—and all created Power Vanity;"

John Hancock

On Wednesday morning, the US House of Representatives convened at 11:00 am. The democrats were rested and somber. It was easy to see who belonged to which party. The Republicans looked like a lot of stockbrokers who had just come in from an all-night bender. They were disheveled and most had razor stubble. None of them had been to sleep yet. They spent the entire night in complete gridlock over who to elect. Roughly half supported Paul Randall, and the others were determined to vote for Juan Marcos. CSPAN owned exclusive coverage rights to the vote, but it was streamed to all the major networks.

It had been a while since all 435 members met together. This was the big one. No one was absent on this occasion. There were 221 Republicans and 214 Democrats. The consensus on the morning news coverage was that whoever was to be selected, it would not be Howe.

The process granted exactly one vote per state. Each representative would cast their vote for their state. The votes of each representative would be tallied for that state and the single vote of each state would go to the chosen presidential candidate.

Once the voting started, it quickly became evident that the Republicans had not reached a consensus overnight. The votes started to come in much diffused among the three candidates. When the vote was over, Marcos held sixteen states and Paul Randall only received fifteen states. Anthony Howe held the remainder of the state votes. Anthony Howe was the president-elect of The United States of America by 19 state votes from the United States House of Representatives.

The vote for the vice president was a separate issue. It went to the Senate. The Senate was controlled by the Democratic Party. There was no division and Howe's running mate, Sidney Hamilton, was elected expeditiously.

As the news was announced in real time, Paul Randall's heart jumped to his throat. His mouth went dry and he felt dizzy. *Breathe,* he thought. *Sit down and breathe.* Paul walked out of the living room of his Texas home and into his office. He sat down on his leather sofa. "Concentrate on breathing—in through the nose, out through the mouth," he whispered to himself.

The shock had so taken everyone off guard that they didn't see Paul walk out of the room. Kimberly was the first to notice he was gone. She came into the office to check on him. She saw his face was white. She went to get him some water and came straight back. "Put your feet up on the couch and drink some water, Paul." Kimberly said. He followed her instructions without a word.

Sonny walked into Paul's office and said, "What are you going to do, sir?"

"I don't know, Sonny," Paul replied. "The people elected me to the office. Congress should have honored their wishes."

The phone rang. "Hello?" Kimberly answered. "One second, here he is." She passed the phone to Paul and said, "General Allen Jefferson."

"Allen," Paul answered as he held the phone to his ear.

"Your orders, sir," Jefferson said sternly. "You have my support, whatever you decide to do. I expect there will be many that will fall in behind me as well. The people elected you. There will be a lot of fallout over this."

"I haven't thought that far in advance, Allen. I didn't see this coming. Give me an hour to think it over. I'll call you back," Paul replied.

Meanwhile at the Bair's house in Florida. Karen was crying and Matt was angry. The provision of the law that allowed this decision failed the people in this situation. The letter of the law had been followed, but the spirit of the law had been thrown to the wayside.

"What's going to happen?" Karen sobbed.

"I don't even want to speculate. It will heavily depend on Paul Randall. It'll depend on whether he gives a concession speech or calls for a coup. I know he has enough support in the Pentagon to pull it off. This is an awful situation for our country. It may tear us apart. It may trigger a civil war," Matt stated bluntly. He realized this was not what she wanted to hear, but he couldn't tell her everything was fine. He put his arms around her and pulled her close to comfort her.

Matt's phone rang. "Hey, Cousin." It was Wesley Bair, the college history professor.

"Hey, Wes," Matt replied. "What do you think about the news?"

"It's a load of horse crap," Wesley said. "The militia sites are blowing up on the internet. There are a lot of people ready to fight."

"Does that include you and your brother?" Matt asked. He knew they had trained with the Eastern Kentucky Liberty Militia before.

"I'll send you an encrypted e-mail later. I don't want to discuss that over the phone. We've already triggered Prism protocol and the NSA is storing this call to be reviewed by an analyst," Wesley warned.

"Sorry, I wasn't thinking," Matt apologized.

"It probably won't matter tomorrow," Wesley stated. "You and Karen should try to get up here. I'd leave today and drive straight through. If there's trouble, you won't want to be traveling. Randall is no quitter; I know he's not going to let this go. I think he owes it to the American people not to let it go."

"Thanks for the offer. I'll keep my ear to the tracks and make a decision by tonight." Matt knew Wesley was right. Things could get deteriorate fast.

Back at the ranch in Texas, Paul Randall was regaining his composure. Sonny walked into his office. "Sir, Juan Marcos is reading his concession speech in ten minutes. Will you be watching it with us?"

"I don't think so, Sonny. You all go ahead." Paul Randall's

thoughts were racing a million miles an hour. The vote was legal, but Congress had not acted in the interest of the American people; they had done what they always do. They acted in their own political interest. He was stuck between a rock and a hard place. To fail to recognize Anthony Howe as the president-elect would be to tear the country in pieces. To recognize Anthony Howe as president would betray those who made him the winner of the popular vote and handed him the highest number of electoral votes.

Calls of support came in from several state governors and other senators. Sheriffs from all over the country called to give Paul Randall their support. Texas Governor Larry Jacobs also called. He told Paul that he would back him 100 percent in any decision he made.

Sonny came back into the room with a look of dire importance. "Paul, President Mustafa Al Mohammad is on the phone."

"I'll take it," Paul responded. "Mr. President," he said as he took the phone.

"Paul, I wanted to call and tell you how sorry I am for the way things worked out. I know better than anybody how hard you worked and what it took to finish the race," President Mohammad said.

"Thank you for your condolences, sir," Paul replied respectfully.

"I am calling Governor Howe as soon as we finish, Paul. Can I let him know when you'll be offering your concession speech?" Al Mohammad asked.

"Our attorneys are looking at everything as we speak, Mr. President. As soon as they conclude whether or not Congress acted in good faith, I'll decide what I'm going to say and when I'm going to say it." Paul spoke in a manner that let the president know he would not be bullied.

The president said, "Paul, there are a lot of inflammatory statements coming out of your supporters. Some of the things that are being said are seditious, and those who are saying them are in jeopardy of federal prosecution. I think the wise thing for you to do is to make a statement that will put this sense of ill will to rest. You know the rules for Congress, and they followed those rules."

Paul Randall replied, "Mr. President, there is some question as to whether or not Congress has a right to vote their own personal opinion in the votes or if they have a fiduciary duty to vote the will of their respective constituents. As soon as I'm advised by our attorneys, I'll issue a statement."

"Now listen, Paul, tread carefully. Don't say anything that adds fuel to the fire your supporters are starting. It may be considered treason if it's construed to be inciting violence against this office or the country. I would watch my words if I were you. We've all been very patient with you and your accusations throughout the campaign. You crossed some lines with some of the things you said in the debates. We all say things during the campaigns. I've been through it twice. I know how nasty it gets, but now it's time to begin the healing process so we can all work together," Mustafa Al Mohammad lectured.

Randall exclaimed, "Every accusation I made in the campaign was true! The Constitutional violations throughout your presidency have been appalling, Mustafa. Now you dare call me and try to suppress my First Amendment right to free speech. How dare you! Do what you have to do, and I'll do what I have to do!"

President Al Mohammad hung up without saying good-bye.

Paul Randall was mad. He knew he shouldn't make a decision

when his emotions were this volatile, but it had to be made soon. He knew what the lawyers would say: It's a grey area. Randall could take it to court, and if he won, Howe would appeal the decision. This would go on and on, all the way to the Supreme Court. Four of the Justices had been appointed by Mustafa Al Mohammad over the past eight years; they would no doubt rule in Howe's favor. People tend to forget when they elect a president for four years that he has the power to elect Supreme Court Justices that may be there for the next four decades. Their decisions have done more to degrade our country into the cesspool that it's become than all the other politicians combined.

Paul Randall spent the next couple of hours talking the situation over with the lawyers and Sonny. He knew he couldn't issue a concession speech nor could he call for a coup. The fact of the matter was that he had neither won nor lost. As the lawyers would tell him, it was a grey area. Paul Randall saw things in black and white. He didn't operate in grey areas and this wasn't a situation he wanted to be in. *Sonny is good with grey areas. Maybe he can write a speech*, Paul thought. He knew better. This had to come from himself; this had to come from the heart.

Later that afternoon, Sonny came in with the phone again. "Governor Jacobs," he said as he handed Paul the phone.

"Larry, good to hear from you again. To what do I owe the pleasure?" Paul asked.

The governor had held several fundraisers for Paul at the Governor's Mansion in Austin. It was only about seventy miles from Randall's Ranch.

"Highway patrol chopper spotted a convoy of six DHS armored vehicles out of Austin headed south on Interstate 35 toward San Antonio. Are you doing anything to make new friends in DC?" Governor Jacobs asked.

"I had a heated conversation with Mustafa a couple hours ago. But I'm not south, I'm west. If they were coming here, they'd have taken US 290 west to State Road 16," Randall replied.

"That's the way you'd come," Jacobs countered. "Those are the backroads to them. DHS is big government; they'd never do anything the most efficient way. They may be headed to San Antonio and then planning to hook back up Interstate 10 toward Kerrville. I'm going to send fifty state troopers to rendezvous at Comfort, Texas, and form a road block on the north side of town. You should get a bag ready and be prepared to bug out. Do you have somewhere you can go? Don't tell me where; you shouldn't say anything on the phone. I'll call you if they're spotted heading north on I-10. You'll only have about thirty minutes if they get around the road block. They can roll right over the squad cars if they're determined. You should start getting things ready now. Wherever you go, make sure it's in Texas. You know we'll protect you here. I'm sending two highway patrolmen to escort you and they'll let me know where you go. I'll arrange plain clothes protection and counter surveillance for wherever you decide to bug out to."

"Thanks, Larry. I guess I'm America's most wanted," Paul said.

"There's no telling what kind of stuff Mustafa will pull. You just keep your head down," Larry said.

Right away, Paul began getting things together. He told Kimberly and the twins to get their bags together. The boys were 18, so they understood when things were urgent without needing all the details. His first thought for a hideout was his ranch foreman's house in Boerne, but that was south, the same direction DHS would be coming from.

Paul's friend and fellow rancher, Jimmy Thompson, had a cabin on Lake Meredith. Paul and Kimberly visited them there before and stayed several days.

As soon as he thought of the cabin, Paul called Larry back. "Larry, would it be too much to ask for a lift in the Highway Patrol helicopter?" he asked.

"I'll do better than that; I'll send you my chopper," Larry replied.

"You don't know how much I appreciate it," Paul said.

"I'm happy to have the opportunity to help you out, Paul," Larry replied.

Jimmy Thompson left an open invitation to use the cabin whenever they wanted. This isn't exactly what he had in mind when he made the offer, but Jimmy was a patriot and would be glad to help if he knew the situation. Paul didn't want to say anything over the phone, so he couldn't exactly call to ask permission. He gave Sonny a list of supplies and some cash so credit card transactions couldn't be tracked. He handed Sonny a map of where the cabin was and told him to come up in two days. Paul sent him out the door right away, so he wouldn't get caught up in the nonsense.

Larry called back about the time the helicopter landed. "The chopper should be there soon."

"It just landed in the backfield," Paul replied.

"The DHS convoy turned north on I-10. They're heading your way. I bet when you were fighting the NDAA indefinite detention clause, you never thought it might be used on you," Larry commented.

"I knew it would be used on Americans, which is why I fought it. It allows the government to hold any citizen without charging them. It's an abomination to the Constitution. You don't build a police state unless you intend to use it," Paul said.

The men cut their conversation short so Paul could get going. The Randalls grabbed their bags and an assortment of rifles, shotguns and pistols. He trusted Texas Governor Larry Jacobs to provide protection for them at the cabin, but Paul, Kimberly and the twins were ready to get involved if need be. Shooting was a regular pastime for them. They all trained together in the back forty of the ranch.

The Randalls boarded the helicopter and headed to the cabin.

CHAPTER 20

"If ye love wealth better than liberty, the tranquility of servitude better than the animating contest of freedom, go home from us in peace. We ask not your counsels or arms. Crouch down and lick the hands which feed you. May your chains set lightly upon you, and may posterity forget that ye were our countrymen."

Samuel Adams

Paul Randall slept only a few hours. He was tired, angry and unhappy about the turn the country had just taken. This speech was not to be a call to arms, nor was it to be a concession speech. It was to be an American Exit Strategy. It was to be the last harbinger to prepare for the coming social and economic meltdown.

Paul installed the encryption software to make sure the Skype message being telecast to the networks could not be used to track his location. He set the recorder so the message could be uploaded to an assortment of social media networks and alternative media websites if the networks shut him down.

Ed Nolan of CNC interrupted the program that was on the air. "Senator Paul Randall will be making a much anticipated statement regarding the outcome of the election. We've had no news of the Senator's whereabouts, nor have we received any advanced notification of a concession speech. We are going to the Skype speech now."

Paul Randall appeared on CNC and the screens of all the major networks.

"America," Paul began, "today is a sad day for us all. I'm being forced to come to you from a remote location, because the present administration is afraid of what I might say.

"DHS agents went to my home to detain me without cause. They came in six armored personnel carriers armed with automatic weapons to hold me under the NDAA. They told my ranch hands at the house that I could be detained because I was a potential terrorist threat. Fortunately, my family and I were not home when they arrived.

"There has been a great intellectual awakening since the previous election. People are educating themselves rather than believing the media and what they're taught in public schools. People are learning about economics and the legitimate role of the federal government as prescribed by the Constitution. They're learning about the prosperity of the past when our nation enjoyed individual liberty and workers kept the fruit of their labor. Because of this awakening, America elected me to be your next president through the popular vote. That opportunity has been taken away by congressional representatives who failed to recognize the will of their constituents. There is the possibility of recourse through the law, but know it would be appealed to the Supreme Court where the efforts would be lost on the liberal majority that would, all but certainly, rule in favor of

Anthony Howe.

"There are those among you who are ready to fight. This would bring about needless bloodshed. I'm not cowering or acknowledging the legitimacy of Anthony Howe's presidency. I do not recognize the legitimacy of the present corrupt administration either. I believe through their acts against the Constitution, they are enemies of the Constitution and therefore enemies of America.

"To those of you who are ready to take up arms, I say stand strong with your arms but do not be the aggressor. I say stand up for your Second Amendment right that Anthony Howe has vowed to steal from you in January. The Second Amendment so eloquently says:

'A well-regulated Militia, being necessary to the security of a free State, the right of the people to keep and bear Arms, shall not be infringed.'

"Our founding fathers knew that without the ability to fight off tyrants, there would not be a free State. Once this liberty is trampled, there will be nothing to stop the fully developed police state from infringing upon your every human right, including life itself.

"So what are we to do if we're not to fight this rogue government? We are to do absolutely nothing. My proposition to you is the American Exit Strategy. The next administration has no plans to alter the course of our country, which has been set by the two previous administrations. Howe will continue to spend our nation into the grave through warfare and welfare. To pay for it, he'll depend on stealing the fruits of your labor through his excessive sixty-percent income tax.

"He'll continue to use the Federal Reserve to pilfer the remainder of the money not taken by the hand of the IRS. Through the continued quantitative easing programs, the Fed creates new dollars that add to those already in circulation. As each new dollar is created, those already in existence are worth less and less. Where does this wealth go when it leaves your wallet or savings account? It goes into the coffers of the Federal Reserve which then funnels it into the budget of the ever-growing federal government. This is inflation. This is why your grocery cart is twice the price and half the weight as it was four years ago. Inflation is a stealth tax that you never see, because you still have the same amount of dollars in your bank account. The problem is, those dollars buy a lot less.

"The endless wars and welfare dependency have cost more than could be extracted from the American people through taxation and inflation, so we have borrowed to the limit of our national credit. No one will buy our new bonds. We're barely able to maintain the interest on the debt without an outright default. When we do finally default, the dollar will go the way of every other fiat currency throughout history. It will have no value at all. Those of you who have all of your wealth in the worthless paper at that point will find yourself as broke as our nation.

"My recommendation is to convert as much as possible into tangible assets. Purchase things you know you'll need to survive the coming collapse. Also focus on items that have value and can be stored and easily traded like ammunition, canned goods, coffee, jewelry and even soap and razors.

"Convert the rest of your dollars into gold and silver to hedge yourself from this mathematically certain event. The supply of gold and silver coins will quickly be depleted if even a fraction of the American people follow my advice. There is also the possibility that the government will outlaw gold as Franklin D. Roosevelt did in 1933 through Executive Order 6102. If that happens, don't turn it in. The legislation that would ban gold would be designed to steal your wealth from you. It would therefore be, just as a ban on guns, an illegitimate law. Hold on to your wealth by any means necessary. If gold and silver are outlawed or depleted from availability, purchase more of the things you know you'll need and can be easily traded though barter networks.

"Even if I had been confirmed as the president-elect, I could not have stopped the storm that is coming. My only ambition for the office was to be your guide through the storm, that we could come out the other side. As I stated throughout my campaign, I hoped that we might avoid much unnecessary human casualties through policies that would have provided a much softer landing for our crashing economy. As much as possible, I still intend to help you weather the coming economic hardship, but I will be doing so with much less resources than I would've had access to as president.

"When Governor Howe becomes your president, his economic policies will quickly take us to the brink of destruction. You must take responsibility to prepare yourself and your family from the collapse. If you live in a city, you should set a goal of being out before Howe takes office. You should seek out like-minded individuals to form communities in rural areas where you can be self-sufficient. Once there, you can establish barter networks and exit the dollar as your primary means of trade. This will allow you to keep the fruits of your labor. Barter transactions will be outside of the capabilities of the IRS to steal through taxation and the capabilities of the Federal Reserve to steal through inflation.

"When relocating, seek out states that have a reputation for freedom. I hope we'll see leadership arise in state governments that will stand up and assert their constitutional sovereignty against this rogue, criminal enemy that is occupying the nation's capital.

"It's my expectation that those who follow my advice will greatly increase their chances of survival. There will be many who do not heed my warning. As I have said before, many of them will die of starvation and violence that cannot be controlled by a bankrupt nation.

"There's not only darkness going forward. A majority of those who have supported the oppressive regime of Al Mohammad and voted for Anthony Howe live in the cities. The cities will have the highest die-off rates due to resource scarcity and violent crime. The more self-sufficient rural areas are predominantly liberty-loving patriots. Those who are most likely to survive will be those who tend towards individual liberty. They will soon find that they have outlasted their oppressor. Once the dollar meets its demise, the federal government, like a parasite without a host, will simply wither away.

"When this happens, there will be no need for a constitutional convention to frame a new nation as our forefathers had; we need only to adhere to the principles that they put together in the original Constitution of America.

"For now, brace yourselves as for a storm, for it is surely coming. Be vigilant in defending the Constitution against the tyrant and be faithful in caring for your fellow patriots. We will continue to post new information and updates to help you navigate through the impending chaos that is to come. Updates will be available through all of our traditional channels as well as our new website which will be hosted on multiple proxy servers outside of the US. Hopefully, this will prevent the government from keeping the site down. Using redirects, we will switch to another server each time the site is disabled through an attack. If you visit us and the site is down, try back in thirty minutes. This whack-a-mole strategy is our best chance at keeping ahead of the NSA.

"Thank you, and good night."

Paul shut down the computer. FOX News had aired the entire message. The other major networks had shut it down just after they knew it wasn't a concession speech.

Back at the White House, President Al Mohammad was seething. He called Anthony Howe. "I tried to have FOX shut the message down, but my requests were refused. I'm having the DOJ draw up paperwork that will label Paul Randall as an enemy combatant. This will allow us to take Randall out as soon as we find him."

Al Mohammad's brand of ruthless murders committed under the Patriot Act had put those of his neocon predecessors to shame.

Anthony Howe responded, "We're on the same page on this issue, Mr. President. I can assure you that my administration will complete any work you begin in reigning in Randall or his faithful followers."

Al Mohammad was happy to be passing on the torch of the iron fist to Howe. The power that had taken so many false flags and so much political wrangling to gain would be in good hands. Al Mohammad would miss the power, but he had enough information on Howe's personal indiscretions to still get things done if they needed to be.

CHAPTER 21

"The time is now near at hand which must probably determine whether Americans are to be freemen or slaves; whether they are to have any property they can call their own; whether their houses and farms are to be pillaged and destroyed, and themselves consigned to a state of wretchedness from which no human efforts will deliver them."

George Washington

Matt looked at Karen a bit stunned. He didn't know what to expect from the Paul Randall speech, but he didn't expect what he just heard. Matt sat with his brow furrowed as he digested the message that had just come from the Senator.

"What are you thinking?" Karen asked.

"I think we should put the house up for sale tomorrow," Matt answered.

"And go where?" Karen asked.

"We'll move to Kentucky, near Adam and Wesley," Matt replied.

"What are we going to do in Kentucky?" Karen asked.

Matt replied, "We'll try to find a small farm and start growing produce; maybe get some bees and some type of livestock. We have to make the transition now. Everything was falling apart already, but since Paul Randall just put it out there, the clock is ticking. We have to get on board with his plan or get left behind."

"How are we going to be farmers? We don't know anything about farming. How can we make money farming?" Karen began.

Matt explained, "There won't be any money pretty soon. We'll barter with the things we produce and trade with the silver and gold that we've purchased. Trust me on this one, Karen. If we stay here, we will die. We won't just pass away in our sleep; we will die the most horrific death you can imagine. Gangs will take over. Once people run out of food, they'll turn to cannibalism. Societies of much higher integrity than ours have resorted to cannibalism when they were starving."

"Like who?" Karen asked.

"Like the Israelites," Matt answered. He grabbed his Bible and looked up the passage. "The Northern Kingdom of Israel was under siege, and no one could get food into the city of Samaria. 2 Kings 6: 25-30 reads:

There was a great famine in the city; the siege lasted so long that a donkey's head sold for eighty shekels of silver, and a quarter of a cab of seed pods for five shekels. As the king of Israel was passing by on the wall, a woman cried to him, "Help me, my lord the king!" The king replied, "If the LORD does not help you, where can I get help for you? From the threshing floor? From the winepress?" Then he asked her, "What's the matter?" She answered, "This woman said to me, 'Give up your son so we may eat him today, and tomorrow we'll eat my son.' So we cooked my son and ate him. The next day I said to her, 'Give up your son so we may eat him,' but she had hidden him." When the king heard the woman's words, he tore his robes.

"This is not some abstract concept. This is what people do. The Donner party was stuck in the Sierra Nevada Mountains in the 1800s, and they resorted to cannibalism. They were members of a much more civil society than ours. These days, people will stab you for your tennis shoes, even though there is absolutely no threat of starvation. It's just the common cruelty of greed and the product of not valuing human life. The wickedness and depravity of this culture is getting ready to blossom into the most unimaginable flower of desolation that has ever been. You won't want to read about the things that go on in cities like these a year from now, much less live in one of them. I love you, Baby, but this subject is not open for discussion. We have to go while we still can."

Karen looked at the floor. "I don't want to move, but I'm afraid of staying here. Most of the things you've said about things over the years are coming true. This all seems very extreme, but so have most of the other things you've predicted over the years. I know you're probably right, but that doesn't make me feel any better."

Matt wanted to move out of the area for several years. He agreed to stay as long as they had jobs. She still had the job at the school, but Matt didn't want her to go back there. It wasn't safe.

More than anything else about moving to Kentucky, Matt knew that Karen hated the cold winters. Florida had beautiful winters. January and February generally had temperatures around 75 degrees. The mountains of Kentucky saw temperatures below freezing most of the winter.

Karen grew up watching *Little House on the Prairie*. The show romanticized the hard scrabble life of the late 1800s. Even now, it was her favorite show. Matt and Karen had the first and second seasons on DVD and watched it often.

Matt said, "Imagine living the life of Laura Ingalls, *Little House on the Prairie*. Imagine selling extra eggs at the town mercantile to buy fabric to make a dress."

She almost smiled, but Matt figured the apprehension must have overpowered the serene thoughts of going back to a lost age. Karen didn't argue about it. It was probably the only choice they had.

Matt's phone rang. It was his cousin, Wesley.

"What did y'all decide?" Wesley asked.

"I don't think we're heading out tonight, Wes," Matt answered. "Randall is calling for a sort of bloodless revolution. I suppose we have a little time. I'm going to put the house on the market tomorrow. We'll try to find a small place up by you and Adam. Do you know of anything for sale around there?"

Wesley said, "The old Blanchard place is up for sale. It's about three miles from Adam's house. I looked at it. I thought about putting in an offer, but it was more renovation than I wanted to do. There's nothing wrong with it, it's just dated. The house has really good bones. The property is very hilly, but most everything around here is. It has a lot of woods. It also has about a half-acre garden near the house that's fairly level."

"What are they asking?" Matt inquired.

"Sixty thousand, but it's been on the market for six months. They'll probably come down," Wesley replied.

"How big is the property?" Matt quizzed.

"If I remember right, about thirty acres. It has a huge creek that feeds into Wood Creek Lake," Wesley answered.

Matt asked, "How far is it from the highway?"

Wesley replied, "If you were walking straight to it, it would be about three miles, but the way the road snakes around those hills, it's about seven miles off the I-75 exit."

"Three miles is a little too close for comfort," Matt commented.

Wesley chuckled. "No one is going to find you that ain't looking for you. Only about half of the ones that are looking for you will find you out there."

Matt's curiosity was sparked. He continued to quiz Wesley about the property. "Does it have any out buildings, any cattle barns?"

Wesley answered, "Like I said, it's mostly woods. There are a couple of steep meadows on the backside, but nowhere big enough to graze any cows. There's an old chicken coop; pretty big, but old. There's also a metal work shed; it's about the size of a three-car garage. It has a good roof. The house is about 300 feet off the road, and heavily wooded. It's very secluded. The nearest neighbor isn't that far, but you'd never see nor hear him as far back in the woods as that house sits. I think you should do it."

"Do you have any pictures you can email to me?" Matt asked.

"Didn't take any, but I'll go out there in the morning and take a few. I'll send them before lunch tomorrow," Wesley replied.

The two cousins said their farewells and Matt started thinking about what he would ask for their house. Similar houses in the neighborhood sold for as much as $270,000 after the Fed had re-inflated the housing bubble through quantitative easing. But just like the bubble before, it popped. As soon as rates started to creep back up, home buyers had trouble getting mortgages and prices receded to lower levels than when the first housing bubble popped. The tax roll estimated their house at $70,000. That would be enough to pay the commissions, taxes and still have enough to buy the Blanchard place in Kentucky. The county appraisal was always low balled to keep people from fighting the appraised value, but Matt and Karen would have to sell at a discount in order to get a quick sell.

The next morning, Matt listed the house for $69,900. He did what he could to get the yard looking neat while Karen cleaned the inside.

Matt and Karen looked at the pictures of the Blanchard place after lunch. It was a really nice place. Like Wesley said, it was a little dated.

Karen said, "I don't really like it. I thought it was going to be some type of cabin from Walnut Grove."

The picture of the chicken coop had a background of red, orange and yellow trees in their autumn glory. The photos had been taken in the morning light, which gave a dramatic contrast in the knot holes and grain of the weathered wooden planks that the chicken coop was constructed of. The hinges on the door were black iron strap hinges that likely weighed a pound each. The latch was a simple wooden handle that lifted a crossbar inside the door. Some farmer had constructed it himself. While there were no berries this time of year, Karen recognized the blackberry bush growing on the side of the chicken coop.

She said, "Those are blackberry bushes. Imagine eating a couple of blackberries early in the morning when you're going in the coop to collect the eggs for breakfast."

A smile subconsciously rose on her face.

Matt noticed and asked a bit surprised, "Do you like it?"

"No," Karen tried to hide her smile. Having been caught, she started to giggle as she turned away from him.

"Yes, you do," Matt laughed. "You like that old beat up chicken coop."

Adam called that evening. "How y'all doin'?" he asked with his thick mountain accent.

We're good," Matt replied.

"Wesley said you're thinking about buying the Blanchard place," Adam said.

Matt replied, "We looked at the pictures Wesley sent us. I like it. It would be nice to have some pasture like you have on your place, but everything else seems suitable."

"Not many folks around here have pasture. I can only support about twenty-five head of cattle on what I have," Adam said. "Lots of folks have taken to raising goats. They do well in the hills and eat just about anything."

"That's a good idea," Matt said as he imagined owning goats.

"You wouldn't be able to do much with solar out there—too many trees," Adam said. "That metal out building backs up to the creek. It is a big ol' creek, too. I bet you could set up a water wheel turbine to generate electricity. Of course, that would only work when the creek is running strong, might not get much in the winter."

"I guess people lived for thousands of years without electricity. I hope it doesn't come to that. But you never know," Matt said.

Adam inquired, "What do you think about buying silver and gold at these prices? I know you've been telling me to do it for years. Randall made a pretty good case for it last night."

"I think you should listen to him. Get out of the dollar, whatever you do. How much cash are you sitting on?" Matt asked.

"Maybe $35,000," Adam said.

"Are you stocked up on all the food and ammo you can handle?" Matt asked.

"All set," Adam answered.

Matt said, "Could you buy some materials for your roofing business? You'll still need to keep doing something after the crash, and people will always need roofs. If supply lines are disrupted, materials could be hard to get a hold of. You should also get as many traditional tools as you can."

"That's a good idea," Adam said. "I could probably store $10,000 worth of materials in the loft of the cattle barn. What do you think about ammo for bartering?"

Matt said, "I think ammo will be the one-dollar bills of the new economy. Silver and gold will be the big bills. Also think about things you can't produce like coffee. You can't grow coffee in Kentucky."

Adam thought for a moment. "Maybe I'll put $5000 in gold, $5000 in silver and $5000 into ammo. I could probably buy a pallet of coffee, a pallet of flour and a pallet of sugar and a few other staples from Walmart for around $5000. I'll hang on to $5000 in cash for paying bills and other things until it hits the fan."

Matt replied, "I think coffee is a great idea. You'll need to make sure everything is in something the critters can't get to. Mylar liners inside of plastic buckets will keep everything safe.

"Five thousand won't even buy a whole ounce of gold. The current spot is $6125 per ounce. You could buy one-tenth-ounce gold coins. With the premium for the smaller coins, $5000 will get you about seven of the one-tenth-ounce coins. Your other option is to sink the full $10,000 that you have allocated for metals, into silver."

"I should have bought gold when it was $1200 an ounce. I could've had four ounces for $5000." Adam spoke with the regret of hindsight.

"No use kicking yourself now," Matt said.

"What's the spot price for silver?" Adam asked.

"It's $175 per ounce," Matt answered.

"Wow, it was under $20 when you told me to buy it!" Adam exclaimed. "Did you buy any at that price?'

"A little." Matt didn't want to rub it in. "I still think it has the most room to grow. Anytime silver and gold have been used as currency, the ratio has been around twenty to one. The ratio now is thirty-five to one. At twenty to one, the silver price would be $306 an ounce if gold remained at its current level. Besides, silver is much more divisible. After the ninety-percent silver market dried up, bullion dealers started selling tenth-ounce silver rounds to simulate the value of the old pre-1965 silver dimes. Of course the tenth-ounce silver bullion rounds have more silver than the old silver dimes, but it offers the divisibility for making smaller transactions in a barter economy. I bought several rolls of those back when silver was $55 an ounce. I was worried the price would go back down, so I didn't buy many. Retrospectively, I should have backed up the truck."

"Is it still okay to buy online?" Adam asked.

"It would have been better before the eve of Armageddon, but the risk of staying in paper is probably much greater. Why don't you split it up? Buy $5000 now, then buy another $5000 worth when your first order shows up." Matt suggested.

"But the silver price is up $11 today. How long will it take to get my order?" Adam asked.

"Probably four to five weeks. If everyone is trying to buy now, maybe longer," Matt said.

"The price could almost double by then," Adam said anxiously.

"Then blow the whole wad at once and don't look back. I would have never given this advice before. I always tried to dollar-cost average by spreading my purchases out over time, but we're running a little short on time. If panic buying hits the metals market, like you said, the price could double by the time you get your order." Matt wanted to give Adam good advice, but this was not the best circumstance. The future was uncertain and giving advice was tricky business in this environment.

Adam replied, "I'm going to let you go. I'll call the online dealer and see what he can promise me."

Matt was mentally worn out from the pressure of trying to make the right decisions to take care of Karen and himself, but there was no way he was going to sleep right now. He went to the office to check out trailers online. Inflation had sent all commodity prices soaring. Even used metal trailers were selling for double what they had been selling for. Most everything he saw was over $10,000. Matt finally found an old horse trailer for $3000. He called and made an appointment to drive out to Davie, Florida, to see it the next morning.

His body was tired, his mind was tired, but sleep was elusive that night.

CHAPTER 22

"The strongest reason for the people to retain the right to keep and bear arms is, as a last resort, to protect themselves against tyranny in government."

Thomas Jefferson

Pastor John Robinson called an emergency board meeting to discuss the Randall Speech.

"Gentlemen, I want to thank everyone for clearing your schedule on such short notice," Robinson began. "I've prayerfully considered what Paul Randall had to say in his speech. I have also considered what Anthony Howe has pledged to do upon his inauguration. I tend to believe him when he says he will put the new restrictions on firearms by executive order. I really believe we need to get out of dollars immediately and entirely. I have been on the phone this morning and negotiated several deals. They're simply pending your approval. I have negotiated what I believe to be a fair price for the farm adjacent to the Howard Young place that was gifted to Liberty Chapel recently. The deal would give us nearly 500 acres between the two farms. I have arranged two separate large bullion purchases with a local dealer and another one in Montana. I have also spoken with the CEO of Castle Arms in the Idaho panhandle. Those folks at Castle are really good people. They're not accepting cash, but they've promised to hold 200 AR-15s and 800 thirty round magazines if we can pay them in bullion. We should be able to do that if all goes well with the metals transaction. In the interest of time, I'll ask you to vote on the entirety of my recommendation. If the vote is not unanimous, we can go back and look at what needs to be changed."

The chairman recommended a vote and it was unanimous. He made a motion to allow the pastor to convert all liquid funds into hard goods by any means he saw fit. That motion also passed unanimously. There was a great deal of trust that had developed between the pastor and the board over the years. They were all in agreement that times were going to get tough in the near term.

Pastor Robinson explained his plan to build barracks on the two farms and his plans to store up as much food as possible. The details would be worked out later. For now, they needed to act on the mission at hand.

As they left the boardroom, Pastor Robinson put Ron White in charge of food storage. "I want you to see how much bulk rice, beans and wheat you can purchase from any nearby distributors. Recruit anyone you need to help drive trucks or make separate purchases. Robert Rust, the range master, is going to start building up the ammunition stores."

Ron asked, "What about Castle Arms? Don't they produce ammo? I thought those folks up in the Idaho panhandle taught their children to reload ammo in homeschool?" Ron was only half joking. He was sure he remembered a story of a woman from Lewiston teaching her kids to reload as part of their curriculum.

"They all shoot and they're all homeschooled up there," Pastor John Robinson replied. "It only stands to reason that the kids probably reload. But no, Castle doesn't produce ammunition. I know a lot of folks up there have a good stockpile of ammo, but no one is selling. They see copper jacketed lead as a precious metal. Albert Rust is good friends with a sales rep from Cabela's. He seems to think he may be able to get a pallet or two of .223 ammo."

"Do you intend to engage the government?" Ron asked somberly.

Pastor John replied, "I pray it never comes to that, Ron, but the Second Amendment is the teeth of the Constitution. It protects our right to worship. If we give that up, we'll let them tell us who we can pray to as well. It's all part of the same Bill of Rights. I'll stand my ground. I don't want to die, but I will not stand idly by while a criminal government desecrates the law of the land and makes our country into a concentration camp. Once they're loading us into the cattle cars, it'll be too late to defend ourselves."

"I saw a documentary on the Holocaust last week," Ron said. "So many of the photos show the Jews being herded into the cattle cars and only two or three armed Nazis with guns. If they'd only known what they were in for, they could've easily overpowered the guards."

Pastor John said, "The Nazis spent years conditioning the Jews to accept ever-increasing encroachments upon their liberty. Each step was just a minor inconvenience more than what they had been conditioned to tolerate from the time before. It was the proverbial 'frog in the boiling water' approach."

"Sounds familiar," Ron returned.

Pastor John continued, "No one with the mind of a free man will walk willingly into a gas chamber, even if you tell him it is a shower. It's a long drawn out process of training a group to think like slaves that takes away their will to fight. Once you've taken that, extermination is simple. That's why we must draw our line in the sand. If we're to die anyway, let us die with dignity and honor. Any man that does not respect your God-given right to defend yourself, does not respect your God-given right to live."

Ron said, "If we must die, let us die free."

"You're a true patriot, Ron," the pastor said. He smiled as they walked together.

Pastor John parted ways with Ron and grabbed two of the single men who were on the church grounds crew. They picked up a box truck from the church motor pool. "You guys packing?" the pastor asked.

They shook their heads and said no.

One of the men, Will Pender, said, "I have my 1911 in the truck. I don't carry it when we're working, because we get so dirty."

Pastor John said, "We'll swing by your truck and grab it. I have a Glock 26 that James can use. We're hauling the widow's mite today, gentlemen." They placed a large bag of cash in the cab of the truck and headed out to purchase the bullion in Kalispell, Montana. It was going to be a long trip.

"I appreciate you men coming on the journey today," the pastor said. He told them they would be gone until the next day. He was trying to keep everything as hush-hush as possible. Now that they were en route, there would be less temptation to tell their friends what they were doing.

Pastor John filled them in on all the details. "Once we purchase the bullion, we are heading to Coeur d'Alene. It's about another five hours from Kalispell. One of the folks at Castle Arms used to go to Liberty Chapel. We'll be staying at his ranch near Coeur d'Alene."

The men stopped in Missoula, just past the Montana border to eat dinner. They ate at The Hitching Post. James and Will snickered a bit when they went inside. It looked more like a bar than a restaurant. They both took pictures with their phones. No one would believe Pastor John was in a bar unless they had hard evidence. They all had the BBQ pork chops. Each had a cup of coffee before they left. There was still more than 100 miles to Kalispell; this was no time to get sleepy.

The men finally made it to the private mint where they picked up boxes filled with silver and gold bullion. Four hours later, they were in Coeur d'Alene.

James McIntosh said, "I'm surprised by the amount of Don't-Tread-on-Me flags flying under the American flag. It seems every car and truck bumper had a sticker with a silhouette of a Minuteman or the Roman numeral III."

Will Pender said, "The Roman numeral III represented the patriots who were willing to fight. Only three percent of the population initially supported the original American Revolution of 1776."

Pastor John said, "There are several Appeal-to-Heaven flags flying. I remember these from my old history book. They flew in the American Revolution also. The flag was inspired by John Locke who spoke about appealing to Heaven when earthly powers deny men of their God-given rights."

The people who were still out in the street on this briskly cool night didn't look like they had a chip on their shoulders. They didn't strike the pastor as people who were readying themselves for war. Nonetheless, there was no mistaking; this community had drawn their line in the sand.

CHAPTER 23

"The LORD your God is with you, he is mighty to save. He will take great delight in you, he will quiet you with his love, he will rejoice over you with singing."

Zephaniah 3:17

Matt had a fitful night. He woke several times wondering if they would be able to sell the house in a hurry. Each time he woke up, he prayed that God would send them a buyer. He got up early and did his morning routine. Then, he retrieved $3000 from the safe, tucked his Glock in the back of his pants and headed to Davie to check out the trailer.

When he arrived, the man who met Matt fit the profile he expected. The man wore boots, a straw cowboy hat, Lee jeans and a checkered shirt. People from Davie looked more like Texans than Floridians. It was nice. It was too bad they didn't have more influence on the rest of the county, that had voted for Al Mohammad by a 2-to-1 ratio in the previous election.

"Howdy," the man said as he walked off the porch toward the

trailer. "Are you haulin' horses?"

"No, personal belongings," Matt replied.

"Are you taking Randall's advice?" the man asked.

"Yeah, we're heading to Kentucky to be near family."

"I don't blame you," the man said. "Folks around here are digging in. We mostly all grew up here. If Howe wants the guns from Davie, Florida, he'll have to take them bullets first."

Matt smiled as he looked the trailer over. It had small rust spots, but it was in good shape. The inside was exceptionally clean. He knew he would be in trouble if he brought home something that smelled like horse manure. "Can you take $2500 for it?" Matt asked.

"You can have it for $2000 if you want to pay me in silver or gold, but if you're paying with federal funny money, I have to have $3000," the man answered.

Matt looked up as he did some quick math in his head and thought about how he could convert the cash back into gold if he went home to get gold to pay the man. He decided the risk of getting stuck with the paper wasn't worth it so he just paid the man with the cash. The man gave Matt a hand getting the trailer hitched to his truck.

"Thanks, fella. Y'all have a safe trip to Kentucky. I better go spend this while it'll still buy something," the man said with a smile as he walked toward his own truck.

Matt stopped at Home Depot to buy a few more five-gallon gas jugs. There were only two left on the shelf. He found five more gas cans, but they only held two gallons each. The last thing he wanted to do was to get stuck halfway between Florida and Kentucky with no gas. Besides, it would be good to have gas stored in Kentucky as backup fuel or a barter item. Gas had jumped from $7.25 the day before Paul's speech to $8.20 today. People were starting to hoard it as they anticipated the price to spike higher. He stopped at the RaceTrac gas station to fill up the truck and the new gas cans. He found four more one gallon cans inside RaceTrac. The truck held 26 gallons; he had 15 gallons in the shed. That plus the new plastic cans, made the total 65 gallons. He figured he would only get about 13 miles to the gallon with the trailer full. He still needed another 15 gallons to be safe. He stopped by an Auto Zone on the way home and found exactly three more five-gallon cans. Once those were filled, he headed home.

Karen came out as he was backing the trailer into the driveway. She had a look of curiosity on her face. "That's the trailer?" she asked.

"That's it" Matt replied.

"It's for horses," Karen stated.

"It'll hold furniture, too," Matt said. "This was $3000 and everything else was $10,000 or more. U-Haul has nothing and won't have anything for weeks."

"We don't even know if we can sell the house," Karen said.

"We still have to leave, even if we don't sell the house," Matt said.

They had a quiet lunch and then Matt asked Karen to go to Publix to get some boxes.

"Are we packing already? Shouldn't we at least wait until we get an offer on the house?" Karen didn't do well with fast changes. Unlike Matt, she needed time to digest things.

"It would nearly tap us out, but we could still buy the farm with our silver and gold, even if we don't sell the house. I don't want to waste two trips to go look at it and then come back and move everything. I don't know if we have that much time. People are hoarding gas; it may trigger a gas shortage. It could be weeks or months before it's resolved. If the farm doesn't work out, we'll have to stay with Adam and his family for a while."

"Why didn't you tell me that before?" Karen said.

"We're kinda doing things on the fly here, Karen. I'm making up the plan as I go along," Matt said. He caught his voice raising. He inhaled and exhaled deeply, then went to hug Karen. The stress of the situation was getting to both of them. "Everything is going to be just fine, baby. I just need you to support my decisions right now. We have to move fast or things are going to get away from us."

Karen didn't say anything, but she gently stroked Matt's earlobe with her finger as he held her. He knew that meant okay.

Karen went to get the boxes and Matt started mapping out what would go where in the trailer. He measured out the dimensions and drew it out on a piece of paper. There was a knock at the door and Matt did what he had been doing over the past weeks. He drew his gun and went out the side door to see who it was. It was Jack Mason from next door.

"I guess you guys are heading out?" Jack asked.

"How did you guess?" Matt responded with a snicker.

"Let's see, was it the For Sale sign on the lawn or the trailer? Oh, it was both." Jack laughed. "You think it's going to get that bad, huh?"

"Mad Max bad, brother," Matt said.

"Well, we'll head up to my mom's in North Carolina if it gets too bad," Jack said.

"Is she stocked up?" Matt asked.

"No, I think we'll have a chance to stock up if we see things starting to slide downhill," Jack said.

"Just like you had a chance last time?" Matt asked in a slightly sarcastic tone.

"You have a point," Jack said.

"Don't wait 'til your house is on fire to start shopping for fire insurance, Jack." Matt learned long ago that people would avoid looking at reality as long as possible. Normalcy bias causes people to believe nothing bad will happen to them because it hasn't happened to them before.

"I'll let you get back to what you were doing. Give me a call if you need any help packing. We'll all miss you here," Jack said.

"We'll miss you guys, too," Matt replied.

Karen returned and Matt started loading dishes and kitchen items into the boxes she had retrieved from Publix. After that, he started loading all of the dry storage food items from the extended pantry he built several years back to accommodate the great deals Karen regularly brought home on her couponing hauls. The day was finished and they went to sleep. Matt slept much better since he'd burned off much of the nervous energy in completing the day's tasks.

The next morning, Matt's phone rang. It was the realtor. She said, "Matt, a representative from Blackstone contacted me about the house. He's offering $55,000. I know this is a lot less than you wanted, but he can close in three days. If you want out fast, this is probably your only opportunity. They've been buying foreclosures for several years now. It's their business model to purchase well below market."

"Doesn't he want to see it?" Matt asked curiously.

She replied, "They'll send an inspector the day after they get a contract. The buyers aren't even in Florida. They base their decision on the appraisal and the inspection report. The fund made a ton of cash in the last housing market dip. They plan to do the same thing again. I'm sure you'll get the $69,900 if you want to hold out for a few months. I expect things will turn back around just like they did last time."

"Good luck with that," Matt said. "I'm going to talk it over with my wife and call you back in an hour."

Karen wasn't happy about the offer at all. She wasn't happy about listing at $69,900 and she certainly wasn't happy that they would have to sell at $55,000. After a forty-five-minute presentation from Matt on how the apocalypse was on their doorstep, she consented to the offer. Matt called the realtor back and she e-mailed the contract to him.

Once the paperwork was done, Matt and Karen started loading a few of the furniture pieces they had chosen to keep. Because of the limited size of the trailer, they had to be very selective on what they could take. Miss Mae, the cat, stayed hidden under the bed. She didn't like the commotion of moving any more than Karen did.

CHAPTER 24

"If there must be trouble, let it be in my day, that my child may have peace."

Thomas Paine

Sonny arrived at the cabin with the supplies Paul Randall requested. It took Paul a moment to register that it was Sonny. He had never seen Sonny in anything other than a formal suit or dress slacks with a button-down shirt. Sonny was wearing a ball cap, jeans and a grey tee-shirt. "Who did you borrow those clothes from, Sonny?" Paul said with a laugh.

"It's my disguise for going on the lam," Sonny replied. "I thought it would be appropriate to make a minor wardrobe adjustment."

"Good thinking, Sonny," Paul replied, "But I didn't intend for you to have to stay out here. You're not in trouble. You should be able to continue your day-to-day life."

"My day-to-day life has been trying to get you in the oval office, sir. Nothing has changed since you were forced underground.

Besides, I don't trust Howe or Al Mohammad. We've all heard about plenty of unfortunate car accidents, disappearances, plane crashes, and untimely heart attacks involving people who didn't see eye to eye with the government over the past few years. There's no need to convict me in the court of public opinion if they want me gone," Sonny said.

"If you want to stay, you're more than welcome," Paul said. "You also know things could get nasty. Have you ever shot a gun?"

"No," Sonny replied, "I'm willing to learn if someone will show me."

"Governor Jacobs sent four guys out here for security. The twins have been talking guns with two of them. They all have suppressed weapons. Maybe they'll trade them out for our guns while we go shoot their suppressed weapons," Paul said.

"I don't quite know what that means, sir," Sonny said.

Paul explained, "Suppressed means they have silencers. We don't want to draw attention to this location with gunfire if we can avoid it. There isn't anybody out here, but the sound of gunshots travel far."

Sonny took his bags into the guest room and Paul Randall made the temporary trade with two of the guards for their suppressed weapons. The guards lent Paul and Sonny a suppressed HK .40 caliber pistol and a suppressed Colt M4 rifle. "Have her home by sundown." The guard joked with Paul about the M4. "That's my baby."

"We'll take good care of her," Paul replied with a wink.

The two men walked down to the lake and found a good sloping hill to shoot into. Paul set up some empty juice bottles at five, ten and fifteen yards.

He instructed Sonny with the HK pistol first. "You want to

create some tension between your hands. Keep both elbows bent and soft. Push slightly with your right hand and pull a little with your left. This will keep your aim steady as you squeeze the trigger. Slowly take up the tension on the trigger. When you're ready to take the shot, squeeze slowly."

Sonny took his first shot. The suppressed pistol only made the sound of the firing pin striking the cartridge, the click of the next round being chambered and the spent round dropping to the ground. His first shot was several feet away from his target. Within minutes of continued coaching, Sonny was hitting the bottles at five yards. "How is that?" he asked with a smile.

"A person is a bigger target than a juice bottle, Sonny. If you can hit that, you can hit a person," Paul said.

Next, they trained with the rifle for a while, then returned to the cabin. When they arrived, the twins were gutting a wild boar they took with a crossbow in the woods. Ryan called out to Sonny, "Do you like roast pig?"

"I can't say I've had the pleasure of trying it before, but I suppose we shall see," Sonny said. "I've never seen an animal being butchered before. It makes you realize your connection to the animal that had to die for you to eat. I guess it gives me a different sense of appreciation."

"I agree," Paul said.

Ryan and Robert finished gutting the pig and dug a pit in the ground to roast it in. They found plenty of dried mesquite wood. It was very abundant in northern Texas.

Kimberly made some cheddar cheese cornbread and a pot of baked beans to serve with the pig. Everyone ate outside around the pit. The four guards, the Randalls and Sonny all sat up late around the campfire talking about what the future would bring and how long they would be out here. The conversation was filled with apprehension, but it also held a sense of hope and a measure of excitement.

CHAPTER 25

"Then let those who are in Judea flee to the mountains, let those in the city get out, and let those in the country not enter the city."

Luke 21:21

Karen recognized the number on Matt's phone as Adam's when it rang. She handed the phone to Matt.

He answered, "Hey, Cousin,"

"Hi, Cousin." It was Adam's wife, Janice.

"Oh, hey Janice. Is everything alright?" Matt asked curiously.

Janice replied, "Everything is fine. I just wanted to talk to Karen and I didn't have her number handy, so I called your phone. I know this must be a little tough for her. We girls are nesters. God didn't build us to go out and hunt and gather like you boys. I thought I could give her a little encouragement by inviting her to come 'nest' with me and the girls."

"Wow, that's awesome. I think she could use some cheering up about now. This is tough for her," Matt said.

"You take it easy on her; you hear me?" Janice said with a chuckle.

"Yes, Ma'am," Matt replied as he handed the phone to Karen.

"Hi Janice," Karen said.

"Hey girl!" Janice replied. "The girls are so excited about you coming here. Carissa keeps asking what day you're going to be here. Mandy has all kinds of plans for you to help her sew a dress and help us can apples from the orchard."

"Really?" Karen asked. She loved doing country stuff with Janice and the girls. Her mind began to drift to the thoughts of *Little House on The Prairie*. It was such a pure lifestyle. When she was in the mountains with them, she never missed the city. "Tell them I can't wait to be there."

"Mandy wants to know if Miss Mae will be coming," Janice said.

"Of course she's coming. She doesn't know it yet, but she's getting a little kitty cocktail to knock her out when we get done packing the trailer. Do you have a room we can keep her in until we close on the farm?"

"Absolutely. Everything is going to be fine. I know the transition is abrupt, but you will be so happy once you get here," Janice continued.

While the girls chatted, Matt went to fill up Karen's car for the trip. RaceTrac was closed. There were big signs that read "NO GAS" at each entrance and a patrol car parked in the lot. Matt headed west as he knew things would be worse as he approached the beach. Three miles up the road he found a BP station still pumping. The advertised price was $12.40 a gallon. The line was fourteen cars long. Two men were fighting in the street because one of them had evidently cut the other man off in the line. How had this happened overnight? Was this local or all over the country? Matt shook his head and turned around to go back home.

He walked in and told Karen what was happening. They turned on the news for a while, which confirmed the shortages were showing up in cities all over America.

The CNC reporter was saying, "It seems OPEC decided to quit settling oil trade in dollars. The decision came after an emergency meeting of OPEC in the middle of the night. The perceived US political tension and instability in the US dollar, combined with the rapid increase in oil priced in US dollars caused the oil cartel to move to gold settlement. The decision was announced as a temporary measure that would be instituted until a different currency could be established for settlement.

"The BRICS nations, Brazil, Russia, India, China and South Africa recently developed the *bric*. It is a monetary unit that derives its value from a basket of the member nations' currencies. The bric is regularly traded on the currency exchanges and has risen heavily against the US dollar and the euro. Unlike the euro, the bric is only used for international trade settlement. The member nations still use their respective currencies within their own borders. The BRICS nations are recommending that the bric be used to settle oil, but OPEC determined gold will be the settlement terms for the time being.

"Oil jumped $90 in early morning trading. The current price is $331 a barrel. The shock is rippling through to the pumps in real time. The oil crisis is being exacerbated by corporate hoarding. We're getting reports that gasoline producers are slowing the release of fuel to retailers because of the anticipated increase in prices. Retailers are doing the same thing.

"We've heard reports claiming that large trucking companies are offering to pay more than the retail pump price to ensure they have fuel to continue business. According to our source, the trucking companies will, in turn, double their freight charges. Grocers are already marking up prices to cover the increase in freight. A new run on grocery stores may begin before they fully recover from the riots.

"Due to the announcement by OPEC, gold also jumped in morning trading. In the previous trading session, gold closed at $6305 an ounce; the current price is $7138. The $833 increase in a matter of hours is a record in both dollar terms and percentage terms for a one-day jump, and the trading day still has several hours to go. So far, the big winner of the day is silver. As increasing gold prices continue to squeeze smaller investors out of the market, investors are pouring into silver. Silver jumped to $241 an ounce. Today's jump has closed the gold-to-silver price ratio from thirty-five to one to under thirty to one."

Matt decided to take the car to the used car dealership and sell it. Karen followed him in the truck to give him a ride home after the sale. The lot offered him $1500 cash. The car was worth $6500 in the Kelly Blue Book, but Matt took it. Today, they had to cut their losses and bug out.

When they returned home from selling the car, they had to make a few cuts. There wasn't room for all of the things in the trailer and the items they intended to take in the car. They pulled out a dresser, the futon and a box of extra dishes that they decided they didn't need. Matt repositioned the trailer so the food, gun safe and gasoline were the most accessible. They intended to let Miss Mae sleep in the back seat of Karen's car, but now she would have to stay on Karen's lap or the floor board by Karen's feet for most of the trip.

Since Blaine was an attorney, Matt granted him power of

attorney and paid him to go to the closing for them on the following day. Blaine briefed Matt on the process before they left. "The money should be wired into your account the day of the closing. If all goes according to plan, the funds will clear in time to close on your farm in three days."

They would only net about $50,000 after brokerage fees, taxes and closing costs, but they could easily cover the difference for the price of the farm in silver or gold; especially now, after the recent rise in the metals prices.

Matt and Karen said their goodbyes to the neighbors and loaded up. Matt put his Ruger LC9 in an ankle holster and put his Glock 21 in the back of his jeans. He wore an oversized plaid shirt over his tee-shirt to help conceal the large frame pistol. Matt instructed Karen to keep her Kel-Tec in her pocket and her Glock 19 in her purse. Matt put the pistol grip on the Mossberg pump action shotgun so it would easily fit behind the seat of his pickup truck. The AR-15 would stay in the safe at the back of the trailer for now. He drilled holes in the trailer so the safe could be bolted to the trailer floor during the trip.

The delays set them back. They planned to get on the road by 10:00 am, but it was after 3:00 pm. Karen picked up Miss Mae, who was now feeling the full effects of her kitty tranquilizer, which Karen had given her three hours prior. She only gave her a small piece with her food, so she was not totally asleep. Mae's eyes were glassy and she had no problems sitting still in Karen's lap.

As they pulled onto the ramp for I-95 north, Matt said, "We should've prayed before we left. If we've ever needed God, it's on this trip."

Karen replied, "Is it too late? God couldn't hear us in the truck?"

Matt smiled. He got the point. "God, we ask that you would

surround us with your favor as with a shield. Watch over and protect us on this journey. You're always so good to us and you always protect us. We are so grateful. Thank you."

I-75 was usually much busier at this time of day. Even on weekends, all the lanes were mostly full until you hit the toll booth past the Indian casino. Matt decided to take I-95 instead of the Florida Turnpike or I-75. I-75 would have taken them through Tampa. The Turnpike would take them through Orlando. If he continued through on I-95, it would take him to Jacksonville, which was probably the worst of the three cities, but Matt intended to get off I-95 at St. Augustine and take the backroads to connect to I-75 north of Tampa. Additionally, Matt's friend Frank lived in St. Augustine. If they got into trouble, Frank's house was a place of refuge.

The plan was good, but this route still took them through Atlanta. Atlanta had never completely returned to what would properly be described as civilized after the SNAP riots. The conundrum was that gas was becoming scarce and they had just enough in the reserve cans to get them to Kentucky. I-285 was a bypass that took them around the city of Atlanta, but it was still too close for comfort in Matt's opinion.

After they drove a little over 250 miles, Matt said, "Get the map and look to see if you can find a campground near the highway south of Atlanta. There's a magnifying glass in the glove compartment."

Matt's eyesight had really deteriorated in the past few years, so he needed a magnifying glass to read the Northern Star Road Atlas. The atlas was very complete, but the icons were extremely small.

Karen said, "The magnifying glass makes it much easier to pick out the tent icon that signifies the campground. How far south of Atlanta?" she asked as she thumbed through the atlas in search of Georgia.

"Preferably about halfway between Macon and Atlanta. The less populated, the better," Matt replied.

"Here's a state park with a campground. It's called High Falls," Karen said.

"How far from Atlanta is it?" Matt asked.

Karen focused on the map. "It looks like it's about fifty miles from downtown Atlanta. It's about thirty miles from the I-285 bypass you said you want to take."

"How many miles is the park from the I-75 exit?" Matt inquired.

"I would say about two miles," Karen replied. "Are we going to sleep in the tent?"

"I think we have to. Someone has to stand guard over the truck while the other sleeps," Matt said. "Things will get a lot worse than during the SNAP riots, and we are in a very vulnerable position by being on the road. The more we can stay away from people, the better off we'll be."

Matt and Karen noticed less and less traffic as the day went on. Most of the traffic they saw were other trucks pulling trailers.

"It looks like everybody is bugging out," Karen said.

"It does seem to be the pastime of the day," Matt said. "I'm going to pull over at the next rest stop so we can go to the bathroom and I'll fill up the gas from the cans in the trailer. The tank is almost empty. Even if the gas stations are pumping, they might be hot zones for civil unrest."

Matt pulled into the rest stop parking lot. Just like the highway, it was a ghost town. There was only one other truck in the entire lot. Matt kept an eye on Karen from the truck while she went to the restroom and she did the same while he went. They had a few pieces of cheese and crackers from the cooler. Karen got back into the truck and Matt went to fill up the truck. He started with the one-gallon containers, because of the way he had to stack them to save space in the trailer. While he was filling the truck, two guys from the other truck in the lot came over.

"Howdy," one of the men greeted Matt.

"How you doin'?" Matt replied.

"Not good; we ran out of gas. Do you have five gallons you can spare?" the man replied.

"I can't do it. I calculated exactly what I need to get where I'm going." Matt hated not being able to help, but there was nothing extra. He needed everything he had.

The two guys seemed like good old boys. They both had on jeans, boots, and ball caps. One of the caps had some tractor brand on it and the other was a camo print.

The second man replied, "How 'bout we just take it all then?" he lifted his shirt to reveal a semi-automatic pistol handle.

Adrenaline rushed into Matt's brain. He dropped the gas can, drew his Glock and shot the man in his chest. The other man was clearly surprised. He fumbled to draw a weapon. Matt breathed out heavily, inhaled again and then slowly exhaled as he lined up the sights with the man's head. The man drew out a nickel plated revolver and Matt squeezed the trigger of the Glock 21. The close range impact of the .45 caliber hollow point bullet left a small hole in the front of the man's head while the back busted open like a rotten melon. The man dropped backwards and lay beside his fallen comrade. The first man rolled over and leveled the semi-auto pistol at Matt. Matt squeezed off two more rounds into the man's chest. The man dropped the gun. Matt walked up to the body and put two more rounds into his head.

Matt grabbed both of the men's guns and threw them into the back of the trailer next to the gas cans. The revolver was a Smith and Wesson .357 Magnum and the semi-automatic was a Berretta 9mm. Matt slammed the trailer door shut and headed toward the truck.

Meanwhile inside the truck, Karen heard the shots and screamed. Even in her kitty drugged out stupor, Miss Mae jumped out of Karen's lap and ran under Karen's seat. Karen drew her Kel-Tec because it was in her pocket and easiest to access. She checked the mirrors to see where the shots came from. She saw Matt standing next to the two bodies. "Thank you Jesus, he's okay," she said with tears already starting to flow.

Matt looked at the two men. The grey matter of their brains lay in chunks, spread around in thick puddles of blood. As Matt got to the door of his truck, his stomach flipped and the contents emptied on the ground. He took ten seconds to catch his breath and calm down, then walked back to the trailer door to get a bottle of water and a ginger ale. He rinsed the vomit out of his mouth with the water and returned to the truck. Karen was pulling her phone from her purse.

"Who are you calling?" Matt asked puzzled.

"911," she replied. She couldn't believe he even had to ask.

"No!" Matt shouted. He was thinking on an entirely different level. Of course she would be calling 911. He should have known that, but he knew this was not the situation for that.

"Why?" she asked.

"There are multiple reasons. I'll explain in a minute. For now, we have to get out of here," Matt said.

Matt jumped back into the truck and sped off. He was careful to not go over the speed limit once on the highway. As soon as they were back on the road, he called Frank.

"Hey, buddy!" Frank answered.

"Hey, man. I just had an incident with a couple of guys at the rest stop. I need to get off the road for a while. I'm just past the rest stop north of Palm Coast," Matt said.

Frank could hear the panic in Matt's voice. "Alright, calm down. You are just one exit before mine. Get off at State Road 206 and take it west to State Road 305. Follow it north to 207 and take a real hard left. In a few yards from there, you'll be on my road. You'll know where you are once you get there. Just focus on driving for now and we'll talk when you get here."

"Got it," Matt said as he hung up the phone.

"Why didn't we call the police?" Karen asked.

Matt replied, "Number one, we don't know if there were more attackers in the area. We had to get out of there. Number two, there's no way we want to get caught up in an investigation when the world is falling apart. Those guys could've been best friends with the town sheriff for all we know. They could be total thugs or they may have been robbing me out of desperation. At any rate, that may have been the town they were from and we could end up getting lynched."

"Why are we going to Frank's?" Karen asked.

Matt answered, "I need to get off the road. Check the scanners, see if anyone called anything in. I also need to take a breather. I'm a little freaked out right now."

Karen said, "I'm freaked out, too. I guess it didn't occurred to me that you'd be shaken up. You just shot two people. You wouldn't be normal if you weren't."

"I also threw their guns in the truck. I need to get rid of those," Matt added.

"Why did you do that?" Karen asked.

"I don't know. Because I'm freaked out I guess. I also have blood all over my shoes. I need to clean them off." Matt started to feel a knot in his throat, but there was no time for getting emotional now. He pushed it back down and kept driving.

They were at Frank's house in about twenty minutes. He was in a semi-rural area. Lots of people kept livestock and the houses were spread out. Frank greeted them and ushered them inside. Frank's wife, Angela, made hamburgers on the grill while Matt explained what happened at the rest stop. Karen put Miss Mae in her cat carrier and brought her inside. The late November air was significantly cooler in north Florida than where they came from.

"You can let the cat walk around inside if you like," Angela told Karen.

"She would probably find somewhere to hide and we would be looking for her when it's time to go. But thank you," Karen replied.

Frank threw Matt's hiking boots into the washing machine. His jeans had blood spattered around the bottom. Matt changed his jeans and threw them in the wash as well. Matt walked Frank over to the trailer and told him about the guns.

"I have no idea why I threw them in the trailer," Matt explained.

"Brother, you were traumatized. You did good. You stayed alive and you kept your wife safe. That's what you were supposed to do. Don't beat yourself up over some small detail like that. If you want to get rid of them, I'll be happy to take them and bury them. I'll always know where they are. They might come in handy someday, you never know," Frank said.

Matt gave them to Frank, who then wrapped them in thick construction garbage bags with a sock full of rice to absorb the moisture. He then placed them in a two-gallon plastic bucket. He wrapped the bucket in more plastic then dug a quick hole behind his tool shed.

"You look like you've done this before." Matt was relieved to have gotten rid of the pistols.

"You know me, brother. I've been prepping since before it was cool. I have stuff buried all over the place," Frank said with a smile.

"You're a regular pirate," Matt said.

The guys rejoined the women inside and ate the wonderful burgers Angela had made. Afterwards, they went to the computer to listen to the local police scanner on Broadcastify.com. There were several reports of looting and robberies, but they heard nothing in reference to the shooting.

"It's just after 9:00 pm," Frank said. "It sounds like the natives are starting to get restless over in town. That's how it was during the riots. I would say the police are going to have their hands full. They won't have time to worry about you. You all are welcome to lay low here as long as you like though."

"Thanks for the offer. I think I'll try to get back on the road around 1:30 in the morning. That will put us in Atlanta at 7:30, just after sunrise. That tends to be the most peaceful time of the day. Atlanta will probably be a mess. We don't have enough fuel to get around it. The bypass should be okay early tomorrow morning, but I have to get through there," Matt said.

Frank replied. "It sounds like you have thought this out."

"Well, I had it all planned out before I almost got robbed," Matt said.

"You're still on track, brother," Frank responded. "It's just a slight detour. Do you want to try to take a nap before you go?"

"No way. I could never go to sleep now," Matt said. "Not after that incident."

"Well," Frank replied, "we'll make you a big pot of extra strong coffee before you pull out. You'll be pretty far from any major cities until you get to Atlanta. Valdosta is the only big town between here and there. Driving at night will probably work out good. Make sure you top off your tank before you head out."

Matt thanked Frank for his hospitality and for helping him out of this tough situation. They moved back and forth between the news radio and the police scanner. Nothing was ever mentioned about the bodies.

They talked about the uncertainty of the future and what the world would look like tomorrow. Times were a-changing.

CHAPTER 26

"I predict future happiness for Americans if they can prevent the government from wasting the labors of the people under the pretense of taking care of them."

Thomas Jefferson

Matt and Karen Bair were ready to leave from Frank's house just west of Saint Augustine at 1:00 in the morning. They took their time getting on the road, because they didn't want to arrive in the Atlanta area until after sunrise. Frank and Angela fed them well before they left, and Matt's clothes were now clean. Matt replaced the Mossberg from behind the truck seat with the AR-15. From now on, stopping to refuel would be a military exercise.

They pulled out of the driveway at 1:30 am with full cups of hot, strong coffee. The adrenaline was high because they knew it was still possible to be questioned about the shooting. It was conceivable that they were seen leaving the rest stop or had been caught by surveillance cameras. In this age of total government intrusion, they must have been caught on film at some point. Their best hope was that the police were too occupied with criminals to be chasing after them.

Matt kept to the speed limit and was soon out of Florida. He was relieved to pass the state line. While a shooting certainly warranted the involvement of police from a neighboring state in ordinary circumstances, Georgia likely had enough problems of their own right now.

After five hours of driving, the adrenaline and caffeine were wearing down and they were both very tired. Karen slept while Matt drove. He woke her up to tell her they needed to pull off the road and fill up the tank again. It was still dark.

"Oh no," she said anxiously.

Matt explained the procedure. "We're going to pull off the road at the state park where we were originally going to sleep. Once we're off the exit ramp, I'll look for a side road with no people. I'll get out of the truck with the AR-15 and you fill up the tanks. If anyone pulls up other than a police car, close the trailer door and get back into the truck. If police pull up, I'll stick the AR-15 in the truck bed under the tarp. Don't say anything to the police except direct answers to what they ask you."

"What if they ask about the rest stop?" Karen asked.

"Did you actually see me shoot those men?" Matt asked.

"No," she said.

"Then you didn't see anything," he replied. "After we refuel, you'll drive through Atlanta, and I'll be watching out for threats with the AR-15."

They arrived at the exit and executed their refueling plan without incident. In minutes, they were back on the road and Karen was driving. They were out of coffee, but they did have some Mountain Dew. Prior to reaching the I-285 Atlanta bypass, Matt started searching for another campground. They needed to get some rest once they were past the city. He soon located one in the Chattahoochee National Forest. It was only about seventy miles north of Atlanta.

They soon reached the I-285 bypass just after sunrise. It was eerily quiet. Matt didn't know what to expect. The news radio reported several fires and some rioting in Atlanta the night before, but there was not much in the way of details. All of the news reports were focused on the oil markets and the stock market, which was shut down again to cauterize the bleeding of wealth into oblivion. The Dow plummeted 840 points the previous day causing the SEC to halt trading before lunch. This was the second time in a month that the circuit breaker rule was used to freeze trading on all the major exchanges.

Just before they got back on I-75 north, Karen pointed out a wreck in the distance. As they got closer Matt could see two cars blocking traffic and a woman's body lying in the road.

"Should we stop to help?" Karen asked.

"Neither one of those cars are damaged." Matt analyzed the scene. "Drive around on the left shoulder in case there are people on the other side of the vehicles lying in ambush. That will put them on my side of the truck so I can return fire if they shoot at us."

"Okay," Karen said with a voice that let Matt know she was determined to get through. Karen was completely feminine, but she could be tough if she had to be. Matt absolutely loved that about her.

As they passed the two cars in the road, Matt noticed two men in ski masks on the backside of the cars. They were sitting with their backs against the cars holding shotguns in their hands. As they passed the two cars, the masked men drew their guns. Matt thumbed off the safety of the AR-15 and stuck it out the window in the direction of the men. He began laying down cover fire to keep their heads down until they were clear of the effective range of the bandits' weapons. Karen smashed the gas pedal to the floor of the truck and they sped off. Miss Mae once again found refuge under the seat.

Fifteen minutes later, the adrenaline wore off from their most recent near miss. After being up so many hours and having so many adrenaline rushes, they were crashing. Everything was starting to feel like a dream. The sun was up and the day was bright. When they reached the campground, Matt pitched the tent and Karen went straight in and fell fast asleep. There was only two other sets of campers at the site. Their gear made it obvious that they were hunters.

Matt started a fire and made some coffee. His body was screaming for sleep, but he had to keep watch while Karen slept. He kept the door of the tent zipped up so Miss Mae wouldn't sneak out of the tent. It was chilly, so it was safe to assume she would crawl in the mule with Karen. The mule was Matt's nickname for Karen's sleeping bag. It was the largest thickest, heaviest sleeping bag ever made. He had come up with the moniker for the subzero rated sleeping bag because it was like trying to move a dead mule. It was bulky and heavy, but the mule was a great thing to have in a tent when it was cold outside. Matt made himself some bacon, eggs and toast over the fire. He heard Miss Mae meowing in the tent. He unzipped it and let her walk outside. She cautiously inspected the scent of the fire before completely coming outside. She slowly walked to the back of the tent to relieve herself, then trotted back to where the bacon and eggs were. Matt sat the plate down and the cat ate her fill. He put her back in the tent and she found her place in the catacombs of the mule.

Matt walked around the fire and threw in the occasional stick. He did this until about noon when he started another batch of bacon and eggs. He started some coffee for Karen and woke her up. She was completely under. He hated to wake her, but he had to have her up so he could sleep a few hours before they completed their trip.

Karen finally came around and took over guard duty while Matt crawled into the tent. The sleeping bag was already warm and Miss Mae was still in a ball in the middle. Matt was snoring within two minutes of lying down.

Karen heard a gunshot in the distance. She thought of waking Matt but didn't. She kept her hand on her pistol inside the waist of her jeans as she surveyed the woods and listened for movement. About thirty minutes later, she found out what the gunshot had been. Two of the hunters from the camp across from them were coming through the woods with an eight-point buck. She watched as they strung the deer up in the tree and began to skin it. She was happy to see they had something to do besides giving her trouble.

Two hours later, one of the hunters came by with a heaping plate full of freshly roasted venison. She was a bit nervous when he approached, but she could quickly see he was a kind-hearted man and meant no harm. It refreshed her hope for humanity and reminded her that everyone wasn't mean. She thanked him and he returned to his camp without saying much. The seasoning on the venison was spectacular. She though it must be something similar to Montreal Steak seasoning, but it had something else in it. She just couldn't figure out what it was.

She woke Matt up at 4:00 pm and they struck the tent. Karen gave Matt some of the roasted venison, which he ate with some salt, vinegar potato chips and celery sticks. Matt made another pot of coffee before he put out the fire. He topped off the magazine for the AR-15 and put three more magazines in the glove compartment of the truck. He never thought he would actually shoot at people with it; of course, he never thought he would have to kill anyone either. Matt didn't think he hit either of the men behind the car on the bypass, but he felt strangely indifferent as if he didn't care whether he had or not. As he thought about it after some rest, he realized he felt no guilt for having killed the two men. There was some worry that he would be caught up in an investigation at this, the worst possible time in history, but no guilt. If he felt anything, he was angry that the men had caused him to deviate from his plan and risked getting him caught up in a legal quagmire. Should he feel guilty? He didn't know. There was no doubt, if he would have hesitated, it would have been him lying in the pool of blood and brain. He thought about what Frank had said. Matt did what he had to do. He was certain there would be no shortage of instant replays of the event in his head as he lay in bed at night trying to forget.

The Bairs filled the tank and got back on the road.

CHAPTER 27

"Do not be yoked together with unbelievers. For what do righteousness and wickedness have in common? Or what fellowship can light have with darkness?"

II Corinthians 6:14

Wesley Bair finished his coffee. He didn't say a word at breakfast.

"What's up, little brother?" Adam asked as he finished a biscuit with jelly.

"Adam, I need to bring Shelly up here. The world is falling apart and if I don't, I'll probably never see her again," Wesley replied.

Adam said, "Hold your horses, Wes. Like I told you, you're welcome to stay here, but you know this isn't going to be no love shack. I mind my own business, but I won't allow people sleeping together under my roof if they aren't married. I ask God to bless me every day. The least I can do is maintain a moral standard in my house."

Carissa was too young to really get the drift of the conversation, but Mandy was 12 and she seemed to know exactly what was going on. She didn't say a word, but she gave her mother a look that said, "Please do something!"

Janice saw that Mandy was embarrassed and interrupted the conversation. "Why don't you boys go check to see if the hens laid any eggs. Plus, you'll be able to finish your conversation in private."

Adam and Wesley both winced as they noticed how the conversation had bothered Mandy. She wasn't a baby anymore and they had to be more careful. They walked out to the yard and Adam continued his speech. "I thought there wasn't anyone serious? Have I even heard of Shelly?"

Wesley replied, "I don't say much about her to anyone. She was in my class last semester. I would've gotten fired if the college knew I was dating a student, even though she isn't in my class anymore. We've been going out for a while. I guess I didn't know it was serious until just now. The thought of never seeing her again is putting a sinking feeling in my stomach."

"You could've told me about her. What did you think? I was going to turn you in to the dean?" Adam inquired.

"Not at all. I was just in secret squirrel mode with the relationship and didn't talk to anyone about it," Wesley answered.

Adam stated, "I understand you like this girl, Wes, but you can't bring a non-Christian up here to live. It's hard enough to raise two girls right. I don't need them having any permanent bad examples around. You hardly ever go to church with us. Your priorities are based on other things besides God's will, but you know right from wrong. I guess I know deep down that you will come around at some point."

"She is a Christian," Wesley interjected.

"Come on, bro. Are you telling me you two have been hanging out at church every Sunday when you go to Berea?" Adam asked.

"Not exactly," Wesley said. "I kept telling her I would go with her, but it's always too late by the time I get down there."

Adam didn't say anything for a while. He was Wesley's brother, not his father, but he stepped into that role without meaning to on some occasions. This was different though. This was about setting a good example for his girls and maintaining the integrity of his home.

"Do you want to marry this girl?" Adam asked.

Wesley was silent for a while.

Adam continued, "If not, I think you should just let her go. We're approaching one of the most interesting periods of our nation's history. Things are about to get nuts. If she ain't the one, she's just going to be extra baggage that you don't need. If she's some crazy chick, she's going to get you distracted, and that might get you killed. We don't know; we may be in the middle of a civil war a month from now. You also can't bring some brainwashed liberal or statist neocon around here either. The time for missionary dating and trying to convince people to wake up from the lies in the mainstream media is over. We have to know we can trust people and we have to know where they stand."

"She's the one," Wesley finally declared. "And she voted for Paul Randall. She's pretty radical. I saw her light into some liberals about the Second Amendment one time. She really knows her stuff. That's why I like her so much."

"Why are you just now figuring that out?" Adam questioned.

"I already knew. I just wasn't ready to commit. I thought I had all the time in the world. I was being selfish," Wesley responded.

"Well, if she comes here, you have to sleep on the couch and give her your room. If that rule gets violated, one of you have to find somewhere else to sleep until you get married. Do you even know if she feels the same way?" Adam asked.

"She does. I've been taking her for granted," Wesley said.

"Alright, go get her. It's eighty miles round trip. Take Janice's car to save gas. Your truck will burn fuel that we don't have to waste," Adam said.

"She'll probably want to bring her stuff," Wesley replied. "I would be better off in a truck."

Adam stated, "Wesley, it could be weeks, months or years before the gas stations have fuel again. I understand this is important to you, but we have to conserve resources. The back seat folds down. You should be able to fit an awful lot of clothes back there. Besides her clothes, we have everything she could possibly need right here."

"You're right," Wesley agreed.

"Take a .45 and a rifle. Those college kids might start getting desperate. You never know," Adam added.

Wesley nodded in agreement. He went inside to the safe and grabbed an AR-15. He stuck a 1911 .45 Colt Commander in a shoulder holster and took two extra magazines for each weapon.

Wesley wasted no time. As he got in the car, Adam shut the door for him. Adam looked at him as he said, "Watch your six."

Adam went back inside and pulled out his phone. Matt and Karen should have arrived by now. He called Matt's number, but all the circuits were busy. Since he couldn't get through on the phone, he shot Matt a text, "U ok?" Even when circuits were overloaded, text messages would usually go through.

Adam, Janice and the girls started doing their chores. There were animals to feed and a few apples left in the orchard to gather.

Three hours later, Wesley and Shelly arrived.

Wesley introduced her to the family and everyone gave her a warm welcome. Janice showed her where she would be sleeping while the guys brought in her personal effects.

Once Shelly was settled, Janice made some sandwiches and everyone ate together.

Janice kept the conversation going to make Shelly feel welcomed. "So how were things at school when you left?"

Shelly answered, "People are afraid. Everyone is going home. My parents were coming to get me tomorrow if Wes hadn't come to pick me up."

The discussion stayed on the topic of the current situation for the rest of the meal.

After lunch they all retired to the family room to watch the news. Mandy usually had no interest in the news, but the world was falling apart. She listened to the adults and started asking questions about the news. Carissa sat near her sister and played with her dolls.

CNC's Patrick James was reporting from Wall Street. "The scene here on Wall Street is eerily reminiscent of a horror movie. There are no people going back and forth. This was to be a short week anyway due to the Thanksgiving holiday, but I've never seen Wall Street so vacant. The SEC determined that US markets will remain closed through the holiday and reopen on Monday. An SEC spokesman told CNC earlier that Thanksgiving week trading is always light because many traders travel for the holiday. He said the reduced amount of traders brings increased volatility into the market. There are less buyers and sellers to absorb the shocks when trading is light.

"The White House released a temporary emergency order to help deal with gasoline shortages and calm fears. Tensions are still high from the riots at the beginning of the month. Those were triggered by temporary budget shortfalls in the SNAP benefits program. The White House was eager to get in front of this latest event to prevent the chaos and bloodshed that erupted from the last economic challenge.

"In the comments given by White House Press Secretary Armando Sanchez, the administration laid out an overview of their plan to manage the present crisis. Sanchez told reporters to expect a longer, more detailed explanation of the plan in a speech that the president will deliver tomorrow morning.

"Sanchez began by saying the White House was in complete control of the situation. He assured Americans that gas stations would be back on line again by tomorrow morning. The US is releasing a large portion of their strategic oil reserves to combat the situation, but Sanchez asked that Americans cancel their plans to travel for the Thanksgiving holiday. Once the gas stations reopen, the US Government will be limiting gasoline purchases to five gallons per week. While law enforcement representatives will be monitoring gas stations to insure that no one purchases more than five gallons at a time, the White House is asking people to respect the restriction on the honor system until Homeland Security can institute a ration system next Monday.

"While the White House Press Secretary made no mention of it in his address, the Department of Energy has notified all US oil producers and gasoline refineries that the US Government would be nationalizing twenty percent of their current production until strategic reserves could be resupplied. The notification, sent to oil and gas industry executives, also included vague language that informed them that essential government services, emergency services, food transportation and public transportation would be supplied with fuel from the strategic reserves until the crisis fully abates.

Wesley Bair snickered to himself at the report.

"What's funny?" Adam asked.

"Fully abates," Wesley answered. "This isn't going to 'fully abate.' The government just nationalized the oil industry."

Adam added, "They'll never quit taking twenty percent. There's nothing temporary about it. "

Janice said, "Maybe twenty percent is temporary. They'll probably have to raise it to thirty percent after a few smaller oil companies go bankrupt from the government takeover."

Wesley commented, "Taking twenty percent of production might bankrupt all of the oil and gas companies. The only ones that will be able to stay solvent will probably be the ones the government bails out. I bet that's the plan. It'll be just like the health insurance industry. The individual mandate had a fine that was lower than the cost of insurance. Everybody waited until they got sick to buy insurance. That bankrupted all of the insurance companies except Medisure, which is every bit as much of a government entity as the DOD or the Social Security Administration. That strategy won the government the single payer system they wanted from the beginning. This move will do the same for the oil industry. The only company that will survive will be the one the government picks. It might be Exxon, BP or whoever they decide to prop up.

"People associated fascism with the Nazis, but fascism is really the intertwined relationship between large corporations and the government. Medisure is the government tentacle of health care, Howe Clancy is the government tentacle of banking and we'll soon see who is to be the government tentacle of the oil and gas industry."

Janice said, "Well, I suppose that won't go over well with oil stocks when the SEC reopens the markets."

"You're right about that," Adam agreed.

"Maybe someone could pick the company the government is going to bail out to run the show. That stock might do well." Shelly said. She was shy, but she was eager to be part of the family.

"Possibly," Wesley said. "But I expect the government to watch them all sink to the bottom so they can come in and bailout the company they want with a large stock purchase. That way, they'll get it dirt cheap and be able to purchase more than fifty-one percent of the stock. That would give them controlling interest."

Adam's phone chirped. It was a text message from Matt. "Be there by 10 we r safe but roads r rough :("

Adam read the text to everyone.

"Praise God, they're safe," Janice said.

Wesley said, "I didn't have any trouble picking up Shelly, but who knows how bad things are in the rest of the country. The news don't exactly cover the highway."

"Did they have to go through Atlanta?" Shelly asked.

Adam answered, "They were planning to take the I-285 Bypass, but they didn't have enough fuel to go any further out of the way than that."

Matt, Karen and Miss Mae arrived at 9:30 that evening. They were received with much affection. They told the tales of their adventure and everyone listened with eyes wide open. Adam had seen much worse while deployed in the sandbox, but everyone else was shocked that things could be so bad here in America.

Janice coordinated the sleeping arrangements. The kids went to sleep around 11 o'clock, and the adults sat up discussing the recent events. All were speculating the timing and severity of the collapse that was upon them.

CHAPTER 28

"He that is good for making excuses is seldom good for anything else."

Benjamin Franklin

Treasury Secretary Chang and Fed Chair Jane Bleecher needed very little evidence of the impending collapse to convince President Al Mohammad of the need for drastic measures.

President Al Mohammad dictated to his aide the list of those who were to attend the crisis control meeting.

"Call Anthony Howe; this is all going to be his problem in eight weeks. He might as well start learning what this job is all about. Get someone from the Department of Defense in here, but not Allen Jefferson; get someone who plays ball. This is too important. I'll lock up anybody who gets in my way. Make sure Gerald Brown is in here from HHS."

"Have Tamara Slocomb from DHS bring a couple of her goons. I have a special project for them. I need chairs all around the back of the room for the Plunge Protection Team traders. I need everyone who is associated with the Plunge Protection Team, all the way down to the NSA analysts who gather intel for the traders. I need Tamara's people to put the fear of God in those traders, so they know how important it is to not speak to anyone about this meeting. The world is falling apart and we have to take any means necessary to hold it together."

The Plunge Protection Team was the nickname assigned to the Working Group on Financial Markets. The group was created in 1987 in response to the market crash that year. It consisted of the Fed Chairman, the Chairman of the Securities and Exchange Commission, or SEC, the Chairman of the Commodity Future Trading Commission, or CFTC and the Secretary of the Treasury. The group had grown to employ an elite force of traders and speculators who operated outside of the government. Most of the traders were tapped from among Howe Clancy's brightest. Their salaries were paid from black-box spending allocated through the NSA. They were awarded huge bonuses deposited into foreign accounts when they were able to manipulate markets successfully to reach specific outcomes.

The thirty traders that acted on behalf of the group were sworn to absolute secrecy. In exchange, they were granted carte blanche on how they accessed their information and how they traded. They were jokingly referred to by support staff and NSA analysts as 007 traders. They operated completely above the law. In financial terms, they had a license to kill.

The access to trading information that the traders received from the NSA was so far beyond anything that could be termed insider trading, the 007 traders referred to it as omniscient trading.

The NSA fed the traders information from tapped e-mails and phone conferences. Company reports on any computer could be hacked by NSA analysts and forwarded to the traders. Microphones on private laptops, tablets and cell phones could be remotely activated to get real time information from conversations by company executives. Company earnings reports, financial difficulties, market shortages, and every conceivable morsel of information regarding statistics and events that affect stock prices was available to the 007 traders. If one could imagine trading today's stock market with tomorrow's Wall Street Journal, one would just begin to grasp the power of the 007 traders.

Treasury Secretary Melinda Chang and Fed Chairwoman Jan Bleecher held a private meeting with the president before the crisis control meeting.

President Al Mohammad displayed his flippant attitude about the crisis to the two women by saying, "Well, I hear Mount Weather is nice this time of year. Actually, it's a pleasant fifty-six degrees all year around."

Both of the women cracked up laughing. Mount Weather, also known as High Point Specialty Facility was the nearby underground emergency management FEMA facility that was designed for continuity of government in the event of nuclear war or other catastrophe. It was well stocked with water, food, energy, and everything needed to sustain life for an extended period of time for about 200 people.

Al Mohammad continued, "All joking aside, ladies, you two are very important to this country and you both have your golden ticket to High Point if we see signs of civil unrest. That said, there is very limited spacing, so you would only be able to bring one immediate family member if you chose to come to High Point. There are other installations around the country that I could arrange to have other members of your family sent to if you want to serve your country from High Point in Virginia.

"So relax. If it does all fall apart, we'll go underground and come out after the zombies have all eaten each other."

Both of the women were relieved to have received the invitation to Mount Weather.

"Thank you very much, Mr. President," Melinda Chang said. "I wish I had better news."

"Now what?" Al Mohammad asked.

"Several sovereign funds, including China, Japan, Brazil, Taiwan, Switzerland and others have contacted the Treasury over concerns about US Bonds. They fear staying in US Treasury bonds, but they know that a large sale by any of the others would trigger a stampede out of Treasuries. They're asking us for a solution since it's in everyone's interest to keep the prices stable," Chang said.

"Did you ladies come up with a solution?" the president asked.

Jane Bleecher responded, "We have a tentative agreement to purchase the bonds at face value and the respective countries will agree to keep the bonds and never sell them."

"So we're going to give them the cash for the bonds and let them keep the bonds?" Al Mohammad asked.

"We have no other choice, sir," Chang said. "If they start dumping bonds, the values will crash anyway. This is our last hope of propping up the dollar."

Al Mohammad's desk phone buzzed. "Yes?" he responded.

"Anthony Howe is here, sir," the voice replied.

"Send him in," Al Mohammad replied.

"Mr. President," Howe greeted with a smile.

"Sit down, Anthony," the president said with a scowl.

The group proceeded to fill Anthony Howe in on the details of their conversation up to that point.

"So did the representatives of the concerned countries agree to the deal?" Howe asked.

Chang replied, "If we settle in gold."

The room was silent as Howe and Al Mohammad processed the implications of the deal. Howe had a better handle on the situation than Al Mohammad.

"And we have about 8000 metric tons of gold?" Howe asked.

"That's what is on the balance sheet, sir, but we don't actually have access to all of that," Bleecher replied. "Some of it was leased out and delivery was taken. The gold we lost possession of was scheduled to be re-accumulated but price volatility has made that impossible. Most all of the remaining gold is presently leased, but we still have physical possession of it."

"How much is that?" Howe asked.

"About 3000 metric tons, sir," Bleecher replied.

"Well, at over $7000 an ounce, that's still a nice sum," Al Mohammad said.

"It is about $680 billion, sir. China's holdings of US debt are near $2 trillion alone," Chang said.

"Could the Plunge Protection Team drive up the value of gold to $14,000 an ounce by the time you actually finalized a deal?" Howe asked.

"It would likely float to that level on its own if we quit suppressing the price, sir," Bleecher replied.

The Plunge Protection Team had been suppressing the gold price for years to provide a false sense of value for the US dollar. The team would slowly make small purchases of gold and gold-futures contracts throughout the trading day using money from the Exchange Stability Fund. They would then dump the gold and the gold contracts in after-hours trading. As there were few buyers in the after-hours markets, each successively lower price buyer would be quickly taken out as they bought the gold and the contracts. The result would often be a $30 or $50 per-ounce price cut in gold. The lower price would be in place at the beginning of the next trading day and would generally set the trading range for the day.

The team also used lease contracts on the gold reserves held by the Fed to manipulate the markets lower. As the free market started to recognize the value of the discounted gold price, delivery was often taken on leases that were anticipated to expire.

Mohammad was not that well versed in finance, but he knew all about manipulation. It was an international language that most everyone in DC could speak fluently.

"So if we pushed it back up, how high could gold go by the time we had to settle?" Mohammad asked.

"I don't know," Bleecher replied, "$15,000 maybe $20,000, but it would absolutely crash the dollar."

"Which is happening anyway." Al Mohammad quickly stepped in to make sure he was still in control of the narrative. "But it would buy us some time."

A deal was struck between the sovereign holders of US Treasuries for a partial settlement in gold and a partial settlement in cash. Additionally, the settlement was pushed back until January 1st of next year. The extra five weeks would give the traders plenty of time to work their magic. In exchange for the deal, the foreign holders of the US debt agreed to never sell the Treasuries but find some other means of creative accounting to liquidate the bonds from their own balance sheets slowly, over time.

The plan was finalized and presented to the attendees of the crisis control meeting. The Federal Reserve was to inject $3 trillion dollars into the Exchange Stability Fund with which the traders would prop up the dollar and the stock market on Monday following the Thanksgiving holiday. Prior to driving up the price of gold, the traders were instructed to acquire as much physical gold as possible. The acquisition was to be made by shell holding companies and held in Zurich. This was to be the most top secret operation in recent US history.

The $3 trillion in newly created Fed monies would never be reported on any balance sheet and were to be retired after the crisis was brought under control. It was completely illegal, but desperate times call for desperate measures.

Al Mohammad readied himself to give his speech to the American public. It was only 11:00 am, but this had already been a very tiresome day.

All the news stations were broadcasting the speech.

"My fellow Americans. We have more to be thankful for tomorrow than we've had on any Thanksgiving Day since the first time the pilgrims celebrated Thanksgiving over 400 year ago. We have finally achieved the American Dream of oil independence. With new technologies being used in the Eagle Ford oil field in Texas and the Bakken oil field in North Dakota, our country is now producing eighty-five percent of the oil that America uses. The other fifteen percent is supplied by countries that are friendly with America, like our good neighbor to the north, Canada.

"This has enabled us to sever ties with hostile regimes in the Middle East and other regions of the globe that treat their citizens unfairly. America can no longer claim the moral high ground while we support governments that abuse women and people with beliefs that are different from theirs. Just as America's first independence required sacrifice, this independence from foreign oil does not come without a cost.

"We're going to be temporarily rationing gasoline until production in our own oil fields can be adjusted. Every American will be allotted five gallons per week for necessary travel. For those who need to travel farther than that, we recommend public transportation and carpooling. Beginning Monday, you'll be able to go on the Department of Energy's website and sign up using your Social Security number to receive your new Gasoline Independence card. The Independence cards will be mailed out within two days of your application. These cards will help us get back to normal.

"America has never been more resilient than it is right now and we'll become even stronger in the days and weeks to come. Being able to shed this addiction on foreign oil will make our future brighter than you can imagine.

"Anytime there's an abrupt event, markets get spooked and indexes plummet. We've seen this time after time throughout history. As we look back, those were some of the best times to have purchased stocks. These things always work themselves out. I wouldn't be a bit surprised to see a major relief rally when markets reopen for trading Monday morning.

"Tomorrow morning, get up and watch the Macy's Thanksgiving Day Parade with your loved ones, eat turkey 'til it comes out of your ears, then sit back and enjoy some football or watch *It's a Wonderful Life*, because it truly is a wonderful life. That's what I'll be doing. Be thankful to the universe and yourselves for all you have. Happy Thanksgiving."

Al Mohammad smiled like he didn't have a care in the world.

For once, it wasn't an act. He couldn't wait to be free of this office. His Thanksgiving would be as wonderful as anyone could imagine. America had always bought his lies before; why wouldn't they buy this one? He gave them the confidence they needed to get through these hard times. He thought, *if they knew what I had just saved them from, they would be thankful to me, rather than some mystic being in the sky.*

CHAPTER 29

"Blessed is the man who does not walk in the counsel of the wicked or stand in the way of sinners or sit in the seat of mockers. But his delight is in the law of the LORD, and on his law he meditates day and night. He is like a tree planted by streams of water, which yields its fruit in season and whose leaf does not wither. Whatever he does prospers."

Psalm 1:1-3

Matthew and Karen Bair woke up much later than everyone else. Janice offered to make them a big breakfast, but they only wanted coffee and toast. Adam had already spent a couple hours cutting wood that morning and was getting ready to watch the president's speech that was scheduled for eleven o'clock. Wesley and Shelly went hunting early that morning. Providence blessed them with a wild turkey. It was cleaned and they were just bringing it in.

"Wow!" Matt said. "That's a big bird you shot, Wes."

"Shelly shot it," Wesley replied.

Adam joked, "If things don't work out between you two, we'll keep Shelly and send Wesley packing."

Shelly smiled and blushed slightly. She fit like a glove in the Bair family. She was nervous about blending in when Wesley picked her up the day before.

Janice commented, "This certainly will make a nice Thanksgiving bird tomorrow."

The president's speech was starting and they all gathered around the television to hear what he had to say.

Karen said, "It's almost pointless to listen to him. Whatever he says, you know it's going to be a lie."

"We have eight years of experience trying to decipher the lies and make an educated guess of what is really going on," Wesley replied.

"Unfortunately, I never perfected that skill," said Janice.

They listened as he explained the gas ration cards. Wesley shot Matt a look as the president mentioned the possibility of a relief rally on Monday.

"Sounds like he might have some inside information," Wesley said to Matt.

"Careful, Wes. There's a thin line between conspiracy theory and treason," Matt joked.

Wesley said, "Yeah, if you can't prove it, it's conspiracy theory. If you have proof, it's treason."

Shelly made a mock gagging gesture as she heard the president close with the part about being thankful to the universe and to yourselves.

"He's claiming that the collapse of the petro-dollar system was the best thing that ever happened to us," Adam commented. "Then why did I spend six years in the sandbox getting shot at to prop it up? If it was so great, we could have let it collapse a long time ago. We could've also saved a trillion bucks a year on defense spending, not to mention the men and women who sacrificed their lives, limbs and minds"

Matt said, "Anthony Howe has a tough act to follow. I don't know if anyone can be as much of a dirt bag as Al Mohammad."

Wesley remarked, "I have a lot of faith in Howe. I think he'll surprise you with what a tremendous dirt bag he can be. He has dirt bag skills you've never dreamed about."

Back in the kitchen, Janice started preparing a few items for the following day's Thanksgiving feast. She started her prep work and made a batch of cornbread for the stuffing. Shelly wanted to make sure she made a good first impression so she went in to help.

"Thank you so much Shelly, but you've already done enough by providing the turkey," Janice said.

"God provided it, I just took the shot," Shelly said.

Janice thought, *this girl is too good to be true*. She was happy to have Shelly around. All of Wesley's girlfriends hadn't been this sweet.

"So I guess the 'universe' had nothing to do with it either?" Janice laughed.

"Not at all," Shelly replied with a chuckle.

Adam and Wesley drove Matt and Karen over to look at the

property they were considering. They walked around and looked over the exterior and the out buildings. They called the real estate agent who gave them the code for the lock box. As providence would have it, they were able to get through to the agent on the phone. Normally, she would have never given out the lock box code but the gas rations made her decide against driving fifteen miles each way to let them in.

Matt was scared to ask, but he did it anyway. "What do you think, Karen?"

"I love it," she replied.

"Really?" he asked.

"Really!" Karen affirmed.

Matt grabbed her and hugged her tight. "Thank you, baby."

"Let's call the realtor," Matt said.

Adam said, "Ya'll don't want to pray about it first?"

Matt replied, "Sure." He lifted his hands and eyes towards Heaven and said, "Lord, open the door if this is your will and close it if it isn't."

Adam smiled and shook his head.

Matt offered $55,000. The agent said she would get the offer ready and e-mail it to Matt to sign. When they returned to Adam's, Matt printed out the contract. He and Karen signed and initialed the contract. Matt scanned it back into the computer and e-mailed it right back.

Wesley checked his phone and said, "Paul Randall is issuing a video response to Al Mohammad's speech."

"You get a text alert on that?" Adam asked.

"Yeah, it's scheduled for 8:30 tonight," Wesley responded.

Janice popped some popcorn for the event. This would be much better that listening to Al Mohammad drone on. Everyone gathered around the computer screen in the office where Karen and Matt were sleeping temporarily. Miss Mae even came out from under the couch to see what the commotion was about. She usually only came out from under the fold-out couch to eat. She took her time feeling out any new environment before getting to know the new neighbors.

Paul Randall began speaking. "Patriots, I know none of you who are listening to me fell for the hogwash dished out by Mustafa Al Mohammad today. Once again, he lied to the American people and told them wrong is right and black is white. What you saw in Monday's market crash was not an answered prayer. It was the inevitable end of confidence in the US dollar. OPEC has lost all faith in our fiat currency and that is triggering a currency collapse. Disregard the lies coming from the administration and do everything you can to get out of US dollar immediately. Purchase anything that will hold value. Buy tools, fuel, canned food, ammo or whatever has a shelf life of over five years.

"Mustafa and his henchmen have doubtlessly concocted some mindless scheme to procrastinate our day of reckoning. Whatever their plan, it's the equivalent of trying to support the Golden Gate Bridge with a roll of duct tape. I have much more faith in duct tape than our administration or the US dollar, but one roll would be far less than what would be required to hold up a bridge.

"I pray you'll all have a blessed Thanksgiving tomorrow. I pray that while many will be separated from friends and family because of the gas shortages, that we'll all be one in the spirit. I will agree that we still have much to be thankful for. We can be thankful that we have a God watching over us that is more powerful that the universe or ourselves. May we be thankful that He always hears our prayers and guides us through difficult times. Happy Thanksgiving, patriots!"

Karen looked up from the computer and said, "Maybe that will keep me from having bad dreams about Al Mohammad."

Everyone chuckled, but she said, "I wasn't joking."

Matt helped Adam bring in some more firewood to keep the fire going all night, then everyone got ready for bed. Adam shot Wesley a look and pointed with two fingers from his own eyes to Wesley. It was the international sign for, "I'll be watching you." Wesley smiled without saying a word. He knew his brother only wanted what was best for him and Shelly, but he also knew he was serious.

The next morning, Janice was up early. She made a huge breakfast for everyone. Karen helped her clean up and the two of them started the Thanksgiving feast. Shelly took Mandy and Carissa out to forage for acorns and brightly colored leaves. When they returned with their treasures, they used them to fashion a center piece for the table.

Carissa ran into the family room where the men were talking. She grabbed Adam and said, "Daddy, Daddy, come see what we made for the table!" Adam was caught. He could go the hard way or the easy way. He decided to make it easy on himself and just do as he had been instructed.

Everyone gathered around the table when the meal was ready. They stood and took turns saying a brief prayer to thank God for something each was grateful for. The circle ended with Adam who said a somewhat longer prayer and asked God to bless the meal and to protect them from the coming storm.

CHAPTER 30

"He said to them, 'But now if you have a purse, take it, and also a bag; and if you don't have a sword, sell your cloak and buy one.'"

Luke 22:36

Matthew Bair hung up the phone with Blaine Phelps. "The house in Florida closed this morning," he announced.

"And the money is in our account?" Karen asked.

"It's in transit. The funds will be cleared on Monday morning," Matt answered. "I just need to send a screen shot of the transaction page to the realtor who listed the farm. That will serve as proof of funds for the farm. The seller wants to see it before he accepts our offer. Hopefully we can close on Monday afternoon."

Everyone was getting ready to head to the flea market. It was a huge metal building with over 200 vendors. In addition to the booths, people sold things out of the back of their cars in the parking lot.

"I can't believe I am going to a flea market on Black Friday!" Shelly exclaimed.

"You'll love it," Wesley told her as he gave her a hug.

Most stores opened on Thanksgiving in recent years and the tradition of people waking up at 4:00 am for doorbuster deals on Black Friday had been replaced by people stopping at the drive thru for Thanksgiving dinner on the way to the mall. Fast food restaurants commonly offered turkey burgers, sweet potato fries and cranberry smoothies to commemorate the once-sacred day. The stores still advertised Black Friday deals to market to the remaining holdouts who still thought a day to give thanks to God was more important than a $5 toaster.

Adam went over the list of items everyone was to be on the lookout for. "Karen and Janice, you ladies are going to keep your eyes out for canning equipment. Look for an extra canner, jars, lids and rings. Also watch for good quality clothes for anyone in our group, especially things that wear out like socks and underwear. We need to find outfits that the girls will be growing into over the next few years. I hope things are back to normal, but I would rather have too much than not enough. And pick up any heirloom seeds that look like they are in good shape. Stay away from hybrid seeds. They either don't produce the same product in the following generations or they may be completely sterile in the second generation of seeds.

"Shelly and Wesley, your first priority is to find a really good bug- out bag for Shelly. Everyone else is good in that department. We hope it never comes to that, but everyone in the group needs to be able to get in the woods and lay low for a few days, just in case. After you get that, look for hand tools in good condition. We have plenty of screwdrivers, hammers and pliers, but we need things that will replace the power tools we've become dependent on. Specifically, look for a hand drill, saws, axes, a garden hoe, a plow and sharpening equipment.

"Matt and I will be looking for deals on guns and tactical equipment. We have plenty of guns, but I would like to have an entire extra arsenal to stash in case we get overrun or if there is a surprise confiscation by our caring government. We should try to stick to the calibers we have. We have a lot of ammo. We should be fine in that department."

Wesley asked, "What about fuel? Do you want to buy gasoline if anyone is selling it?

"Good question, Wes," Adam said. "I think Al Mohammad will get the gas stations back on line, at least temporarily. When he does, we'll all get Gas Independence cards. Even Mandy and Carissa will be entitled to cards. Matt has plenty of plastic gas cans to fill up. There are eight of us; that gives us forty gallons a week at five gallons per ration card. I think if we conserve that, it should do us. Anyone selling at the flea market right now is going to be price gouging. I don't blame them, it's a free market, we just don't need the gas bad enough to pay prices inflated higher than what we pay at the pump already."

"What calibers of ammo do you all have stockpiled?" Shelly asked.

Adam responded, "I've got 12 gauge, .223, 7.62x39, .308, .22, 9mm, .45, .40, and .38."

Matt added, "We also have a couple hundred rounds of .32 auto."

Everyone piled into one of the two trucks. Matt unhitched his trailer and took his truck. Adam drove his work truck and pulled his work trailer. He put all of his roofing equipment in the barn the night before. This made plenty of room for any big finds.

The adults all had some cash and each carried a concealed weapon. Matt brought along a few silver and gold coins.

Once they arrived, Janice asked Mandy if she wanted to go with Karen and herself.

"No, I want to go with Dad," she answered.

"I'm going with whoever Mandy goes with." Carissa shouted.

"Okay," Janice agreed, "but you have to watch your little sister. They're men and they aren't capable of doing two things at once. Shopping and watching kids are two things to them."

Adam chirped back, "I can watch Carissa."

"No you can't," Janice said as she walked away.

Matt, Adam and the girls walked along the backside of the building to check out some of the large farm equipment before going in. Matt's sharp eye caught a booth selling fudge near the exit.

"Let's get the girls some fudge," he said. It was a great cover story—no one would suspect it was really his own sweet tooth he was concerned with. They bought the fudge and the girls walked around to the front of the entrance to eat their treat while the guys checked out a booth of odds and ends.

Mandy saw a beautiful grey horse. The horse was strong and muscular. She asked the owner if she could give the horse a bite of her maple walnut fudge. He gave a gentle nod, and Mandy slowly offered the candy to the majestic creature. The horse ate it and nuzzled Mandy's hand. Carissa came over to pet the horse too.

The girls returned to where Adam and Matt were. Adam was looking over some camo gear. He found a couple of tactical vests with cross draw pistol holsters and rifle magazine pouches. The merchant was asking $200 each. They were good quality, but that was a rotten deal. Adam offered him $400 for three of the vests. The man countered at $500 and let Adam know that was his final offer. Adam took the vests. He didn't expect to find anything else like that at the market, and the money wouldn't be good for anything except starting a fire within a few weeks anyway.

Matt asked the man about Kevlar helmets and ballistic plates. The vests Adam had bought had plate carrier pouches for ballistic body armor plates. The man shook his head no.

The next booth had some older shotguns and rifles. There was a bolt action .270, a lever action 30-06, a single-shot 20 gauge and a pump-action 20 gauge. There was also a bolt-action .308 with a black synthetic stock and a good 3-to-9x40 scope.

"Do you have a good long distance rifle?" Adam asked Matt.

"No," Matt answered.

"It's nothing fancy, but this one will do you good," Adam said as he passed the .308 bolt action rifle to Matt for his inspection.

"I might have shot it twenty or thirty times," the seller added. "It's a good gun."

Matt didn't negotiate with the man. He handed him the $350 he was asking.

"This here 20 gauge is perfect for that youngin'," the man said as he nodded toward Mandy.

"I don't have ammo for it," Adam replied.

"I'll give you three boxes of shells, the 20 gauge pump and the 20 gauge single shot for $250," the man offered.

Adam called Mandy over to ask if she liked the shotgun. She had a Ruger 10/22 and was a great shot.

"I like it, but I would rather have a horse," Mandy said.

"Well, there are no horses here," Adam said.

Carissa was fast to correct him. "There's one in the front!"

Adam was stuck. He bought the guns and ammo and walked to the front to see the horse. It truly was a nice looking horse. "How much?" he asked.

"Half ounce of gold or the equivalent in silver." the man said.

"That's pretty steep," Adam answered.

"Think of it as a two-for-one deal," the man countered.

"She's pregnant?" Adam asked.

"Yes, sir," the man replied.

"Well, I don't have any gold or silver yet," Adam walked away.

Mandy was disappointed, but she understood.

Matt called Adam close. "When is your metals order getting here?"

"Next week," Adam answered.

"If you want to accept the risk on the pregnancy, I'll put up the half ounce. You pay me a quarter ounce when you get your gold and I'll take the foal when it's born. If there's no foal, you pay me the other quarter ounce of gold," Matt said.

"It would be good to have a horse. Let me explain this to Mandy." Adam called Mandy over. "Sweetie, we're going to buy the horse, but she's going to be the family horse. You can spend as much time as you like with it, but it's going to have to do some work on the farm. Is that understood?"

"Yes, sir!" Mandy said excitedly.

They walked back over to the man with the horse. Matt produced a half-ounce Gold Eagle coin. The man asked to see it so he could verify the coin's authenticity. He put it on the scale to check the weight. The weight or the size was always off on the counterfeits. The half-ounce American Gold Eagle was real. It was just under seventeen grams. Gold Eagle coins were 22 karat which was ninety-two percent gold. The alloy metals of silver and copper made up the other eight percent and were in addition to the 15.55 grams or one-half Troy ounce of gold contained in the coin.

"Can you throw in the saddle? We have to ride her home. If it's alright to ride her while she is pregnant, that is," Matt asked.

The man agreed to throw in the saddle. "She's about two months pregnant; she should be okay to ride until the last month or two. They carry a foal for a total of eleven months, so you have a while. If you see her getting tired easily, stay off her until a few weeks after the foal arrives."

Everyone shook hands on the deal and they wished each other well. Mandy led the horse to the truck where she and Carissa stayed with her for the rest of the afternoon. Mandy soon had the animal named. Smokey was to be the horse's name because of the deep grey color of her coat.

The guys found a 9mm Beretta, and a Taurus Judge .38. They were both worn, but in great working condition. They quickly paid the full asking price for the pistols; $400 for the Berretta and $275 for the Judge.

The final deal of the day for Adam and Matt were six 55-gallon black plastic barrels. They would make great rain catch barrels. They were labeled as having been used for pickles. They had an odor of vinegar, but it would fade in time. When purchasing barrels that would be used to catch water for human consumption, they had to be sure the barrels were never used for toxic chemicals. The faint scent of vinegar was a reassurance of the fact that they were safe.

The ladies returned with two large boxes of mason jars and three boxes of reusable Tattler lids. They paid a premium for the lids, but they would last for years. They didn't find any canners, but they each had one already. Janice had an old heavy-duty stainless steel canner. Karen's was a newer aluminum canner. It was light and well made, but one had to be careful with it to avoid warping the thinner lightweight aluminum. It would have been nice to find another stainless steel canner like Janice's.

They found three new packages of socks and some clothes for the girls. The clothing was used, but just barely.

Karen found a complete set of home school curriculum for 9th through 12th grade. She looked it over to make sure it taught creation and accurate American history. She bought the entire set with the intention of starting a school if things didn't get back to normal soon.

Wesley and Shelly found a used US military ALICE pack in good condition. They were hard to come by. There were plenty of replicas made in China, but the durability and ruggedness of the US military all-purpose lightweight individual carrying equipment packs would last a lifetime. They found a good tent from the same seller. Shelly spotted a US army field medical kit. Wesley told her that Matt and Karen had an entire hospital at the house, but she bought it anyway because of the compact design.

They found a guy willing to sell his full size Glock 17 for silver bullion. Wesley had quite a few silver coins he bought on Matt's recommendation over the years. Being a student of history, Wesley knew silver and gold were the money of the ages. The Glock would be Shelly's everyday carry weapon.

Shelly found an old coffee grinder. It was one of the larger ones that would have likely been used in an old store. Because of its size, it could be used to grind corn as well.

Wesley bought a few old saws and a large ax, but he was unable to find a hand drill.

Janice drove Adam's truck and Adam rode the horse home. They were about ten miles from the farm. It was a long trip for the horse that obviously had not been taken out much. Adam took it very slow and let her rest and drink every time they were near a water source.

The group returned to Adam's farm and each displayed their loot to the others. Mandy waited in the drive for Adam to return with Smokey. When he arrived, he explained that Smokey was too tired for Mandy to ride that night. Mandy didn't seem to care; she was content to simply pet the new horse.

The next morning, Matt and Adam made a few caches to bury. Matt thought they should bury them near the house, but Adam recommended taking them far back in the woods.

Adam explained his reasoning. "If the farmhouse is overrun by looters or military, we want a fallback position deep in the woods."

"That makes sense," Matt agreed.

They made cache tubes with large plumbing PVC pipe, which Adam had saved from when he put in his septic tank. They put the two pistols they purchased at the flea market with several rounds of ammunition for each in the cache tubes. Adam put in the single-shot shotgun and one box of 20 gauge ammo for it. Finally, he put in a very basic AR-15 that he had bought for Janice. He kept out his AR-15 that was fully tricked out as well as his .308 AR-10. The .308 was configured as a long range weapon, but he could quickly change the scope out for a reflex sight and use the AR-10 as a close range battle rifle.

He put six thirty-round magazines in the tube with the AR-15 and 300 rounds of ammunition. He made a separate tube for his AK-47. He included four thirty-round magazines and 500 rounds of ammunition for the AK.

They made sure all of the weapons were well oiled before wrapping each one individually with thick contractor garbage bags. Matt inserted an old sock filled with rice which would help remove any moisture in the tubes when they were sealed.

Wesley had a similar arsenal. He owned an AR-10 which he used for hunting as well as an AR-15 and an AK-47. If times got tough, he would use the AR-10, Shelly would use the AR-15.

They made a separate tube with some MREs, canned pasta, bottled water, and water purification tablets. Matt would make other caches for his farm after he closed on the property and moved in.

Matt and Adam discussed what they would do for church the next day. The church was eighteen miles away. They couldn't justify going every week with the current gas situation, but they realized how important it was to stay connected. They decided everyone would go to church once a month until the gas situation changed. Tomorrow, they would watch Pastor John Robinson's service online, which was broadcast over the internet from Idaho.

CHAPTER 31

"With the coming of dawn, the angels urged Lot, saying, 'Hurry! Take your wife and your two daughters who are here, or you will be swept away when the city is punished.'"

Genesis 19:15

Pastor John Robinson prayed and began his Sunday morning message.

"I hope everyone had a great Thanksgiving. We have a lot of empty seats today. I expect a lot of folks stayed home and are watching online because of the gas shortage. I'm very proud of those of you who decided to come anyway, but I also want those of you who stayed home to know that I think it was probably a wise decision.

"Our internet listeners have grown tremendously over the past three years. We have listeners each week from every state. Today's message is for those of you who are still living in major metropolitan areas. I firmly believe that the time for you to get out of there is now."

Pastor Robinson read the account of Lot leaving Sodom and Gomorrah from Genesis 19 then continued his message.

"Now Lot was considered righteous by God and the angels came to warn him to get out of the city before they destroyed it. Lot escaped only with his life. It sounds like a pretty good story. After all, Lot survived, right? But what did he lose? Lot lost almost everything but his life!

"Let's take a closer look at Lot's experience. His wife was unable to leave Sodom without one last look. This act of disobedience caused her to be turned to salt. Tragic for her to say the least, but now Lot was on his own—a single parent with two daughters.

"When Lot and Abraham parted ways in Genesis 13, it was because the two of them had become so wealthy that they could not both graze their livestock in the same place. Abraham let Lot choose the direction he would travel and Abraham took the other direction. Lot chose to pitch his tent near Sodom. When the angels escorted him out of the city, we aren't told that Lot brought one single worldly possession when he had to bug out. It's my guess that Lot lost much wealth in the destruction of the city.

"Now, let's see if there were any warning sign. Is it possible that God was giving Lot some gentle nudges in the years leading up to the destruction of Sodom? Evidently, Sodom was rather infested with wickedness. After all, God saw fit to bring about quite a violent end to the city. Perhaps it wasn't so bad when Lot first moved there. Maybe the neighborhood just started sliding down hill slowly. First they opened a little bar at the end of the street. A year later there was a palm reading shop next to a smoke shop that sold water bongs and drug paraphernalia. The following year Sodom opened a strip club and the old church became a Goth nightclub. As you read this, the change is very obvious but perhaps for Lot, it was too slow to notice the severity of the change. He may have been the proverbial boiling frog. When you look in the mirror day after day, you aren't likely to see your own hair growing but your friend who you see twice a year may say, 'Wow, your hair grew a lot!'

"Perhaps poor Lot was just never motivated enough by the slow decline to say, 'That's enough, I am moving out of here.' Maybe it was just too inconvenient to take the girls out of school and start over. Isn't it just easier to deal with things than to sell the house, find a new job and uproot the family? Besides that, the wife loves Sodom. It's really going to be a hard sell to convince her they need to move.

"I'm convinced, however, that God gave Lot a pretty good nudge to get out of town back in Genesis 14. In that chapter we read about Lot being kidnapped by foreign invaders. Abraham hears about the incident and comes to rescue his nephew. Lot narrowly escapes this encounter with his life. Could God have allowed this event in hopes that Lot would take it as a warning sign and sell his house to seek greener pasture?

"Maybe Lot thought he was being a good husband by staying in Sodom. After all, his wife loved it so much that she had to have just one more look before they left. In the end, he failed his wife as a husband. She ended up dead. He also failed as a father by not getting his children out of town sooner. You can read the rest of the story yourself to see how the girls were affected by the loose morals of the city. They make some very troubling sexual choices at the end of Chapter 19.

"Recent events should be more than a gentle nudge for you who are still living in the cities. Do whatever you can to get out now, even if you have to leave everything behind. Try to make alliances with friends or family who live in rural or lightly populated areas. If you have nowhere to go, you can come here, but I must warn you that the winters are tough and you'll need to bring your own shelter such as an RV or camper. You won't make it in a tent. Also bring enough food for six months. We have a lot of farmland to work next spring for those of you who have no other alternative, but you'll need food to get by until harvest.

"Make your move now. Don't get stuck bugging out in the middle of the night like Lot. Remember, everyone in his party didn't make it."

CHAPTER 32

"God is our refuge and strength, an ever-present help in trouble. Therefore we will not fear, though the earth give way and the mountains fall into the heart of the sea, though its waters roar and foam and the mountains quake with their surging."

Psalm 46:1-3

After breakfast, everyone took turns on Adam's computer signing up for their Gas Independence cards. Adam was sure to sign up Mandy and Carissa since the only requirement was a Social Security number.

Matt and Karen went to meet the attorney at the realtor's office for the closing. The office was in London, Kentucky, so it wasn't that far. They drove there with Janice's car to save gas. Wesley and Adam would meet them at their new home with Matt's truck and trailer, which contained all of their worldly possessions. Wes and Adam could then return to Adam's farm in Janice's car after they helped Matt and Karen get moved in.

The house was in good condition, but Karen insisted on cleaning before they moved anything in. She started in the bedroom. The guys got everything out of the truck and onto the porch. They moved in the belongings of each room as Karen finished cleaning it.

Everything was still in boxes, but it was in the room where it belonged. The day was soon over and everyone was tired.

On Tuesday, Matt and Karen began taking inventory of their food stocks and supplies as they unloaded each box. The power was switched over to their name and Matt put in the order for internet service. There was only DSL out here, but the service was sufficient at Adam's. They were sure it would be fine. They had Comcast internet back in Florida, so they were used to poor service. The phone company told them it could be several weeks before the technician would make it out to turn on their internet. Matt didn't like being in the dark. He was an information junkie and accustomed to being very connected to news and events.

They couldn't get any of the local channels on their television yet. It would require a digital converter antenna to pick up local channels unless they subscribed to satellite service. To top it all off, the phone signals were inconsistent. At times, they had two or three bars, and at other times, only one. Matt would have to acclimate to a simpler, less-informed lifestyle.

For calling Adam, they could use walkie-talkies. Adam had a set similar to Matt's. The walkies had a range of thirty-six miles and the two farms were only two miles apart. It was three miles from Adam's to Matt's new farm by road because of the way it snaked down the hill and back up. The houses were both near the top of the hills they sat on, with not much in between to stop the signal from the walkies. The thirty-six-mile range ascribed to the walkie-talkies was in a straight line with no objects between them. These are typical conditions for the open ocean or in the desert. That topography did not exist in Eastern Kentucky, so the walkie-talkies would never have an effective range of more than a couple of miles.

Matt happened to find a very good conservative news radio channel out of Lexington, Kentucky. It had a strong signal and came in great on his AM/FM/shortwave receiver.

Matt and Karen brought all of the rice and beans they purchased prior to the riots. He had those sealed in Mylar liners and inside of five-gallon buckets so they would stack up easily. He took the buckets to the metal work shed. The buckets were mostly old latex paint buckets which he had salvaged and cleaned out. He would never store food in a bucket that had held paint without the Mylar liners. The liners were impervious to air, bugs and anything else that might otherwise leach into the food from the buckets. The good thing about the buckets being mostly old paint buckets was that they camouflaged the food stores. Even though they weren't readily recognizable as food, Matt still intended to bury about half of the 30 five-gallon buckets. The majority of which were filled with rice and beans.

Matt and Karen brought the seeds they used for their garden in Florida. Some of them may not produce well is such a different climate. Others would do better in the cooler mountain weather. The plot of land they would be using for a garden dwarfed the small raised-bed garden boxes they had in Florida. The soil here was as black as coal. Matt looked forward to gardening in the rich soil. In Florida, the only soil they had was what they made from composting. Below the raised beds was just sand and rock.

The seeds he brought with him were for green beans, tomatoes, mustard greens, bell peppers, jalapenos, cabbage, mixed field greens and peas. Matt needed more seeds for the other items he hoped to grow here. He never had any success growing squash, melons and corn in Florida. He looked for those seeds when he was at the flea market, but none were available.

He looked for anything that could have been used for solar as well. He brought his small system from Florida. It consisted of two

100-watt solar panels, a charging controller, one deep cell battery and a 1200-watt inverter. He used it in Florida to keep his power-tool batteries charged. It was better than nothing, but he wanted more than what the small system offered. Besides being used as a component for the solar set up, the inverter could be used to hook up to the truck battery to keep the fridge going when the power went out due to hurricanes in Florida. Now, gas was too precious of a commodity to use for powering a fridge.

Matt had always felt fairly prepared until now. He had always been so much more prepared than anyone else he talked to on a day-to-day basis, but now he realized just how little it took to be more prepared than everybody else. Retrospectively, being more prepared than the Joneses was not a good metric for gauging your preparedness.

Well, there was no use kicking himself now. He always tried to keep a proper balance between prepping for the apocalypse and living a normal life. They had food, shelter, a good water source, family, weapons, each other and a God who always looked out for them. They were going to be fine.

Matt put together a wish list to take to town the next day. Hopefully, Adam would be able to go with him to watch his back. Among the items he hoped to get were a chain saw, bar and chain oil, more solar panels and several deep-cycle batteries to build a battery bank. He would also like to have some night vision equipment and some motion detectors to establish a perimeter. The house could use a fresh coat of paint as well. He also wanted a fish trap for the creek. Matt needed livestock like chickens and goats.

Matt realized how much information was no longer available to him without the internet. There were a lot of lost skills that he wanted to look up and print out from Adam's computer while he still had the chance.

A few things he wanted to know was how to raise sugar cane and make molasses, how to make soap, how to build a water turbine to generate electricity from the creek and how to build and use a smokehouse. There was so much to do and to learn and there seemed to be so little time.

CHAPTER 33

"Government can do something for the people only in proportion as it can do something to the people."

Thomas Jefferson

President-elect Howe and President Al Mohammad sat in the boardroom with Al Mohammad's top advisors and the IMF director to discuss a bailout deal from the IMF. The deal demanded extreme austerity. Across-the-board cuts to every area of the national budget were required to secure the bailout funds.

"No way!" Howe demanded. "Six weeks before I take office, and all of a sudden, we get fiscal religion? We have Paul Randall trying to instigate a civil war. I need the full support of the military. There is no way I can authorize a fifteen-percent pay cut to the military right now. Take it from somewhere else. If we have to cut their pay, we can do it after I've instituted the weapons ban. Besides that, our currency is on the brink of disaster. If the currency fails, we'll need the military to keep the population under control. If soldiers start deserting, who will maintain the relief camps in a currency crisis?

"Everything is coming to a head and it's going to all boil over at once, right into my lap. You did a real good job of kicking this down the road until you were almost out of here, Al Mohammad."

Al Mohammad was furious. "Ladies and gentlemen, can the governor and I have the room for just a few minutes?"

Director of the International Monetary Fund Stanley Klauser looked surprised. The Fed Chair, the IMF director, Chang and all the other advisors got up and left the meeting room.

Once they were alone, Al Mohammad stood up out of his chair while Howe sat and listened. "Anthony, you address me as Mr. President. You're in this meeting as my guest. I have tolerated your input even though you have absolutely no say in any of these matters. The only reason you're still here is for the good of the country.

"These terms are being dictated to us by the International Monetary Fund. If we don't play ball, we don't get the funding to keep the machine rolling. If that happens, cuts will be much larger than fifteen percent. Everyone on government payroll is getting a fifteen-percent cut. Congress, the IRS, the Department of Defense, everyone on Social Security, SNAP, and all the other assistance programs are getting cut fifteen percent. Even my staff and I are taking the cuts. There are no sacred cows. These are the terms, no negotiations.

"There's no way I would've allowed Randall or Marcos to attend these meetings if they'd won the election. You start showing some gratitude or get out and come back on January 20th. At that time, I'll have my staff drop a twenty-five-pound box of memos so you can read about what we're doing. And while I'm being so transparent, let me just tell you that your little 'business' trip to Brazil before the campaign was not out of the reach of the NSA. I have all the details of that trip and enough of it is on video.

"Now that we have those unpleasant matters out of the way, go tell everyone they can come back in and you sit down and shut up. I don't want to hear you say one word for the rest of the meeting. Am I clear?"

Howe was fuming. His father's firm, Howe Clancy, had footed a huge chunk of the campaign funds that put Al Mohammad in office. Now Al Mohammad was blackmailing him?

"Yes, Mr. President." Howe forced himself to suck up his pride and anger.

The meeting resumed and IMF Director Stanley Klauser was noticeably annoyed at having been asked to step out of the room.

Klauser was the first to speak in his thick Swiss German accent. "I will remind all of you that the IMF was invited here by the United States. If you find our terms disagreeable, you are more than welcome to try to secure the funds you need to keep your government afloat through other channels. The IMF recognizes the importance of America to global financial stability. For that reason, we have gone to great lengths to put together the funds you have requested.

"The only way we can justify this level of assistance is by requiring that America reduce its liabilities to a more sustainable level.

"In addition to the measures we have already laid out, the IMF is asking that you eliminate all negative taxation in your tax code, particularly the refundable portions of the Earned Income Tax Credit and the Additional Child Tax Credit. You cannot continue to pay out money from your treasury to people who have paid nothing in.

"You should also begin walking back your FDIC insurance limits. In the event that you would require further assistance, we would need to exact a portion of your citizen's bank deposits as we had to do in Cyprus years back and more recently, Spain, Italy and

Portugal. We have run analysis that suggest deposits over $50,000 would need to be seized in order to secure approval for additional funds from the IMF administrators.

"Mr. Howe, this will most likely fall into your hands, but all of you should consider reducing the deposit insurance amounts now."

Howe barely looked up as he nodded at the IMF director. He didn't dare open his mouth after Al Mohammad's warning.

President Al Mohammad said, "Director Klauser, with all due respect, I have to get this through Congress. Is there any way we could spread the austerity measures out over a longer time period? That might make it more palatable."

Director Klauser stacked up his notes and stuck them in his briefcase. He simply answered no. As he walked out the door, he said, "Good day, ladies and gentlemen."

It was no secret that Klauser believed the entire global meltdown had been triggered by the United States via their profligate lifestyle of debt and their insistence on imposing themselves into everyone else's business. He had stated as much in several public speeches. It was likely that he enjoyed being the one to put these arrogant Americans in their place.

"What are you going to do, Mr. President?" Fed Chair Jane Bleecher asked.

The president's chief political advisor, James Mackie said, "I don't think we can get this through the House or the Senate."

"Then I'll do it through executive order," the president announced. "Armando, have your people start getting a speech ready for tomorrow morning. I want to get in front of this so we don't have any more riots. Let the folks know what's going on without making it sound like the nation is broke."

"Yes, Mr. President," Armando Sanchez said.

The meeting broke and everyone returned to dealing with the crisis at hand. Anthony Howe left, unable to do anything except sit back and watch the catastrophe unfold.

CHAPTER 34

"There are two ways to conquer and enslave a country. One is by the sword. The other is by debt."

John Adams

Texas Governor Larry Jacobs made Paul Randall as secure as possible in his hideout. He provided him with encrypted communication equipment, counter surveillance and a very large contingency of Texas National Guardsmen stationed in two separate positions that could reach Randall in fifteen minutes if his cabin came under assault by a federal agency. The two security teams kept their distance to deter suspicion which could be triggered by a mass of troops in a single location.

"How are you holding up Paul?" General Allen Jefferson asked over the secured satellite phone.

"I'm good Allen, thanks for asking," Randall answered.

Jefferson continued, "I'm glad to get to speak to you, but I know how important it is to keep the conversation short, so I'll get right to the details. Al Mohammad has closed several key military bases around the world. We're recalling submarines and aircraft carriers as well."

"Any specific area?" Paul asked.

Allen answered, "Bases are being closed all over the globe, but we're recalling all the assets from the Pacific. I suspect China played a role in making it a requirement to the IMF bailout that Al Mohammad is begging for. China may have footed part of the bill. As far as I know, the IMF doesn't have access to the quantity of funds that Al Mohammad needs to keep things going."

"What else is on the chopping block?" Paul asked.

"We're being briefed late tonight, but I hear the cuts are pretty draconian. I expect the White House to announce something by tomorrow," Allen Jefferson explained.

"What are you using to defend against drone detection?" the general asked.

"I think the guys Jacobs sent have something called a *Skygrabber*, which overrides the controls and puts the drone into a holding pattern or sends it home," Paul answered.

General Jefferson replied, "That's great for the big boys that are working via satellite signal, but you have to watch out for the bugs. Bugs are micro-drones that are about the size of a quarter. They operate as a swarm which gathers information from a twenty-five-mile radius. Bugs have a small hive that's about the size of a large coffee can. The hive collects solar energy to recharge the micro-drones. The NSA has probably dropped thousands of these hives all over Texas to look in windows and cars to try to identify people through facial recognition software. They're operating on a C-band signal which is transmitted from the hive. Skygrabber is strictly for satellite controlled drones, it has no effect on the bugs. To disrupt bugs, you need to construct spark-gap generators. You should have

Jacobs put several around you to disrupt hives in your area, but also all over the state to cause interference. If the NSA sees interference only in your area, you might as well just email them your latitude and longitude now. I'm doing everything I can to get specific information about what they're doing to find you, but they've locked me out of the loop."

"I appreciate your help," Randall said.

"I'm going to get off here; we've already been on too long. I know what type of proxy system you're set up on and it's only effective for short conversations," the general said.

The men said their goodbyes and Paul Randall took the notes on spark-gap generator to the guard that would be rotating out that night. The guards would return to the governor to be debriefed after a seventy-two-hour shift at the cabin. The guards acted as couriers between Governor Jacobs and Paul Randall. This kept their communications sterilized from electronic surveillance.

Jacobs arranged for two men to keep an eye out for Sonny while he visited his parents for Thanksgiving. His parents lived in Austin, which was a blessing and a curse. It was a major metropolitan area, which made it easy to blend in, but it also made it easy for the enemy to blend in. Another negative factor was that there were several federal agencies with offices in Austin, including the modern equivalent to the East German Stasi, DHS. Sonny would be returning to the cabin tomorrow, but tonight, the Randalls were having a family night.

The Randalls sat near the fireplace. They ate popcorn as they watched an old family favorite. Hiding out had started to feel a little like a vacation. Paul liked being out in nature, it was a welcome change from the constant stress of the campaign.

Suddenly, one of the guards ran into the TV room yelling,

"Upstairs now! Safe room now!"

The Randalls were startled. Kimberly froze. Paul grabbed her and forced her to walk up the stairs to the room that was predetermined to be a safe room in case of an attack. The two inside guards ran up the stairs behind them. Once in the safe room, everyone put on their gas masks and Ryan and Robert grabbed their AR-15s. Paul held Kimberly with one hand as she sat catatonic behind the bed. In the other hand he held his .40 cal. Sig Sauer pistol.

A shotgun blast was followed by two large explosions that boomed from downstairs. The door was breached and flash bangs were deployed. Two more pops rang out. No doubt, those were tear gas grenades being activated.

The two outside guards assigned to protecting the Randalls were down. One was hit, lying in the woods, and the other was dead. The one in the woods notified the backup teams to come in. He used the radio to let the two interior guards know that the assault team was a twelve-man team. The two interior guards took up positions at the top of the stairs.

Ryan and Robert took prone positions just inside the doorway of the safe room. Paul kept one hand on his wife and the other rested on the bed with the gun sights aimed at the center of the door. The Randalls could hear rapid-fire gunshots from the other side of the safe room door.

The guards at the top of the steps held the tactical assault team for about five minutes before they advanced up the stairs. The only shots that mattered were head shots. The assault team was covered in body armor. To get a kill, the Randalls' guards had to shoot the assailants in the face. The two guards managed to take out three members of the tactical team before they were both killed.

When the shooting stopped, Paul Randall knew the guards were dead and it was a matter of time before the door would be kicked open. Robert quickly shoved the writing desk in front of the door to slow them down. Ryan overturned a bookshelf to use as cover for his prone shooting position. Robert did the same with a chair. The overturned furniture offered absolutely no ballistic protection from the 5.56mm ammunition, but it did provide visual cover.

"Remember to keep one eye shut guys," Paul yelled to his sons through the gas mask. "They'll probably throw a flash bang in here when they breach the door. That will temporarily blind the eye you have open. Once the flash passes, open the other eye."

A shotgun blast blew off the door knob to the safe room. Two of the tactical team members began bashing the door to push back the desk blocking it from inside. As soon as Ryan saw a body part, he took a shot. He hit one of the invaders in the shoulder. The hit team backed up and the Randalls saw the flash bang being pushed through the crack. All the Randall men were able to close both eyes when the bright light from the device detonated. Robert began firing even before he opened his eyes. The hit team dropped to the ground to avoid the erratic fire from Robert's AR-15. One of the invaders was hit in the head by Robert before he could take cover. The door was a kill zone for the invaders. Anyone who came through had to escape the cross fire from the twins' AR-15s. The invaders cleared the desk at the expense of another team member who was shot by Paul Randall. The tactical team fired into the room as they tried to make a traditional stacked entry but two more of them were quickly executed by the Randall twins.

"Boys, change your magazines!" Paul yelled as the invasion team retreated to the hallway. Ryan quickly complied but Robert did not. "Robert," Paul yelled, "change your magazine!"

A dark red pool of blood was forming on the wooden floor beneath Roberts's body. Paul would have to grieve later. Now he had to defend the remainder of his family. Paul pushed the Sig Sauer into his wife's hand. She took it but was unresponsive. He took Robert's position to maintain the crossfire kill zone. He rolled Robert over and changed the magazine of the AR-15.

"How many are left?" Ryan asked his father.

"I don't know," Paul said. Since they had not been told by the guards, Paul Randall had no idea how many team members there were to begin with.

A firefight began outside in the hallway. It lasted for a couple of minutes, but none of the assault team came back into the safe room. The shooting eventually stopped.

A voice yelled from the hallway at the top of the stairs. "Paul Randall, I am with the Texas National Guard. We've finished off your assailants. I am coming into the room unarmed with my hands up until you can verify my credentials."

The Guardsman walked in very slowly by himself. Paul approached him with his weapon trained on him and inspected his ID. Kimberly crawled out from behind the bed to her dead son's body. She took Robert's head into her lap and stroked his blood soaked hair. She didn't say anything, but she was moving.

"Mom," Ryan said as he began to cry.

Paul surveyed the damage. He was thankful that his wife and Ryan were unharmed, but the horror of Robert's death was just starting to hit him.

A medic rushed in to check them. Kimberly motioned for the medic to go away when he tried to check Robert for a pulse. Robert was gone.

"Senator Randall," the Guardsman said, "we have to move you immediately. Please come with us right away. We'll transport your son's body to the location where we're taking you. You'll be able to give him a proper funeral there."

The man ordered two medics to move Robert's body to the same chopper in which they were taking the Randalls. It was the only way Kimberly would agree to leave the room. Two other Guardsmen collected some of their personal things.

The Randalls were taken to one of the largest Texas National Guard armories. The facility was well staffed with troops. Governor Jacobs instructed the National Guard to defend the Randalls and the armory to the last man.

Three adjacent offices were cleared out to make a living area and two separate sleeping areas for the Randalls. Paul and Ryan arranged the furniture the troops provided for them. The furnishings were sparse. They had a foldout table and chairs in the living area along with a well-stocked refrigerator and a television. They did manage to get nice quality mattresses, even though they were just placed on the floor with no box springs or bed frames.

Kimberly lay on the mattress in the room where the troops had brought her things. Paul came in and sat by her. Neither said a word. Ryan situated his things in his room and then came over to Paul and Kimberly. He sat next to them on the mattress.

Several minutes later, Kimberly spoke for the first time since the assault. "The cost is too great," she said.

Paul sighed as he held her close. He had been willing to die for his country, but had he been willing to sacrifice his son? For now, the pain was simply unbearable. What made the situation even worse was that none of the extended family could be told yet; and none of them would be able to come in order to comfort them.

The next day, a memorial service was arranged. Sonny was escorted to the armory by a detail that Jacobs assigned to protect him while he was away from the cabin. Larry Jacobs came to the service. He traveled to the National Guard armory in an unmarked car and dressed in the uniform of the Texas National Guard as a disguise.

Governor Jacobs embraced Paul when he saw him. He gave Kimberly a big hug as he said, "I'm so sorry for your loss. Robert is a hero and a patriot."

Jacobs sat at a table in the rec room for a while with Paul after the service. "I'm sending a guy over to take care of meals while you're here. The quarters aren't very comfortable, but I can make sure you eat well while you're here."

"We can eat what the troops eat," Paul replied.

"This is not open for negotiation, Paul," Jacobs said. "We're going to have to come up with a plan about what to do with federal offices in Texas. I can't exactly start handing out eviction notices to all of the DHS, IRS and FBI field offices.

"We don't have the strength to march on all of the military bases here. The National Guard couldn't even take Fort Hood."

"Have you heard from Mustafa?" Paul asked. "Do you think he wants to declare war on Texas or just me?"

"I haven't heard a word from Al Mohammad. I am thinking about how to address this with him," Jacobs replied.

"I don't want to spark a civil war," Paul said.

Jacobs reassured Paul, "You aren't sparking anything, Paul. Al Mohammad pulled this stunt and the people of Texas are behind you."

"The people of Texas don't know anything about the attack," Paul replied.

"They'll know soon enough, and when they do, they'll want to do whatever is necessary. I know their hearts," Larry Jacobs rebutted.

Paul said, "When you speak with Al Mohammad, try to not spark World War III just yet. Let me speak with General Allen Jefferson and see if he can make a few changes in key leadership positions at some of the larger bases around here like Fort Hood and Corpus Christi. If he could put some true patriots in the right bases, it might make it easier if worse comes to worse. In the event that Al Mohammad initiates aggression against Texas, troops could be given the option of standing with Texas or staying loyal to the crown."

"Sounds like a good plan," Jacobs commented. "I would just say that staying loyal would require them to stand with Texas. All of these soldiers took an oath to defend the Constitution. Mustafa Al Mohammad is a blatant enemy of the Constitution."

A soldier approached their table. "Pardon me for interrupting, sir."

"What've you got for me, soldier?" Jacobs asked.

The soldier reported, "No identifying information could be found on the bodies of the assailants, sir. No IDs, no dog tags, no military branch patches. We checked for serial numbers on the weapons and looked for manufacturing information on the spent brass. Everything was completely scrubbed. Their prints didn't return any information. No facial recognition software was able to identify any of the men."

Larry asked the soldier, "What does your gut tell you? Do you think they were CIA, SEALs or Delta?"

The young sergeant shook his head. "I couldn't say for sure, sir. If I had to guess, I would say private contractors whose identities have been scrubbed by CIA."

"That makes sense," Paul said. "Mustafa isn't trying to start a war; he just wants to eliminate me. And he'll deny everything, just like he has for the last eight years."

"Mustafa won't call me," Larry said. "And I sure won't call him. I don't want to tip my hand to what we're doing."

Larry Jacobs called General Allen Jefferson to invite him to Texas. Repositioning leadership in key commands of US military bases located in Texas was something the three of them would want to discuss at length and in person.

CHAPTER 35

"...for there is no truth in him. When he lies, he speaks his native language, for he is a liar and the father of lies."

John 8:44

Adam arrived at Matt's house just after 8:00 am. Matt was still having breakfast. Adam had been on farmer time for several years. He was accustomed to getting up early when he was in the military. After he got sober, he returned to his early-to-bed, early-to-rise routine. It was a necessity for working on the farm and roofing. Outdoor work required sun light. If you didn't get a jump on the day, it would be over before you were finished with a day's worth of work. Matt was still adjusting to this schedule.

They planned to go to town to see if they could get any of the items on Matt's wish list. Additionally, they were going to get their weekly rations of gas. Today was Wednesday. Thursday was the day they originally chose to purchase gas each week. They were going a day earlier, because tomorrow was December 1st and EBT cards would be reloading tonight. Mondays were crazy at the pumps with people making sure they got their gas. Tuesdays were unreliable as many pumps would be empty from the Monday rush for gas. Most pumps would be refilled on Wednesday, but Thursday had proven to be the best day to go over the past few weeks. Folks in London, Kentucky, were fairly well behaved, but you never knew when something would happen to spark more unrest. It just seemed wise to get it done the day before SNAP benefits were reloaded.

"You better get a move on if you want to get back in time to hear your buddy's speech at 11:30," Adam joked.

"Al Mohammad ain't my buddy!" Matt snapped. "I just want to hear the speech so I can try to decipher his BS."

Matt slugged his coffee down, brushed his teeth quickly and rinsed with mouthwash as he put on his shoes. He grabbed his list, a wad of cash and his Glock. The cool weather meant he always wore a jacket and the full size pistol was easily concealed under the long tail of the jacket.

Their first stop was the gas station to fill up Adam's truck. Five gallons filled it up since they hadn't driven much that week. The remaining twenty-five gallons allotted on Adam's other five ration cards went in the gas cans. Once he returned home, they would be poured into a fifty-five gallon drum and mixed with Stabil fuel stabilizer to make sure the gas stayed fresh. Matt would keep his ten gallons in the cans and would also add stabilizer.

Adam locked the fuel in the tool boxes in the back of his truck. He didn't keep his roofing tools in the lockable metal tool boxes to reduce the chances of them being broken into and his tools stolen.

The next stop was Allen's New and Used Boat Shop. Not many people were buying boats since the crisis and the store was only open half days, three days a week, Wednesdays, Fridays and Saturdays. Allen's also did maintenance and repairs. They maintained a brisk business in the years before the new depression. Even in the past few years, they did some repair work for folks who wanted to keep their small fishing boats in good shape. Fishing was a popular pastime at the nearby Wood Creek Lake. It was an affordable pastime that also provided fish for dinner.

Matt and Adam found seven deep-cycle batteries at the boat shop. Deep-cycle batteries used for boats are essentially the same as a car battery, but they're designed to be regularly discharged, using up most of their capacity.

Matt bought them all. He found some cables to use to connect the batteries in parallel to provide backup power for his home. If he was able to find additional solar panels, the batteries would be charged using the solar panels. If not, he could still recharge them using a regular car-battery charger. Of course, he would still need electricity for that, but the battery bank would help out in the case of brownouts.

Matt once listened to a Prepper Recon Podcast interview of a modern survivalist named Ferfal on the aftermath of the 2001 currency collapse in Argentina. Ferfal lived through the collapse and described a prolonged period of brownouts in Argentina during the crisis. Ferfal told about "dirty power," which was periods when the wattage was too low to power many appliances. Having a battery backup would allow Matt to charge the batteries during times when wattage was running at regular strength. He could use that power when the grid wasn't producing enough current or when it was completely down.

Their next stop was the local home improvement store. Several items, like batteries and flashlights, were stripped off of the shelves. People around London, Kentucky, were definitely expecting things to get worse. He found bar-and-chain oil for chainsaws, but the chainsaws were out of stock. He bought the oil in case he was able to find a chainsaw somewhere else. He picked up several different types of oil for small engines. If this stuff ran out, it would be as good as gold for anyone who needed it.

Matt found a solar kit. It was overpriced, but he bought it anyway. The four panels in the kit produced only 60 watts. That was just over half of what one of Matt's 100-watt panels produced. Still, it would be additional electricity. The kit had a piece-of-junk charging regulator and a rinky-dink 200-watt inverter to change the voltage from DC in the battery bank to AC that could be used by household appliances. The charging regulator and the 1200-watt inverter Matt already had were good components. "Well, at least I'll have backups." Matt said to himself.

He tried ordering solar panels from a couple of different sellers on Amazon, but they all had backorder notices. He didn't know if they would ever arrive or not. He paid for the backordered solar panels with his credit card, so he wouldn't be out any cash if they didn't arrive. Paying with credit cards was quickly becoming obsolete. Credit card companies were getting hit with record numbers of defaults, even from their most qualified customers. Most everyone had their credit limits reduced by seventy-five percent. Some were reduced by ninety-five percent and others completely cancelled.

Matt found some battery-operated alarms for doors and windows, but nothing for a perimeter alarm system. Adam had a quick solution using mouse traps to fabricate simple perimeter alarms. Adam explained the ridiculously simple concept of the device to Matt. The area just under the striking position of the mouse trap bar would be drilled out to accept a .22 caliber nail gun load. Then, he would attach a small strip of plastic to hold a shortened roofing nail in place over the nail gun load. The device could be attached to a tree at shin height and a trip line ran to an adjacent tree. If anyone tripped the line, the shot would ring out to alert Matt of the intrusion and likely scare off the intruder. They found the aisle containing pest control products and picked up a box of mouse traps. They picked up a few more odds and ends at the home improvement store then headed to the checkout lane.

The last stop before returning home was Eli Miller's. Mr. Miller was an old-timer who knew a lot of lost arts. Adam stopped by Mr. Miller's place often to visit and trade. They had been bartering for years. Mr. Miller regularly sold his excess produce, eggs, honey and milk. When Adam would slaughter a bull, he often traded beef for Mr. Miller's items.

Eli Miller came out of his farmhouse as Adam's truck drove up the long dirt path from the main road. Mr. Miller had on well-worn overalls, a nice shirt and grey ball cap. Several years ago, Mr. Miller had a hand painted sign near his drive that read, "Eggs, milk, honey, fruits and vegetables." He took it down after the FDA fined him $500 for not complying with regulations he knew nothing about. People still traded with Mr. Miller. Word of mouth was all the advertisement he needed.

Adam asked Mr. Miller, "Would you sell a few hens and a rooster to my cousin?"

"I might have a few hens I'd sell, but ain't got no roosters to sell. I only got two of 'em right now," Eli stated.

"How much?" Matt inquired.

Eli stroked his beard as he spoke. "Well, I could probably sell five. You can have 'em for twenty-five cents each. Of course, that'll be in silver money from before '64. That paper money ain't gonna be worth nothin' in a week or two. If you ain't got silver, we can trade something else. Folks talk about inflation, but a silver quarter is what I paid for a live chicken in 1940. Prices ain't changed; just the value of that paper money has gone to the devil."

Matt and Adam laughed at the man's unique perspective on economics. As simple as Mr. Miller was, he knew more about money than the Federal Reserve Chairman.

Matt said, "I don't' have silver quarters, but I have a one ounce Silver Eagle. One Silver Eagle actually has about 3 grams more silver than five silver quarters."

"I don't know how I'd make change for that. I'll give you a pint of honey if that'd be alright," Eli said.

Matt said, "Oh no, sir, I don't need change. I would be very happy to pay an ounce for five hens."

"You're gettin' the honey, too. I don't sleep good if I feel like I cheated somebody," Mr. Miller said. "Stop by in a couple weeks. I'll let some eggs hatch and we'll see if we don't get a rooster for ya."

"Thank you very much, sir," Matt said. "Would you have any goats to sell?"

"I'll sell you a nanny for another one of those Silver Eagles. Same thing with the buck though. I don't have none to sell. If any of 'em give a buck next spring, I'll sell it to you," Miller said.

Matt was excited to be getting a few animals. "That would be great. Here's the silver for the female goat and the hens. Can I give you a deposit for the rooster or the buck goat?"

"I don't need a deposit, son. We'll shake on it and that's that," Miller replied.

Matt realized at that moment that this was the way things were supposed to be. The rat race he lived in for years corrupted his mind to accept as normal the viscous way people treated each other in South Florida. It was like that in big cities all over America. He felt such gratitude in his heart to have met Mr. Miller. If the world was going to fall apart, it was much better to be near folks like Mr. Miller than the mean people he left behind in Florida.

They concluded their business with Mr. Miller and headed home. Adam convinced Matt that he would not be finding any type of night vision equipment in the gun shops or outdoor shops around London. Most of the gun shops weren't even open. They hadn't been able to stock weapons or ammunition since the SNAP riots. The only things they held in stock were holsters and slings; it was hard to justify opening up just for that. Night vision equipment was one more thing that Matt knew he should've bought when he had the chance.

Matt and Adam returned to Matt's house. It was already after 11:30 am by the time he put the chickens in the old coop. Matt tied the goat to a nearby tree and went in to watch the speech.

Karen had the speech tuned on the television. The signal was out of Lexington and the quality was acceptable. It was the best channel they picked up with the digital antenna. Matt decided to stick with the digital antenna rather than go through the hassle of getting satellite. The satellite company had stated delays similar to the phone company. There was still no word from the phone company as to when they would get their DSL internet and landline phone.

"What did we miss?" Matt asked Karen.

"Nothing, he just started speaking," she replied.

Adam put on a pot of coffee then joined them in the living room.

Mustafa Al Mohammad was saying, "As I promised, I'm bringing troops home this week. We've closed several unnecessary military bases around the world. Our relations with other nations around the world have improved through my administration, and we can bring many of our men and women home from the places they're no longer needed. Through trade and diplomacy, our friendship with China has never been stronger. This allows us to not only close all of our bases on foreign soil in the Pacific, but we're also recalling all of our fleets of submarines, battle cruisers and aircraft carriers from the

Pacific.

"We'll be able to dedicate the resources that have been wasted on monitoring a world that is at peace to more productive tasks which will make our future bright and our country strong.

"In addition to these changes, we've made across-the-board cuts to all military and federal employee salaries. I've seen the belt-tightening that everyday Americans had to do over the last decade and decided it is high time Washington made some sacrifices, too. It's not fair to watch Americans struggle while we sit in Washington and live high on the hog.

"We've also made some significant changes to ensure that vital programs like Social Security, Medicare and the SNAP food assistance program can remain solvent well into the future. By making what seems like minor adjustments in the payouts of these programs today, we'll be able to see these programs continue to care for America's most vulnerable tomorrow.

"To grant added security to Americans who depend on these programs, we've received a commitment from the IMF to sure up these programs, should we ever require their help.

"These new temporary payout rates will take effect tomorrow and will guarantee recipients will receive no less than eighty-five percent of the benefits they've been promised.

"We've fought to get the rich to pay their fair share over the past eight years. We had some success, but today, we're instituting a new kind of stimulus program. Rather than have the middle-class taxpayer foot the bill, we're asking those who have more, to do a little more and pay back the country that has made them wealthy. The FDIC will be lowering the insured bank-deposit amount to $75,000 per depositor.

"Not only will this reduce the burden on low and middle income taxpayers of insuring the wealth of the rich, it will also stimulate our economy. The economists who helped us develop this stimulus model projected that this move will cause those with deposits higher than $75,000 to spend more. Spending will create economic activity and kick start America into a new age of prosperity. Things are getting better every day. This little boost should get us back to achieving our full potential.

"Keep looking up America. The future is bright!"

Al Mohammad waved to the hall of college students he was speaking to. The crowd cheered as if they bought every word he spoke.

"These liberal kids from George Washington University were the only people left on earth that would cheer for this loser, so I guess the speech had to be there," Karen said.

"Did he just cut SNAP, Social Security and Medicare by fifteen percent and tell the American people he did them a favor?" Matt was amazed by the audacity of this false hope.

"He sure did," Adam added. "He didn't specify how much the military pay cuts would be, but he just made it easier for a patriot soldier to walk away if it ever comes to choosing sides."

Matt said sarcastically, "Well, at least the new rates are only temporary."

Karen replied, "The rates are temporary, all right. There won't be any SNAP, Social Security or Medicare at all in a month or two."

Matt said, "Paul Randall has been warning everyone for years that this day was coming. If we would've started to phase in the cuts a long time ago, it would have been so much more tolerable. I don't buy that baloney about trying to stimulate the economy by lowering the FDIC limits. They're setting us up for a bail-in like they had in Cyprus, Spain and Italy."

Karen asked for clarification. "A bail-in is where they confiscate the citizens' money from their bank accounts?"

"Yes," Matt answered. "They'll take all deposits above the FDIC insured amounts."

"Why would they tip their hand and lower the FDIC insurance amount? Won't that trigger a run on the banks?" Adam asked.

Matt answered, "Anything they confiscate below the FDIC limit would have to be paid back from the insurance fund. It essentially would be an exercise in futility; not that the government has shied away from those in the past.

"It sounds like they expect a lot of people to withdraw their money. It may actually spark a brief period of economic activity like Al Mohammad said. The majority of people who still have more than $75,000 in the banking system are so oblivious to the problems that are unfolding right now, nothing will wake them up. They're in a normalcy-bias comma. Because they weren't around for the bank runs in the 1930s, they don't believe anything like that could ever happen in America. They think we're immune. Worse than that, they trust the system."

Adam requested more information on the matter. "So they actually have the money in the FDIC insurance fund to pay people if this triggers a bank run and the banks can't pay?"

Matt chuckled. "Not at all. Current reserve limits set by the Fed require banks to keep around ten percent of their deposits liquid. Although what they consider liquid is not all cash that could be handed out to depositors in a run. Realistically, banks could give depositors about five percent of their deposit before they went belly up. Problem number two is that there's only about $1.1 trillion in paper money and most of that is not in a bank to be handed out. I don't know the exact numbers, because so many people have been sticking the actual cash under their mattress lately. Let's be generous. Let's say half of the $1.1 trillion is actually in the banks and not under mattresses and in wallets. That leaves $550 billion in the banking system. Quantitative easing has caused the M2 money supply to explode and it's now near $14 trillion dollars. That's what depositors will be demanding from banks in a run. So after they pay out the $550 billion, there will be $13.45 trillion that the FDIC will be responsible for covering. The FDIC has about $33 billion in the insurance fund. That's a rounding error in the terms we are talking about and changes our $13.45 trillion to $13.42 trillion that the banks and FDIC are short of being able to pay out in a bank run."

"But the Fed could just print the money, right?" Adam inquired further.

Matt answered, "They would have to print the $33 billion from the insurance fund first; it doesn't exist in physical form. A pallet of $100 dollar bills is about $1 billion dollars. To make $1 trillion, you need a football field of pallets of $100 dollar bills, stacked two pallets high. You're talking about 14 football fields of $100 bills on pallets stacked two high to pay out the entire $14 trillion. That would take years to produce in physical form. It could never happen."

"Well, the dollar won't be worth the paper it's not printed on in a few months anyway, so it's a moot point," Karen said in a very matter-of-fact manner.

The guys laughed. She didn't say it to be funny, but the point had shown them what an absurd waste of time it was to discuss the matter further.

CHAPTER 36

"The nature of the encroachment upon American constitution is such, as to grow every day more and more encroaching. Like a cancer; it eats faster and faster every hour. The revenue creates pensioners, and the pensioners urge for more revenue. The people grow less steady, spirited and virtuous, the seekers more numerous and more corrupt, and every day increases the circles of their dependents and expectants, until virtue, integrity, public spirit, simplicity and frugality become the objects of ridicule and scorn, and vanity, luxury, foppery, selfishness, meanness, and downright venality swallow up the whole of society."

John Adams

Matt and Karen woke up early Thursday morning. Matt was determined to start getting up before the sun so he could maximize his day. Fortunately, in December, the sun came up a little later than the rest of the year.

Matt fed the chickens and the goat. He didn't find any eggs, but Mr. Miller said they might take a few days to get used to the new environment. The goat seemed to like the little bed Matt made for her in the metal work barn. He put down an old blanket so the animal wouldn't be on the concrete floor. He didn't have any fence to keep her contained, so he was just tying her up to a nearby tree to forage during the day. He fed her some of the leftover rice and beans from the previous evening meal. She seemed to enjoy those just as much as the chickens did.

Karen had a day planned with the girls and Janice. They were going to make homemade Christmas cookies. Christmas was still three weeks away, but there would be more cookies to be made over the coming weeks.

The chores were done and they were out the door by 8:30. Matt and Karen walked the road to Adams' both to save gas and for the exercise. Wesley met Matt and Karen at the door when they arrived.

"Want to help me pick out a tree?" Wesley asked Matt.

Matt completely forgot about getting a Christmas tree. The move, thinking about the economy and everything else completely filled up his mind. Picking out a good Christmas tree would be a great distraction to clear his mind from all the troubles.

"Sure, Wes. Let me just stick my head in the door and say hi to the family," Matt answered.

Wes and Adam walked to the barn to get an ax. It had been a long time since either one of them swung an ax. They were trying to conserve the chainsaw and fuel for when they really needed it; besides, it would be nice to actually chop down a Christmas tree.

They found a nice looking pine that looked full and natural. It didn't have the perfectly manicured shape of a commercial tree, but it was pretty.

"Shelly and I are getting married on the day after Christmas," Wesley announced.

"Wow! That's quick." Matt was surprised.

"Yeah, well, technically we're living together. We're trying to stay pure, but being under the same roof isn't easy," Wesley explained.

"That's understandable, but it's not the best reason to get married. You need to know that she's the person you want to be with forever." Matt wanted to be sure Wesley wasn't making a hasty mistake.

"I know she's the one. It's the reason I brought her here," Wesley said.

Matt patted Wes on the back. "Then may God bless your wedding and your marriage."

When they arrived back at the house with the tree, they trimmed it to even out some wild limbs. They took the tree inside. Shelly was showing off her ring. It was rather small, but she couldn't have been happier with it if the diamond was ten times bigger. The ring was Adam and Wesley's mom's engagement ring. Adam had kept it since she passed several years earlier. He never intended to sell it. This was a nice way to keep it in the family. Everyone celebrated with warm cookies and hot cocoa.

Matt was anxious to see what was going on in the world. Since he had no satellite or internet at his home, Adam's house was the portal to the information super highway.

"Do you mind if we try to catch some news?" he asked Adam.

Adam clicked on the news, but surprisingly, there were no reports of widespread rioting. However, all was not well in the land of America.

Amy Stein was reporting outside a large bank in Lower Manhattan.

The few people who were spooked by the lowering of the FDIC limits were withdrawing cash from their accounts en masse. Over one hundred people were in a line that snaked out the door and into the street where it was beginning to snow. Amy finally got one of the people who were coming out of the door to speak to her.

"What's going on inside the bank?" Amy asked the man.

The man replied, "People are trying to access their cash and they're being told they can only get $500 dollars in cash. The bank is offering to give depositors bank checks or cashier's checks with no fee instead of more cash."

Amy inquired, "Why can't they get more than $500 in cash?"

The man answered, "The tellers are saying they don't have enough cash in the vaults to hand out more than that. A bank manager was explaining to the lady in front of me that several depositors entered the bank early that morning and made huge withdraws. She asked how much, but the manager wouldn't give any more details."

Amy Stein thanked the man for talking with her as he walked away. She continued her report. "We're hearing that most all ATMs are completely drained of cash. New York Fed President Sydney Roth assured CNC in a telephone interview earlier today that the trucks would be running to get the banks resupplied with cash tomorrow morning. Today's shortage has produced a sense of uneasiness in depositors. Many of the people we spoke with in the bank lines today were not depositors with more than $75,000 in the bank. Even though their deposit amounts were below the limit, they were concerned that there could be a bank run and they wanted to make sure they had some cash on hand."

CNC went back to the studio where Ed Nolan was reporting.

"Gold jumped to $8,650 today," Ed said. "The yellow metal quickly rebounded and made new highs after the twenty-percent correction, which took it down below $6000 on Monday. While this type of volatility is pure adrenaline for traders, the common man can really get hurt trying to dabble in the gold market. Today, we have Wall Street trader Dan Ingles in the studio to tell us what's going on in the metals market.

"Dan, how are you?"

The camera panned out to bring Dan Ingles into the shot.

"I'm great Ed," Dan replied.

Ed asked, "What happened? When the markets reopened on Monday, gold crashed. It lost more than $1200 of the per-ounce price in early morning trading before the markets opened. We saw a short pop Tuesday morning, but gold finished the day down another $320. All of a sudden, it shot up like a rocket this morning. Gold regained all of its losses by the time the markets opened, then it took off to make new highs all day."

Dan answered, "It's hard to say what caused the volatility the rest of the week, but today's action came from individual investors who are having trouble getting cash out of the banks. I think a lot of investors are looking for any vehicle that they can use to get that money out of the bank. As Amy reported a few minutes ago, depositors can't get their cash out of their accounts because banks simply don't have enough paper currency to hand out. Gold investors can go online and purchase bullion by using a wire transfer, a personal check, or even a credit card. Many of the online dealers charge a higher fee for credit-card orders and they have limits on how much can be purchased using a credit card, but it's still an option."

"Is using gold as a means to get your cash out of the bank a good plan?" Ed asked.

"I wouldn't do it," Dan replied. "As soon as the banks are

restocked with currency, the price could go right back down. My suggestion is to hang on. This will get resolved soon."

Adam commented sarcastically, "Yeah, everything will be just fine."

Matt was in utter unbelief. "I can't believe the media would say something so stupid! The biggest risk is to stay in the banking system or stay in dollars. The risk in gold price volatility is nothing compared to that."

CNC's Patrick James was reporting live from DC.

The good Reverend Terrence Sharpe had organized a march on DC. There were thousands carrying signs and chanting in protest to the benefits cuts.

Patrick James didn't have to look long to find Terrence Sharpe. In fact, when he made visual contact, the reverend was already making a bee line for the cameras.

"Reverend Sharpe, can you tell America why you are protesting today?" James quizzed.

"Patrick, what has been done to America's poor today is unconscionable," Sharpe began. "These are the very people President Al Mohammad has sworn to protect and help, and after they put him in power for eight years, he makes this cowardly move."

"Do you think it's possible that the president had no choice but to enact the fifteen-percent cuts? It's much better than the fifty-percent shortfall in the SNAP budget at the beginning of last month. Wouldn't you agree?" Patrick James rebutted.

"Patrick, is the man that steals fifteen percent of the food off of your table any less of a thief than the man that steals fifty percent of the bread from your mouth? The amounts are not the issue here. The issue is that these are the people who can least afford to make a sacrifice. If cuts must be made, they must be taken from those who can afford them. Poor folk in America already don't have the assistance they need to survive. A family of four has been receiving $668 per month in food assistance for years now. Despite the rapid increases in food costs, they haven't seen any increase in assistance. Now, in a time when they most need an increase, they're getting their benefits cut. What are they supposed to do, eat beans and rice for breakfast, lunch and dinner?" Sharpe protested. "Babies can't live on beans and rice, Patrick."

Patrick said, "But the president didn't cut the WIC program, which gives mothers of children age five and below food benefits in addition to the SNAP program. We've done reports in nations where the children do live on rice. They may only eat rice once or twice a day, in fact. The poor in America live at a higher standard than most of the world."

Sharpe retaliated, "What about Social Security, Patrick? Those people have worked hard, paid into that system, and are now being cheated out of what they thought was going to be a good retirement."

"I don't disagree with you, Reverend," Patrick James replied. "I'm just trying to look at the issue from the administration's perspective. From what I understand, the country has reached the limit on our credit card. We're now faced with the task of learning to live on what we make. Many families have gone through the same thing, and they often come out on the other side stronger than before. They emerge with a new skill set of being able to do more with less. Many families with the best money management skills are those who have gone through bankruptcy.

"It's not just the poor and the retired, Reverend; the military, Congress and even the president himself have been subjected to the cuts."

Sharpe continued his protest. "People who have enough to survive might make it out on the other side stronger, but many of these folks are going to starve, Patrick. We also heard a rumor that all Earned Income Credits and Additional Child Tax Credits will be canceled next year."

Patrick said, "We heard the same thing concerning those credits. We're still in the process of verifying the validity of that claim, but our source close to the president has told us that it's only the refundable portion of those credits that will be canceled. For example, if you had a $250 tax liability at the end of the year, and a $1000 EIC credit, the credit would only be worth the $250 to eliminate your tax liability. You wouldn't get a check for the remaining $750. This would prevent negative taxation. Negative taxation allows people to get a bigger tax refund check than the amount they paid in the previous year."

"Folks depend on that money, Patrick," Sharpe said.

The rest of the family wandered into the room where Matt and Adam were watching the news.

"Sounds like a bonus for doing nothing," Janice commented on the EIC tax credits.

"Paid for by those who do something," Adam added.

CNC showed that the crowd continued to grow in DC. The estimates at 5:00 pm were over 200,000 protesters.

As the sun began to set, CNC showed several instances of rioting that grew out of the protests. It seemed more like the bad elements that were taking advantage of the situation than the true believers from the previous SNAP riots.

The sun set around 5:30, and the evening turned cold soon after. Matt and Karen headed home to get a fire going in the wood burning stove. Miss Mae was resourceful. She would dig a tunnel under the covers on Matt and Karen's bed to keep warm when there was no fire in the stove, but they didn't feel right leaving her unattended in the cold evenings. Furthermore, they didn't want to be walking on the road when it was completely dark.

CHAPTER 37

"Let us therefore animate and encourage each other, and show the whole world that a Freeman, contending for liberty on his own ground, is superior to any slavish mercenary on earth."

George Washington

Paul Randall began his first video address since the attack on the cabin.

"America, my family and I have gone dark because there was a military-style attack on our previous refuge two weeks ago. My son, Robert, was killed defending his mother and myself. He and my other son, Ryan, killed several of the attackers while we waited for our backup security team to arrive.

"They killed Robert, but his patriotism will live on in the rest of us. Our resolve has never been stronger. Christmas is next week. It will be a very difficult time for our family without Robert. We hope that you'll remember us in your prayers this holiday season. We'll certainly be praying for you.

"We have sought peace at every occasion, but now violence has been forced upon us. I am certain that our enemies will not cease until their murderous ambition is satisfied.

"Our attackers wore no distinguishing identification, so we have no evidence to show other than our word, but the stench of Mustafa Al Mohammad is all over this attack.

Anthony Howe has voiced his resolve to take your guns after the inauguration in January. I urge you to decide what you will do now. I urge you to decide how you will do it. Make up your mind this day as to whether you will hand over your freedom or stand your ground. Remember, if you decide to stand, you are not the criminal. The tyrant that oppresses you and violates the Constitution, which is the law of the land, is the criminal. It's not about your right to defend yourself, it is about your duty to defend your country.

"If God will protect us, my family and I hope to mourn the loss of our son over the holidays. In the new year, I'll return to my regular video messages. We'll stand by your side as you draw a line in the sand and say 'No further!'

"Remember, it's always darkest just before the dawn. May God grant you peace, love and joy as we celebrate the birth of our Savior. Merry Christmas, America."

After Paul put down his headset, Kimberly gave him a huge hug. They had not thought much about Christmas. It was so painful to just wake up and find that Robert wasn't there.

The soldiers assigned to the armory did their best to make sure it was decorated for Christmas. The chef Larry Jacobs sent was a Texan and had made so many of the traditional Christmas cookies and treats they all grew up with. The Randalls weren't in the mood to eat much, but the soldiers appreciated the great food.

Ryan was distant. He signed up for the Texas Air National Guard. He was headed to Kelly Field in San Antonio the day after Christmas. He had to be here; he couldn't abandon his mom before

Christmas, but mentally, he was already at Kelly Field. He knew a fight was coming and he wanted a front row seat.

CHAPTER 38

"Happiness depends more on the inward disposition of mind than on outward circumstances."

Benjamin Franklin

Karen walked into the work shed situated back, near the creek where Matt was occupied with a new project.

"What are you working on?" she asked.

"A dollhouse for Mandy and Carissa," Matt answered. "There are no toys at Walmart. If I want to give them anything, I'll have to make it."

"It's adorable," Karen said. The dollhouse was a mess. Karen was not in the habit of saying she liked something if she didn't. She was brutally honest most of the time. This time, she was still being honest. The house was a mess, but the thought and the time that Matt was putting into the project was adorable to her.

Christmas was only three days away, so Matt was working feverishly to get the dollhouse finished today. He never hesitated to try something new. It usually didn't turn out as grand as what he set out to do, but you could never say he didn't try.

The days of the Barbie Dream House were over. When the dollar started crashing, Walmarts all over the country began to close. Ninety-eight percent of everything sold at Walmart was imported from China. The loss of value in the dollar meant they could no longer purchase China's cheaply produced products. Walmart's costs began to skyrocket as the dollar plunged. They tried to increase prices to keep up with rising costs, but consumers simply could not pay the new prices. Inflation was running rampant and those who still had jobs spent every last dime on food and housing.

Grocery prices more than doubled since the October riots. Gas was now fifteen dollars per gallon. The ration cards were still the law, but they were no longer needed. Few people had money to buy more that the five-gallon allotment.

"What could I make for the girls?" Karen asked.

"Janice is making corn husk dolls for them. Why don't you make some dresses for the dolls?" Matt suggested.

"Oh, that's a great idea. Can we go over there tonight so I can get the measurements?" Karen asked.

"We need to conserve gas. Let's walk over there first thing in the morning. I wouldn't mind catching some news online at Adam's while we're there," Matt answered.

Phone and internet services still weren't connected at Matt's home. The companies quit sending out servicemen to connect new service or repair outages. Many customers stopped paying their bills due to economic conditions, and the communication companies had to lay off most of their workers. The local phone company was still operating. It provided service for paying customers, but if you had an outage, you were on your own. When folks had outages because of line trouble, they did without and closed their accounts. It was the same story with satellite and cable providers all over the country. Water and electric utilities were still in good repair except where rioting and fires destroyed critical infrastructure.

The next morning, Matt and Karen walked to Adam's farm. When they arrived, they noticed the gifts beneath the tree. The gifts were wrapped in bright, colorful store bought wrapping paper. Matt suddenly realized how far things had deteriorated. To see that wrapping paper and know that it wouldn't be on sale after Christmas this year made him consider how America had crossed over into uncharted territory.

Matt asked Adam if they could catch a few minutes of the news. The local channel Matt received played world news at night for half an hour, but thirty minutes couldn't adequately cover the quantity and magnitude of the ongoing economic meltdown.

The guys made a pot of coffee and went to the living room. CNC was reporting on the same old story, so they went to the office computer to see what RT was reporting. The alternative news station was covering chaotic conditions popping up in some of America's big cities. The reporter covering the story was a new face that neither Matt nor Adam recognized.

The reporter said, "Cleveland, Chicago, San Diego, Buffalo, Newark and several other large municipalities have taken bankruptcy over the past few years. They followed the Detroit template in reorganizing. The president's massive bailout program called City Protection Relief or CPR attempted to fund the bankrupt cities' police and fire departments. Money for that program dried up in November, and the municipal patients flat lined.

"To cut costs in several of the bankrupt cities, police officers were fired. Those who wanted their jobs back had to agree to come back on the force with no benefits and work on salary, which meant no overtime pay and a minimum of fifty hours per week. Most decent cops left the cities. The ones who stayed were the ones who had some method of supplementing their income. Drug protection, extortion, and cash 'discounts' for speeding tickets are among the top forms of supplemental income.

"With the lack of a sufficient or honest police force, pockets of those cities erupted in horrific violence. Gangs are fighting for control of larger and larger parts of the cities. Thugs are no longer content to sell crack on the corner. They're pulling home invasions in affluent neighborhoods and setting up shop in the captured properties."

Karen pulled Janice to the side to secretly get the measurements of the dolls. They stayed in the kitchen to chat.

"Would you want to make the cake for the wedding?" Janice asked.

"I would love, too!" Karen said. "Are Shelly's parents coming to the wedding?"

"As long as the gas pumps are still pumping, Mr. and Mrs. Simpson intend to come. They're in Louisville; it's really rough there," Janice answered.

"Shouldn't they try to sell their house and move out if they can?" Karen asked.

Janice replied, "They think this is just temporary. They think everything will sort itself out and go back to normal."

Karen poured herself a cup of coffee. "Are they delusional?"

Janice also served herself a cup of coffee and joined Karen at the table. "Shelly told me they voted for Howe, and they think he's going to get everything back together when he gets in office. So yes, I guess they are delusional."

"Some people just believe whatever they are told," said Karen.

Janice left her cup on the table and stood back up. "That's why we're in this mess."

Janice went into her bedroom and came back holding a long white dress. "I made this for Shelly. I'm going to give it to her for Christmas."

Karen crossed her hands over her chest. "Oh, it's beautiful! She's going to love it. Does she know about it?"

"No, I took the measurements from her clothes," Janice said.

"So, she's going to think she doesn't have a wedding dress until the day before the wedding," Karen said.

"I'm mean, ain't I?" Janice grinned slyly.

The two laughed and continued planning the wedding. It was nice to have a wedding to keep their minds off of the problems of the day. It was something that felt normal in a world that wasn't.

CHAPTER 39

"There is nothing so likely to produce peace as to be well prepared to meet an enemy."

George Washington

Pastor John Robinson walked to the pulpit. He prayed, then addressed the congregation.

"Folks, I know this Christmas is tough. I know that many of you made a sacrifice to be here tonight for the Christmas Eve service. Many of you haven't been able to attend regularly because of fuel prices and other hardships brought on by the ongoing economic collapse. I'm proud to see so many of you tonight. This is the biggest turnout we've had in weeks. It shows that you have remembered the true reason for the season."

Pastor John went on to read the Christmas story from The Book of Matthew. After reading the scripture, he continued "We just read in Matthew 2 that Jesus' father had a dream where an angel told him to take Jesus to Egypt to escape the evil King Herod who vowed to kill him.

"Folks, in three weeks, Anthony Howe will be taking office. He has vowed to disarm us. As you've heard Paul Randall say, you don't build a police state unless you intend to use it. I anticipate that once arms are no longer an issue for Howe, he'll attack our right to worship. I have no intention of being herded into a cattle car peacefully while a criminal occupies the White House and breaks the law of our land.

"God provided for Jesus' family to bug out to Egypt through the gifts of the wise men. One of the gifts they brought was gold. That sustained Jesus' family during their exile in Egypt.

"God has provided for us as well. We've converted what liquid assets the church held into gold so that its value can be preserved. We've also purchased an adjacent farm next to the property that was left to the church by Howard Young. We've already begun building rudimentary living quarters there. We've stockpiled food, weapons and ammunition.

"We've decided that the two farms will be the place where we'll draw our line in the sand. After much prayer, thought and consideration, we think it is far more defendable than the church property. We think the terrain is much easier to use to our advantage. We also think it's wise to get out of Boise. We expect that cities will be primary targets for arms confiscation.

"I think all of you know our range master, Albert Rust. Albert is also the commander of the 12th Battalion of the Idaho Free Militia. Albert is going to say a few words. Albert come on up."

Albert walked up to the pulpit and began speaking. "Folks, I know Christmas Eve is not the best time to be talking about militias and strongholds, but it's the time when we have the most people here at once.

"I came to Pastor John and volunteered to take the leadership role for our tactical response to whatever Howe intends to do in January. I wanted to make sure that Pastor John was free to continue being our spiritual leader. We'll need his guidance more than ever.

"I have also spoken with the 29th Battalion out of Coeur d'Alene, the 35th out of Lewiston and our friends in the 43rd Battalion out of Moscow. In the event of a standoff, they've all committed to come to the base camp which we've decided to call Young Field, in honor of Howard Young who donated the property. The number of militiamen totals just over 500. I'll be at a table in the back to take volunteers for those who would like to sign up for the Idaho Free Militia.

"As a side note, the Militia was offered a position to stand alongside of the Idaho National Guard. We declined because of the differences in what we considered appropriate rules of engagement.

"I will say the governor of Idaho has committed to resist any federal troops on Idahoan soil. He affirmed his commitment to defend the Constitution and more specifically, the Second Amendment. However, the governor said that his orders to the National Guard will be to fire only when fired upon. The Idaho Free Militia commanders decided that federal troops invading Idaho is an act of aggression sufficient to justify the use of lethal force. The Militia's orders are fire on sight. Please keep this in mind when you decide if you're ready to join.

"Of course, we should all continue to pray for peace, but if the enemy will thrust violence upon us, we have no other choice than to defend our families, our freedom and the law of our land, which is the Constitution.

"Thank you so much. Merry Christmas."

People began to clap. It started low and rose to a roaring standing ovation. There was much to do, much training, and much preparation. But in their hearts, Liberty Chapel was ready.

CHAPTER 40

"For this reason a man will leave his father and mother and be united to his wife, and the two will become one flesh."

Ephesians 5:31

Matt and Karen went to Adam's for breakfast on Christmas morning. They enjoyed a feast of grits, biscuits, scrambled eggs, country ham, red-eye gravy and homemade strawberry preserves.

After breakfast, everyone went into the living room to open presents. Gifts were a bit sparse, but Janice made sure everyone had something to open.

Janice handed a beautifully wrapped box to Karen. She opened the present carefully to keep the paper intact. There may not be any more Christmas wrapping paper for a while. Perhaps it could be reused.

"It's Risk!" Karen exclaimed. Janice had bought several board games to give as presents before Walmart closed down. She anticipated that these items might become scarce.

Matt opened the box Janice handed him. "Monopoly," he said.

Janice said, "I know that's probably not what you asked Santa for, but I figured if we ever lose television and internet, we'll need some form of entertainment."

"That was a great idea Janice," Matt said. "We love the games."

Shelly opened her box and found the beautiful wedding dress that Janice had made. She gasped with surprise. She began to cry as the emotion overwhelmed her. Shelly grabbed Janice and held her tight. She was finally able to say, "Thank you so much."

Normally, Christmas evening was a time for just relaxing. Not this year. Everyone was chipping in to get the house ready for the wedding on the following day. Janice straightened up the house. Karen was in charge of the cake. Matt made the appetizers for the reception. Adam and Wesley were helping Matt, but doing more sampling than production. Shelly tried on her dress for Mandy and Carissa.

The day of the wedding arrived. About twenty people from the church the Bairs attended came. Shelly's mother and father also came.

Shelly's parents brought her a couple of small Christmas gifts. Her mother, Mrs. Simpson, took her for a walk prior to the ceremony.

"Shelly," Mrs. Simpson began, "your father and I want you to be happy, but I hope you know what you're doing. If you change your mind, you can come back home with us tonight."

"Mom," Shelly replied, "I love Wes."

Mrs. Simpson continued, "I know you do, dear, but your father and I have the feeling that you're doing this because of all this end-of-the-world nonsense. I know that Wes and his family think things are going to get worse, but they're being pessimistic. Once Anthony Howe takes office, everything will get back to normal. It always does. People thought the end of the world would happen in 2000. They had some idea that the computers were going to shut down and we were going to start living in caves. We want you to think for yourself. Be rational."

"I am being rational, Mom," Shelly retorted. "You and Dad are in denial. Wes didn't convince me things are going to get worse. It's just common sense. Mom, there are no more Walmarts, we're on a five-gallon per week gas ration and people can't afford more than five gallons a week anyway. Social Security has been cut by fifteen percent, the dollar is crashing, cities are burning to the ground or being taken over by gangs, and people are dying just like Paul Randall predicted."

"Paul Randall triggered this, Shelly. He caused a massive panic and that's what set all of this off," Mrs. Simpson said. "Now he's inciting insurrection against the government. That man is a terrorist. Please tell me you are not getting involved in that cult."

"Mom, you can't be serious. Paul Randall, a terrorist? Where did you get that?" Shelly quizzed.

Mrs. Simpson replied, "All of the news channels are saying he's a terrorist. The man is trying to start a civil war. We have enough trouble without Paul Randall starting another war."

Shelly said, "You're the one who needs to think for yourself. Those are the same news channels who have been telling you everything is going to be fine. You and Dad need to get out of Louisville while you still can."

"Well, I guess we'll just have to agree to disagree," Mrs. Simpson said. "But promise me that if Wes or his family start taking sides with Paul Randall, you'll come home. We'll come pick you up. Just call us."

Shelly didn't say anything else. She knew it would just lead to more arguing. She returned to her side of the house. She and Wes were kept apart to avoid seeing each other before the wedding. Janice insisted on it.

Shelly ran into Adam. "Are you ready?" Adam asked.

"Hair and makeup are all set; I just have to put my dress on," Shelly replied.

"I can see that. You look stunning, but I was referring to mentally and emotionally," Adam said.

"Absolutely!" Shelly exclaimed.

"All right, then," Adam said. "We're sure ready to have you as part of our family."

"Thanks, that means so much to me," Shelly said.

Adam said, "Oh, and a heads up, I may have made your father mad. Wes warned me not to talk about guns and such, but we got into what I thought was a civil discussion about politics, and he walked away. Sorry, I didn't mean to cause any friction for you today."

"Don't even think about it," Shelly said. "I know it wasn't your fault. They believe what they want to believe."

Adam went to get dressed and Shelly finished getting ready as well. Her father came into the room after she was dressed. He gave her a big hug and started to repeat a similar lecture to what she just heard from her mom.

Shelly stopped him. "Dad, we have been trying to change each other's minds for a couple of years now. Today, can we accept each other and enjoy the day?"

Mr. Simpson agreed and he walked out to the yard.

On the wide open lawn, an archway was set up where the couple would exchange vows. Chairs were lined up on either side of the aisle. The archway way was decorated with pine boughs and natural mistletoe that Wesley had shot out of the tree tops.

It looked more like Christmas than a wedding, but there were no flower shops still open. Imported flowers were already a thing of the past. They had to work with what they had. It was a chilly forty-two degrees outside where the wedding was, but the sun was bright and everyone was warm from being inside around the fireplace prior to the ceremony.

Adam officiated the wedding. No formal registration was made with the courthouse. As far as Shelly and Wes were concerned, a wedding was a promise between two people and God. Those who attended were the witnesses. In their opinion, the government should've never been involved in marriage certificates. Like so many other areas of life where the government had interjected themselves, a wedding was none of their business.

During the reception, Mr. and Mrs. Simpson kept to themselves. Adam tried to be friendly, but he could tell they weren't interested in small talk.

Adam and Matt walked around to the barn with a couple of the guys from church who showed up for the wedding. Matt had met Eddie Cooper and Franklin Johnson at church, but only in passing.

Adam said to Matt, "Franklin here is the commander of the

Eastern Kentucky Liberty Militia."

Matt replied, "I remember you were telling me you trained with them a few times."

Adam said, "Maybe more than a few times. We were always on the phone, so I didn't like to say much. I know 'militia' is a keyword for the NSA Prism program. The entire conversation gets stored in the NSA mega-computer in Utah for review once certain keywords trigger the conversation."

Eddie added, "Adam was our tactical commander because of his experience as a Marine in Afghanistan."

Franklin said, "We're going to start training two days a week if you'd be interested. When I say two days, I mean 48 hours. Sleeping out in the cold and getting ready for whatever is coming. It makes more sense than training four or five days a week for a few hours at a time. Everyone has a family and things to do. This allows them to do both until the time comes to make a stand."

"I'm going to talk it over with my wife before I give you a commitment, but I'm definitely interested," Matt said. "How many guys are we talking about?"

Franklin said, "We were eighty-five in November. We postponed training for the month of December. Everyone needed a break for Christmas and New Year's. We'll start back up on January 2nd. So far, we're looking at around 400 men, including the new recruits."

"I guess people are more motivated to get involved than before Howe was elected." Matt said.

"Yes," Franklin said, "but we have to be more careful than ever who we discuss the militia with."

"Why is that?" Matt asked. "The Second Amendment prescribes the need of the militia. I would argue along the same lines as Paul

Randall. It's not about a right. I think the Second Amendment was spelling out a duty of the citizen to join a militia."

"I would agree with you," Franklin said. "But the government has convinced the Tories that the Bill of Rights is an obsolete document."

"What are Tories?" Matt asked.

Eddie answered, "In the American Revolution, the Tories were the colonists who were loyal to the crown."

Adam said, "We like the term because it's so descriptive of our modern loyalists and because it's unrecognizable to most of them. Very few of them have any knowledge of history beyond 1960."

"If they did, they wouldn't be Tories," Eddie said.

The men all laughed. They continued to fill Matt in on what level of training they had done, up to this point, and what type of training they intended to begin in January.

Meetings like these were going on all over the country. Brothers, cousins, friends, church congregations and co-workers were spreading the word. A decentralized militia was swelling. The people in the heartland of America were in a much better position than those in the cities. They were prepared for the worst. They didn't want war nor did they seek violence, but if it was to be shoved into their lap, they would meet their aggressors with a valiant effort.

After the reception, Matt and Karen went home to get Miss Mae and came back to Adam's to stay for a few days. They gave their house to the newlyweds so they could have a simple honeymoon. Karen did her best to fix up the house and put out some nice candles and things for Wes and Shelly.

Adam offered to let Shelly's parents stay the night before heading back to Louisville. They refused and headed home. Mr. and

Mrs. Simpson never arrived home and no one ever heard from them again.

CHAPTER 41

"To contract new debts is not the way to pay old ones."

George Washington

Anthony Howe peered out the window of the New York Governor's Mansion in Albany. The snow was a blanket of purity over the grounds. He thought of the snow as a symbol of a clean start to the New Year. Christmas was gone now, but looking out the window of the opulent home, into the snow, reminded him of the Christmas carol, "Good King Wenceslas." It was rather like that. "I am something of a king," he said to himself. "In just over two weeks, I will go from being King of New York to being King of America."

He hoped and dreamed of someday being King of the World. "I suppose that dream has been beaten into submission and snatched from my palm," he muttered under his breath.

Despite the lies he told the press, Howe knew there was no way out of this mess. He had seen the intricacy of the debt. He knew the true cost of the wars and the precious dependents of the state that kept his party in power for so long.

The snow and brutal cold weather in the north calmed some of the violent riots. But, news stories of theft and murder for goods and property kept rolling in. As he considered the chaos being reported in the major cities, he thought perhaps Paul Randall could be right about the die-off. If he was right about the majority of the deaths being in the major population centers, Howe would have to devise another method of retaining power besides the election. Ninety-five percent of the counties that voted for him were in large metropolitan areas.

Howe recalled his conversation with Al Mohammad from the White House New Year's Eve party the night before.

"Howe," the president had said. "I'm not going to sugar coat this. The Treasury is going to be tapped out on February 1st. You'll have to hit the ground running. You'll have ten days after the inauguration to secure another loan from the IMF. I think you learned your lesson, but don't try to dictate terms to the director. Klauser is short on funds and short on temper.

"You're lucky to have someone like me to coach you through this thing. When I came into office, I got a note from my predecessor and a briefing from my staff."

Howe told the president that his continued "coaching" wouldn't be necessary after the inauguration.

The president insisted in such a way to let Howe know that he wasn't taking no for an answer. He was very polite about it, but with a tone which told Howe that if he had to threaten him again with releasing the information on Howe's personal indiscretions, it wouldn't be pretty.

Howe contemplated in his mind how he might find a permanent solution for this present conundrum, but he dare not even murmur it with his lips. Perhaps an accident, or maybe an assassination intended to take his own life would befall Al Mohammad. That would certainly remove all suspicion of his involvement.

There were plenty of positions of power to be awarded to those who would prove their loyalty to Howe's throne. He would have to be very careful about who he enlisted. Anyone who wouldn't kill for him was undeserving of a seat at the table.

His mind wandered back to the issue of the collapse at hand. Unemployment was now well above thirty percent, even with the creative calculations of the Bureau of Labor and Statistics. Howe knew that number was just to instill a sense of false hope. The real number was closer to seventy percent. Additionally, inflation on consumer staples had surpassed 100 percent since the election.

Howe knew the IMF would ask for a bail-in, if America was to secure more credit. There was no other option. He had to keep the country running at any cost.

What other assets did the country hold? What else could the US Federal Government seize to keep the Titanic afloat for one more month?

FDR bought the people's gold in the 1930s. Perhaps he could do that. He could exchange an emergency issue of Treasury bonds that paid the market rate for privately held gold. It might be difficult to get the small holder to turn in his gold, but there were plenty of ETFs, gold funds and gold IRAs to raid. Besides raising money, gold confiscation would be a slap in Paul Randall's face. The 007 traders could suppress the price until the exchange was made, then push the price back up.

The 401k plans were also fair game. After all, it was untaxed money. A simple emergency rule change would allow Howe to exchange them for more government bonds. And Howe Clancy could facilitate it all for a reasonable fee.

Howe said to himself, "This is a bigger job than I signed up for. But if anyone can do this, it's me. When the smoke clears, Howe

Clancy will emerge as the most influential company in the world. Then, I'll be the de facto King of the World."

Thank you for reading
American Exit Strategy,
Book One of
The Economic Collapse Chronicles.

Reviews are the best way to help get the book noticed. If you liked
the book, please take a moment to leave a five-star review on
Amazon and Goodreads.

I love hearing from readers! So whether it's to say you enjoyed the
book, point out a typo that we missed, or ask to be put on the
notification list for future books, drop me a line.
prepperrecon@gmail.com

Continue the adventure by reading
American Meltdown, Book Two of
The Economic Collapse Chronicles

and
American Reset, Book Three of
The Economic Collapse Chronicles.

Stay tuned to **PrepperRecon.com** for the latest news about my
upcoming books, and great interviews on the
Prepper Recon Podcast.

If you liked *The Economic Collapse Chronicles*, you'll love my second fiction series!

In ***The Days of Noah, Book One: Conspiracy***, The founding precepts of America have been destroyed by a conspiracy that dates back hundreds of years. The signs can no longer be ignored and Noah Parker is forced to prepare for the cataclysmic period of financial and political upheaval ahead.

Watch through the eyes of Noah as a global empire takes shape, ancient writings are fulfilled, and the last days fall upon the once great, United States of America.

And my latest book:
Behold, Darkness and Sorrow

Ambitious college student, Daniel Walker, has his world turned upside down when he begins having prophetic dreams about the judgment coming upon America. Through one of his dreams, Daniel learns about an imminent threat of an EMP attack which will wipe out America's electric grid, sending the country into a technological dark age.

Living in a nation where all life-sustaining systems of support are completely dependent on electricity and computers, the odds for survival are dismal. If he wants to live through the most catastrophic period in American history, Daniel will have to race against time to get prepared, before the lights go out.

Coming Soon!
The Days of Elijah

This follow-up series to *The Days of Noah* chronicles the struggles of ex-CIA analyst and new believer, Everett Carrol, as he tries to survive the total onslaught of ruin brought on by the tribulation, a coming period of wrath promised by the Bible to be unparalleled in destruction and suffering.